P9-DBN-178

CAT ME IF YOU CAN

Berkley Prime Crime titles by Miranda James

Cat in the Stacks Mysteries

MURDER PAST DUE

CLASSIFIED AS MURDER

FILE M FOR MURDER

OUT OF CIRCULATION

THE SILENCE OF THE LIBRARY

ARSENIC AND OLD BOOKS

NO CATS ALLOWED

TWELVE ANGRY LIBRARIANS

CLAWS FOR CONCERN

SIX CATS A SLAYIN'

THE PAWFUL TRUTH

CARELESS WHISKERS

CAT ME IF YOU CAN

Southern Ladies Mysteries

BLESS HER DEAD LITTLE HEART

DEAD WITH THE WIND

DIGGING UP THE DIRT

FIXING TO DIE

A Cat in the Stacks Mystery

CAT ME IF YOU CAN

Miranda James

Berkley Prime Crime
New York

BERKLEY PRIME CRIME
Published by Berkley
An imprint of Penguin Random House LLC
penguinrandomhouse.com

Library of Congress Cataloging-in-Publication Data

Names: James, Miranda, author.
Title: Cat me if you can / Miranda James.
Description: First edition. | New York: Berkley Prime Crime, 2020. |
Series: Cat in the stacks mysteries
Identifiers: LCCN 2020014871 (print) | LCCN 2020014872 (ebook) |
ISBN 9780451491183 (hardcover) | ISBN 9780451491190 (ebook)
Subjects: GSAFD: Mystery fiction.
Classification: LCC PS3610.A43 C38 2020 (print) |
LCC PS3610.A43 (ebook) | DDC 813/.6—dc23
LC record available at https://lccn.loc.gov/2020014871
LC ebook record available at https://lccn.loc.gov/2020014872

Printed in the United States
1 3 5 7 9 10 8 6 4 2

Cover art by Dan Craig
Book design by Tiffany Estreicher

For Nancy Yost

La fanciulla del West

Thanks for more than two decades of representation and support (and I hope you enjoy the joke).

CAT ME IF YOU CAN

ONE

"Do you regret saying yes so quickly when I asked you to do this?" I glanced over at Helen Louise Brady, taking my eyes briefly from the highway ahead. I had to be careful because I wasn't used to driving in the mountains.

Helen Louise laughed, and in the backseat, Diesel, my Maine Coon cat, chirped loudly.

"I do admit to having second thoughts, maybe even third," Helen Louise replied, a note of mischief in her tone. "You caught me by surprise that night. I certainly wasn't expecting that question."

"No way you could have," I replied, my attention once again focused on driving. "I hadn't really planned it. You know how I am. Occasionally a thought hits me, and out of my mouth it leaps." I shot her a wry grin.

Helen Louise laughed again. "I do know how you are, and your ability to surprise me is one of the qualities I love about you. Asking me to go along with you on this, especially after popping that other question, came out of the blue."

I had asked Helen Louise to marry me a couple of months ago, and to my delight she had said yes. I had given thought to that question before I posed it to her. There was nothing spontaneous about it. We hadn't yet set the date, though the family knew a wedding was in the offing. Everyone seemed happy about the pending nuptials.

"I hope this isn't pushing you too far outside your comfort zone."

"It's been years since I've done any such thing," Helen Louise said. "Other than make occasional speeches at one of the local clubs or in a church committee, that is, but I used to do it frequently when I was practicing law."

"You feel comfortable with the subject, don't you?" I still felt anxious, worried that I had pressured her, though I had tried hard not to.

"Talking about books I love to other readers?" Helen Louise grinned. "I'm not a librarian doing readers' advisory, my love, but I think I can manage."

"I know you can," I said. "As long as you're sure you're okay with doing this, and I didn't push you into it, I'm happy."

"Then be happy, Charlie. You've never pushed me into doing anything before, and I doubt you will in the future. I'm not all that pushable." Helen Louise tapped my shoulder lightly. "I'm happy to talk about Elizabeth Cadell to the group. Frankly, I'm curious to find out whether anyone in the group is familiar with her work."

"I vaguely remember Cadell from my early public library days. I never read her, though, until you insisted."

"And you liked her."

I ignored the smugness and said simply, "Yes." Cadell's gentle blend of mystery and romance had charmed me, especially when I was in the mood for a cozy read.

Diesel again chirped from behind us, evidently in need of being noticed. Helen Louise twisted herself around to reach back and rub his head. He rewarded her with his deep purr, the source of his name.

"This is my first visit to North Carolina," I said when Helen Louise settled back into her seat and faced forward again. "I've always heard that the Asheville area is beautiful."

"I went there once, probably thirty years ago," Helen Louise replied. "Before I gave up law and headed to Paris to study French cuisine, of course. Had to depose someone who lived there. It is a beautiful area. I love mountains."

"After all those years in Houston, where the only thing close to a hill or a mountain is a freeway overpass," I said, my tone wry, "I am certainly enjoying the different terrain." I grimaced. "Though having to learn to drive in the mountains as we go is a bit nerve-racking."

"You're doing fine," Helen Louise said. "You had no problem during the pass down from the Gatlinburg area into Cherokee." Cherokee, North Carolina, was a town on the reservation of the Eastern Band of the Cherokee Nation, in the western part of the state just over the Tennessee border. We had stopped there briefly to look around before continuing our journey. We both wanted to return to Cherokee after our sojourn in Asheville to explore a bit more.

"Thanks," I said. "Honestly, though, I was so tense coming down, especially with that one guy in the truck going about three miles an hour. I felt like ramming him out of the way."

"I could tell," Helen Louise said, the barest tremor of amusement in her voice. "I'm glad you didn't succumb to temptation." She glanced at her phone and its GPS. "We're not that far from Asheville now. Only about another half hour, maybe forty minutes."

"That's good," I said. "This scenery is spectacular, I must say, but I'm not able to enjoy it as much as I'd like."

"I told you I'd be happy to drive," Helen Louise replied.

"I know, and I appreciate it," I said. "But I do better with heights if I'm at the wheel. Otherwise I can get a little too freaked out."

"Charlie Harris, you are a mess, a psychological mess," Helen Louise said in a mock-tragic tone.

"But you still love me anyway," I replied airily.

"Lord help me, I do." Helen Louise giggled.

A sound suspiciously like a snort came from the backseat. If cats could snort in derision, Diesel would certainly do it.

"That's enough from the peanut gallery," I said.

Diesel warbled in response. He always seemed to know when I was speaking directly to him.

"Ramses wanted to come, too, and he wasn't happy at being left behind." Ramses was a Christmas present from a young friend. He was still too kittenish to trust out of his home environment. Diesel was several years older and well seasoned.

"I'm sure he wasn't," Helen Louise said, "but Azalea will spoil him even more rotten than she already does."

"I've no doubt of that." Azalea Berry, my housekeeper, had become devoted to Ramses after claiming for years that she didn't like cats in the house. She even displayed affection for

Diesel, calling him Mr. Cat for some reason known only to herself. Diesel didn't appear to mind.

"This should be a lot of fun," Helen Louise said. "It's nice to get away from the everyday routine for a few days."

"I'm happy to be having this time with you, and neither one of us distracted by work," I said.

"Henry promised to call me only in the case of an extreme emergency," Helen Louise replied. Henry managed Helen Louise's French bistro in Athena, and he was more than capable of running the business and baking up to Helen Louise's Paris-trained standards.

"That's good," I said. "I promise not to look for mysteries anywhere."

Helen Louise laughed. "We'll be talking a lot about mysteries every day, thankfully all fictional. That's enough for a vacation."

"No argument here." In recent years I had found myself involved in several murder investigations, and though I fancied I had a knack for solving them, I wouldn't mind if I didn't encounter another one for quite some time.

We chatted in desultory fashion, with the occasional feline comment thrown in, the rest of the way to Asheville. As soon as the highway exit came in sight, Helen Louise switched into navigator mode. She fed me the directions step by step to the boutique hotel where we would be spending the week.

"That's where we would turn to go to Biltmore." Helen Louise pointed to the left not long after we exited the highway. Biltmore, the Vanderbilt estate, was the major tourist attraction in Asheville. We would view it sometime this week, depending on the schedule set up by Miss An'gel and Miss Dickce Ducote, sponsors for the mystery week. The sisters, the leading lights of Athena society, were dear friends of ours, and it was thanks to their connections we would have a special tour of the Vanderbilt estate.

"Take the next left," Helen Louise said, "and then the first right after that. The hotel should be on the right about a block later."

"Easy enough." A few minutes later, I pulled the car into a circular drive before a lovely redbrick building. According to the information we had found online, the Hindman Hotel was originally built as a home for a local family of prosperous merchants in the late nineteenth century. At some point the family fortunes shifted and the house became the property of an ambitious hotelier. Alas, this building was all that was left of his once hopeful empire.

The Ducote sisters had reserved the entire hotel, with its twenty bedrooms, several of which were luxurious suites, for the week of our gathering. The pictures we saw online promised a beautiful setting for our stay here, and I had selected one of the small suites for Helen Louise, Diesel, and me. Miss An'gel had assured me that Diesel would be welcome at the hotel. I would have left him home otherwise, albeit reluctantly.

I opened my door, got out, then stuck my head in to ask Helen Louise if she wanted to go in with me. Diesel took that as his signal to jump into my vacated seat and then out onto the driveway. "You stay right there, boy," I told him in a stern tone. He warbled.

"You two go on in," Helen Louise said. "I'll stay here."

"Okay." I shut the door and glanced down at my cat. "You stay right by my side, you hear?"

Diesel warbled again, and he stuck by me all the way to the reception desk inside. He looked around the whole time, his nose occasionally quivering as it caught some intriguing scent. When I stopped at the desk, however, he sat by my feet and stayed there.

A young man stepped up to the desk from a door in the back. "Good morning, sir." He gave me a toothsome smile. "How may I assist you?" His name tag read Arthur. Tall, muscular, and handsome, he looked to be in his early twenties.

"Good morning, Arthur." I introduced myself. "I have a reservation for this week."

Arthur nodded. "Yes, Mr. Harris." His fingers tapped at the keyboard, and after a moment he said, "A reservation for yourself and Miss Brady, as well as a cat." He frowned. "There must be some mistake. We don't allow animals unless they are service animals. Is your cat a service animal?"

"No, he is not," I said.

"Then I'm afraid we can't allow him." Arthur frowned.

"I was assured that I would be allowed to bring the cat. Miss An'gel Ducote, who arranged to reserve the whole hotel for the week, told me so."

Arthur swallowed as his eyes grew wide. "Oh yes, Miss Ducote," he said, his voice almost a whisper. "Then there is no problem, Mr. Harris. My apologies." Arthur now became obsequious almost to the point of irritation. He babbled about numerous amenities, then tapped a bell for a bellman, and kept assuring me that I would love the hotel and so on.

I suppressed a grin. I had seen this effect before. Miss An'gel had a forceful personality, and not many, certainly not this youth, could withstand it.

The bellman, a man about forty, appeared, and Arthur directed him to the car. "Suite four," he said. "Thomas will bring your bags up to your suite, and if you'll leave him your keys, he will also park your car for you. Valet service is included."

"Thank you, Thomas," I said. "The keys are in the car along with the other member of our party, my fiancée, Helen Louise Brady."

Thomas nodded, his eyes fixed on Diesel, who had approached him to sniff at his shoes. "Does he bite or scratch?" Thomas asked, his voice steady.

"No," I said. "He's friendly."

Thomas rubbed Diesel's head after the cat sniffed his fingers. "He's the biggest cat I've ever seen outside of a zoo."

I explained about the Maine Coon breed, and Thomas nodded. I noticed that Arthur appeared rooted behind the desk, though he was peering over it at my cat.

Thomas left to take care of the bags and the car, and Helen Louise appeared moments later. Arthur escorted us to our suite on the second floor. He opened the door with a flourish and stepped aside, waving us into the room. "I'm sure you'll be very happy with your accommodations."

Diesel preceded us into the suite, and at first glance, I decided Arthur was correct. The suite had beautiful furnishings, reminiscent of a bygone era of luxury. Everything looked perfect.

Except for the body sprawled on the sofa.

Helen Louise bumped into me when I stopped suddenly, aghast at the sight of an apparent corpse on the sofa. The woman lay supine on the sofa, her head turned into the back cushions, her right arm dangling onto the floor.

Oh no, not again, I thought. *We've only just arrived, and already . . .*

"What's wrong?" Helen Louise asked as she stepped around me. "Oh, good heavens. Is she dead?"

"Dead?" Arthur hurriedly moved past us, accompanied by Diesel. The cat trotted over to sniff at the hand lying on the carpet.

"She's not dead, not even dead drunk," Arthur said in an irritated tone as he bent over the body and gave it a shake. "Cora, wake up. Wake up, right this minute."

Relieved that we hadn't stumbled onto a corpse our first few minutes in Asheville, I watched in fascination as Cora woke slowly from her nap and pushed herself up gingerly into a sitting position. Obviously disoriented, she blinked at Arthur, then at us. Diesel rubbed his head against her legs, and she emitted a squeak of surprise. When she saw the cat, she smiled. She wore a scrap of cloth embroidered with lace on the top of her head, held in place with a large jeweled pin that reminded me of my grandmother's hatpins. The effect was decidedly old-fashioned, and she smoothed it into place with one hand while she continued to stroke Diesel with the other, with mixed results.

"I must apologize for this." Arthur frowned. "Cora has narcolepsy, you see."

"I'm real sorry." Cora's voice had a nasal twang. She got up from the sofa, her expression one of embarrassment. "Sometimes it just comes over me, and I can't help myself."

Helen Louise said, "We certainly understand. I'm sure it must be difficult for you."

Arthur continued to frown. He hissed something at Cora under his breath, and she turned an indignant look on him. "Of course I finished the room, Mr. Smarty Arty. I don't never fall asleep when I'm working. It happens when I stop. You oughta know that by now." She looked at us. "I sat down, only for a minute, you see, and before I knew it I was so tired I passed out like that."

Diesel meowed in sympathy, and Cora smiled at him. Arthur eyed the cat with a moue of distaste. He obviously was no ailurophile.

"There's really no harm done," I said in as patient a tone as I could muster. "If you'll excuse us now. We'd like to freshen up after our drive this morning."

Arthur started. "Certainly. Come along, Cora." He hurried

her along in front of him and pulled the door shut softly behind them.

Helen Louise laughed. "That gave me quite a start, I don't mind telling you. I was afraid we'd walked right into another murder investigation."

I had to laugh also. Diesel warbled and jumped onto the sofa. He regarded us quizzically, as if he wondered what we found so amusing. "I'd never have guessed she was a narcoleptic housekeeper. Poor woman."

"No, how could you?" Helen Louise giggled.

"I wonder if Miss An'gel and Miss Dickce have encountered Cora in her sleep state." I surveyed the room, furnished comfortably in an English country house style I found attractive. The sitting room of the suite was about the size of my den at home. Not large, but of a pleasing size that could accommodate a small group of eight or ten, perhaps. I spotted a door to the right and headed for it.

"Come look at the bedroom," I said.

Helen Louise came to stand beside me, and together we beheld the beautiful canopied bed. The furnishings in this room followed the theme of the sitting room, and the space was again a comfortable size. A large wardrobe stood against one wall beside a large window. On the opposite wall I noticed a door that must lead into the bathroom.

"Lovely room," Helen Louise said. "I think we'll be fine here for the week."

I went over to sit on the bed. "Nice and firm. No back problems sleeping on this mattress, I should think." Diesel joined me on the bed and stretched out.

A knock sounded at the suite door, and I went to admit the

bellman with our luggage on a large cart. He brought everything into the bedroom. I gave him a healthy tip, and he smiled his thanks as he handed over the car keys. "The car is parked behind the hotel, sir."

I saw him out, and when I returned to the bedroom, Helen Louise was busy unpacking. Diesel remained on the bed, seemingly quite comfortable, but I knew I needed to get his litter box set up. I filled his water and dry food bowls as well.

That task accomplished, I unpacked my own things. When I finished, I checked the time. A few minutes to one. I realized I was hungry.

"How about lunch?" I asked.

"I think I could manage a bite or two," Helen Louise said.

Diesel meowed.

"You'll have to stay here, boy," I said, "but you've got everything you need. Come and see."

The cat followed me into the bathroom, and I pointed out his food and water bowls. He immediately headed to the bowls, and I left him and returned to Helen Louise in the sitting room.

She held the remote control for the television and was surfing the channels. She paused on a channel with a program about animals and turned the sound up a couple of levels, and we left the suite to go in search of lunch.

"I checked into the restaurant's ratings," Helen Louise remarked as we walked down the stairs in the center of the hallway. "Consistently excellent reviews, so I think we should be well fed this week. Apparently it's quite a popular spot with locals."

Downstairs we found Arthur once again resident behind the front desk. He directed us to the dining room, down the hall near reception.

To our great pleasure we found our friends Miss An'gel and Miss Dickce there along with their ward, Benjy Stephens. Benjy rose at once in greeting when he saw us, and the sisters professed their happiness at our safe arrival.

After shaking hands with Benjy and giving Miss An'gel and Miss Dickce quick hugs, Helen Louise and I took seats at their table as they insisted we do. They had come down for lunch only a few minutes ahead of us. We exchanged remarks on the beauty of the area and responded to queries about our drive from the Gatlinburg area to Asheville. The sisters and Benjy had driven from Athena by way of Atlanta and had arrived yesterday.

"Was there any problem with bringing Diesel into the hotel?" Miss An'gel asked.

"Not after we mentioned your name," Helen Louise said with an impish grin.

"Good," Miss An'gel said. "We left Peanut and Endora at home to keep Clementine company." Clementine was the Ducotes' housekeeper. "In fact, she insisted."

"She doesn't like being alone in the house," Benjy said.

"I must say I'm relieved that we didn't bring them," Miss Dickce said. "As much as I miss having them nearby, I hate to think of having to lock them up in the room here whenever we leave the hotel."

For a moment I felt terribly guilty for leaving Diesel in our room, but I doubted the hotel's graciousness toward his presence would extend to his appearance in the dining room.

"Is the whole group here now?" I asked, feeling the need to change the subject.

"There are a few who should be arriving this afternoon," Miss Dickce said. "Then we'll all be present and accounted for."

Our server approached with menus for Helen Louise and me, and after taking our drink orders, left with a promise to return shortly. Helen Louise was already busy inspecting the menu, and I knew she would select something we would both enjoy.

"We had the oddest experience when we walked into our suite," I said. Before I could continue, Miss Dickce giggled, and Miss An'gel stiffened.

Benjy grinned. "Let me guess. You found a body on the sofa."

I had to laugh. "I see you've met Cora as well."

"Gave me the fright of my life," Miss Dickce said. "A body sprawled out on the sofa."

"The poor girl." Miss An'gel shook her head. "I know that her condition must be a sad trial to her, but it is mighty disconcerting to hotel guests."

"Was she employed here when you last visited?" Helen Louise closed the menu and laid it aside.

The server returned with our sweet teas and asked if we were ready to order.

Helen Louise responded. "We will both have the smothered chicken, along with the braised mixed vegetables and the house salad with the balsamic vinaigrette dressing on the side."

The server, a young man barely out of high school, or so he appeared to me, glanced nervously at me. I smiled reassuringly. He then nodded and walked away. I supposed he wasn't used to women ordering for the men accompanying them. I always found such reactions amusing, albeit a bit antiquated.

"Now, back to Cora." Helen Louise repeated her question.

"No, she was not," Miss An'gel said. "We were last here, what? Three years ago?" She looked at her sister.

"Four, I believe," Miss Dickce said, her tone decisive.

"It sure is a beautiful hotel," Benjy said. "And from what little I've seen of Asheville, there's history everywhere."

"Yes indeed," Miss An'gel said. "We'll have some opportunities to experience an important part of the town's history when we visit Biltmore."

We chatted for a few minutes about the Vanderbilt family and their history. Our server arrived with salads and a fresh basket of bread. Benjy, at twenty, had a healthy appetite and a metabolism to match, and he had been steadily depleting the original basket of its contents while we talked.

The cuisine sustained the reputation Helen Louise had found online. We all enjoyed the meal thoroughly, along with the conversation. I regretfully declined the chance of pecan praline pie for dessert, though I promised myself at least one slice before the week was out.

As we left the table, Miss An'gel offered to show us the meeting room allotted to the group during our stay here. "It was originally the parlor, but it has been modified somewhat to suit the needs of the hotel for meeting spaces. Still, I think you'll find it comfortable."

We followed Miss An'gel from the dining room across the entryway, nodding at Arthur in reception along the way. He appeared to be standing at rigid attention upon sight of Miss An'gel, and I suppressed a chuckle. I could have sworn I heard his exhalation of relief once he was out of Miss An'gel's sight.

Benjy stepped forward to open the door, then stood back to let the rest of us precede him into the room. The thick door and walls had evidently muffled the sound of the argument that burst upon us the moment Benjy opened the door. A young man and an older woman stood only a few feet apart. I had trouble understanding them because they spoke at the same time. Neither appeared to be listening to the other.

Miss An'gel cleared her throat loudly, and the combatants stopped, turning expressions of mixed hostility and surprise toward us.

I recognized them—Zac Ryan and Ellie Arnold, both members of the Athena Public Library mystery group. Zac, a young man in his later twenties, had recently moved to Athena to teach art history at Athena College. Apparently he was something of a wunderkind, having earned his PhD at twenty-four and worked for two famous East Coast museums for a few years. Ellie, perhaps a decade older than Zac, had lived most of her life in my hometown. She worked in the largest bank in town as a loan officer. Helen Louise knew her from church, but I knew her only through the group. I wouldn't have thought Ellie and Zac were acquainted well enough to be arguing like this. Maybe Zac had applied for a loan and had been turned down. I was surprised to see Ellie. I hadn't known she planned to join the group this week.

Ellie glared at Miss An'gel, then turned her focus back to Zac Ryan. "I'll settle up with you later, you little rat." She pushed her way abruptly through our group in the doorway and disappeared up the stairs.

THREE

I hoped the coming week wouldn't be fraught with tension between Zac and Ellie. One of the purposes of this so-called mystery retreat was for the group to get to know one another better. Our two monthly meetings thus far hadn't given us much time to socialize. The other was to share the mutual love of mystery fiction by talking about our favorite writers. The Ducote sisters, founders of the group, had underwritten the trip, unbeknownst to most of the members, to make it affordable for those who couldn't have come up with the money for a week in a boutique hotel like the Hindman. I hoped the sisters wouldn't be rewarded for their generosity by bad behavior and dissension throughout the week.

Zac Ryan, his handsome face now flushed red, stood awkwardly in front of us. I suspected he wanted to run out of the room himself, but for some reason felt unable to.

"Good afternoon, Zac," Miss An'gel said. "I do hope you and Ellie can mend your differences so that we can enjoy ourselves this week." Though her tone was benign, there was yet the air of command about the words.

Zac's expression of chagrin at Miss An'gel's subtle rebuke earned him my sympathy. "I'm sure everyone will do their best to make our time here enjoyable," I said.

Zac threw me a look of gratitude. "Yes, of course, Miss An'gel. Only a little private disagreement between Ellie and me. I promise I won't let it interfere with our plans."

"Thank you." Miss An'gel turned to face the rest of the group. "As I told you, this is a comfortable room, and it is ours exclusively this week. I am really looking forward to our talks." She glanced at her watch. "I'm afraid you'll have to excuse Sister and me. We have an appointment with a dear friend this afternoon. We'll be back in time for our meeting at seven."

Once the sisters left the room, Zac eyed the rest of us a trifle askance. I had encountered him a couple of times on campus since he joined the Athena faculty, once during his orientation tour and another time at a reception for a retiring faculty member from his department. He had always come across as an affable, intelligent, well-spoken young man, and I wondered what had caused the obvious discord between him and Ellie Arnold.

None of my business, however. The best we could do at the moment was to ignore the fact that we had found him in an embarrassing situation.

"Zac, it's good to see you again." I stepped forward and thrust out my hand. "Charlie Harris. I'm the archivist and rare books cataloger at the college." I turned to indicate Helen Louise and introduced her as my fiancée.

Zac nodded in acknowledgment of my introductions. "I've eaten several times at your bistro." He smiled at Helen Louise. "The food is always delicious."

"Thank you," Helen Louise said. "I've seen you in the bistro, and it's nice now to have a name to go with the face."

Zac's gaze shifted past Helen Louise and me and settled on Benjy. I motioned for Benjy to step forward, and he did so, a bit shyly as was his wont. I tended to think of Benjy as a boy, because he had been young for his age when he first came to stay with Miss An'gel and Miss Dickce. But after nearly two years with them, he had developed into a man, nearly as tall as Zac, with excellent manners and a respectful deference to his seniors. I made the introduction, and Benjy shook hands. Zac greeted him warmly and the two stood there smiling intently at each other.

"So this is where we're going to be meeting." The booming voice came from somewhere behind me, and I turned quickly to see Johnny Ray Floyd striding toward the group. Johnny Ray with his compact, broad torso was probably a foot shorter than I was, and I topped off at about six foot one. His powerful shoulders strained the seams of his ill-fitting dress shirt, and the rolled-up sleeves exposed his muscular arms. I hadn't seen him in anything other than his work clothes before today because he usually came right from work to the group meetings at the public library. He ran his own highly successful plumbing company, and his mother was one of my housekeeper's close friends. Whenever there was any kind of plumbing issue at my house, Johnny

Ray came himself. He had the friendliness of an overgrown puppy, and despite the occasional coarse expression he dropped into conversation, he was a bright, articulate member of the group.

I stepped forward to offer my hand. "Hi, Johnny Ray. Glad you could make it. How's the family?"

"Hey there, Charlie, and Helen Louise." He winked at her, and Helen Louise laughed. He was an incorrigible flirt. "Family's doing great. Lou's upstairs with the twins. When I left to come down here, she was thinking about tying them to chairs in the suite to keep 'em quiet, and the oldest is in his room reading."

"He takes after his dad," Helen Louise said.

Johnny Ray chuckled. "He sure does. Rather have a book any day than something else. Just like me when I was a kid."

Zac and Benjy broke off their conversation to greet the newcomer, and Johnny Ray shook their hands and exchanged pleasantries. "Who else is here?" Johnny Ray asked.

"The Ducotes, of course," I said, nodding toward Benjy, "and Ellie Arnold. I think everyone is supposed to be here by this afternoon."

I glanced over Johnny Ray's shoulder to see two more members of the group approaching. Burdine and Elmore Gregory, a long-married couple in their early seventies, strode into the room in their usual hearty fashion. They had retired a few months ago from a successful chiropractic practice. I remembered Aunt Dottie talking about Burdine and how good a chiropractor she was. By the time I moved back, they had shut down to retire.

Based on my own experiences with the couple, the best adjective I could ever find to describe the pair was enthusiastic. They loved books, and nature, and British television crime shows, and they shared their love of these with anyone and everyone they met, whether the persons they encountered wanted them to or not.

The Gregorys meant no harm, and I tolerated them as best as I could, but after a while, that unending enthusiasm wore me down. They were indefatigable members of the group, and I would simply have to be patient. Not one of my strengths, but I could use the practice, the Lord only knew.

Another round of greetings ensued, and when I had the opportunity, I explained that the Ducotes would join us this evening and that Ellie Arnold was here as well.

"We saw Melba earlier in the dining room," Burdine said. "She was eating with Paul Bowen." She tittered. "I can tell Melba is smitten. He is a hunk, even if he is a bit younger than she is. Can't say I blame her. If it weren't for Elmore, this gal would be going after Paul herself."

Elmore looked pained. His wife's occasional displays of vulgarity bothered him, I knew, but they appeared devoted to each other nevertheless.

Paul Bowen, a banker who worked at the same bank as Ellie Arnold, was probably in his early to mid-forties, whereas Melba Gilley, my longtime friend, was my age, early fifties. Melba had a history of bad luck with men, and I could only hope that Paul, should he be interested in her, would be a good match. I loved Melba like a sister, but she seemed jinxed sometimes.

I didn't know Paul, except through the group, but he had always seemed like a pleasant man. His contributions to the group revealed his ability to articulate his thoughts with clarity and conciseness. He possessed a wry sense of humor as well, and his favorite crime writer was Craig Rice, known for her humorous hard-boiled novels.

I mentally ticked off the members of the group who had agreed to this trip, and all were accounted for now except one, Celia Bernardi. A widow of many years, Celia was nearest the Ducote sisters in age, though she acted like a woman close to her deathbed in marked contrast to the sisters' vitality. She bemoaned her ailments during the group's meetings, but no one had the heart to tell her to stop except for Miss An'gel. Miss An'gel managed to quell Celia when necessary and did so in a polite but no-nonsense fashion. To others, Celia appeared perfectly healthy, with a rosy complexion and no obvious physical issues. I suspected that she made hypochondria her hobby, particularly since she appeared to have no family to occupy her time and interest.

"Has anyone seen Celia today?" I asked. Perhaps she had changed her mind at the last minute and decided to stay home. She had appeared to be excited about the trip and the group activities at the last meeting in Athena, though, so I hoped that wasn't the case.

"Yes, she was in the dining room earlier," Elmore Gregory said, "moaning about arthritis or rheumatism. Can't remember which, poor old girl." He shook his head.

Burdine snorted. "Nothing poor about her. I keep telling you, she's perfectly healthy for her age. She could keep up with you and me on the trail any day, if she'd just get up out of that recliner and move around. Don't be wasting any sympathy on her."

Elmore glowered at his wife. "You're too hard on her, Burdy.

Poor woman all alone like that. And I'd like to know when and where you got your medical training, diagnosing everybody like you do."

I uttered silent thanks that Burdine did not deign to respond to this challenge from Elmore; otherwise we would have had to stand there while they argued. My impression of their relationship was that they thrived on conflict with each other. I had known other couples who had a similar dynamic. The arguments kept them invigorated rather than exhausted, as I would have been. Helen Louise and I had quite a different relationship, one based on harmony and mutual love and respect.

"I wonder if anyone has told Celia where we'll be meeting," Helen Louise said to me in an undertone while Johnny Ray chatted with the Gregorys. Once again Zac and Benjy were chatting, apart from the group.

"Surely Arthur did," I said. "He impresses me as the type of person who fulfills instructions to the letter. Wouldn't you say so?"

Helen Louise nodded. "Yes, and if it weren't for Miss An'gel, Diesel would have to sleep in the car."

I laughed. "Thank goodness for Miss An'gel."

"And Miss Dickce," Helen Louise added. "She's as formidable in her way as Miss An'gel."

"True," I said. "Especially behind the wheel."

Helen Louise snickered. "Benjy told me he insists on driving whenever he's in the car with her. She scares him to death."

"She'd terrify a Formula One racer," I said, recalling with a shudder the one short car trip I had made with her.

"She swears that, in over sixty years of driving, she's never had an accident," Helen Louise said.

“I wonder if Miss An’gel would concur,” I said wryly.

Any further consideration of Miss Dickce’s driving record ended abruptly as the sound of shrill screams penetrated the room.

Everyone froze momentarily; then in a burst of movement, we all headed for the door at the same time.

FOUR

We all managed to get out of the room without trampling one another, but we came to an abrupt halt outside. I tried to determine where the screams had come from.

They started again, then suddenly choked off. The sound lasted long enough, however, to indicate the place of origin. Up the main staircase on the second floor. Zac and Benjy reacted more quickly than anyone else and bounded up the stairs two or three at a time.

Helen Louise and I followed more carefully, one step at a time. From behind me I heard Johnny Ray Floyd insisting to the Gregorys that the three of them should remain downstairs, and I silently blessed him for that.

Helen Louise and I found Zac and Benjy in the doorway of the guest room closest to the landing. They moved into the room as we approached. The occupant turned out to be Celia Bernardi and she had apparently found Cora asleep in a chair. Having thought the maid was dead, as she now explained to Zac and Benjy, she had screamed. The screams woke Cora, and her resulting movements startled Celia so much that she screamed again before Cora could reassure her that she was perfectly all right.

Celia suddenly collapsed toward Benjy, who stood nearest her, and he managed to catch her before she fell to the floor. With Zac's assistance, Benjy maneuvered the now swooning woman to the chair vacated by Cora, who stood looking worried near the door into the hall. Helen Louise suggested that I get Celia a glass of water, and I hurried into the bathroom.

I returned moments later and found Celia coming to, with Helen Louise chafing her hands. Helen Louise took the glass of water and held it to the woman's lips. She told Celia to have a sip, and the woman complied. The color had returned to Celia's face, and she appeared to be mostly recovered. Benjy and Zac indicated that they would be downstairs, and I nodded as they made their escape.

Cora, after one last muttered apology, hurried after the young men. I knew little about narcolepsy, but it seemed to me that Cora's case could be a severe one, if she dropped off every time she sat down on the job. If she kept startling guests this way, I would expect the owner of the hotel might rethink the decision to hire her. She might be an exceptionally competent maid, but this might not be the best working environment for her.

"I feel such a fool," Celia said wearily as she handed the empty glass to Helen Louise.

"Why on earth should you?" Helen Louise said in a tone of surprise. "Neither Charlie nor I screamed when we found Cora asleep on the sofa in our room, but I can tell you I was hard-pressed not to."

A weak smile rewarded Helen Louise's statement. "Thank you, my dear." Celia's eyes held a momentary twinkle as she looked up at me. "I should think by now Charlie at least would be used to stumbling over corpses."

"I never expect to find one," I said, my tone a bit stiff. "And actually I haven't found that many dead bodies, although I have assisted in several murder investigations."

"I see." Celia regarded me with what I interpreted as a skeptical mien. "That's as may be, but I'd be perfectly happy for you not to find one this week. I don't think my nerves could stand the real thing, after the fright I've had with a pretend corpse."

"Can we get you anything before we go?" Helen Louise said, and I silently blessed her. I wanted to get out of Celia's room before she made any other remarks about my sleuthing. She always managed to annoy me. I shouldn't have let her get to me, but I'd known her for years. She had been a friend of my mother's, though considerably younger. Even when my mother was still alive, Celia had a gift for poking at a sore spot.

"No, thank you," Celia said. "I'm quite recovered now. You could tell me, however, are An'gel and Dickce here?"

"They've gone to visit friends," I said. "They'll be back in time for the group gathering this evening at seven downstairs." I described the location of the room, and Celia nodded.

"Thank you," she said when I finished. "Now, I'm sure you have far better things to do than minister to my needs."

Resisting the urge to respond with a tart *You bet we do,* I simply nodded, and Helen Louise smiled. We left her to her own devices.

In the hall outside, I paused to ask Helen Louise what she'd like to do next, after ascertaining that none of the group was waiting for us. A quick look down the stairs assured me that they hadn't lingered there for us.

"I'd like to go to the room and relax for a while," Helen Louise said.

"Same here." We headed for our room. "I know Diesel will be delighted to have us back with him. I don't really like leaving him completely alone, even with the television on, for too long at a time."

Diesel was sitting right inside the door when we walked into the room. He glared up at me and warbled several times.

"Yes, I know," I said, my tone apologetic. "We didn't mean to leave you all by yourself for quite this long." I rubbed his head, and Helen Louise stroked his back. That appeased him, and he ambled over to the sofa with us, stretching out across our laps after we seated ourselves. Helen Louise got his head in her lap, while I got the legs and the huge fluffy tail that twitched in my face.

"I hope you're happy now," I told the cat. He meowed, shifted onto his back, and gazed up at Helen Louise. She stroked his belly, and he began to purr.

"He's exacting penance from us, you know," Helen Louise said with a snort of laughter.

"And we're being penitent enough to let him get away with it," I replied.

After a minute or so of this treatment, Diesel tired of it and shifted his position again so that he lay on his side across our laps. He closed his eyes and appeared to go to sleep.

Helen Louise and I stared at each other. I shrugged. I was comfortable as I was, and she indicated that she was, too. *At least for now*, I thought.

"This is definitely an interesting group you've got," Helen Louise said. "I wonder how we're all going to get along, spending so much time together this week."

"I haven't the foggiest," I said. "At some point I might be tempted to glue Burdine's lips together to keep her quiet."

Helen Louise giggled. "Charlie, that's terrible. But I understand how you feel. She and Elmore bicker like some people breathe, I swear."

My mind had already shifted to another member of the group. "Did you notice the way that Zac seemed to glom onto Benjy? They seemed to really hit it off."

"Well, I'm fairly certain Zac is gay," Helen Louise said. "He may well be attracted to Benjy. I haven't thought about this until now, but I don't think Benjy has really decided exactly what he is yet. He's a smart young man, and he'll figure it all out when he's ready. Miss An'gel and Miss Dickce will support him, no matter what."

"Now that he's going to Athena College," I said, "he's getting plenty of exposure to others his age through his classes. That should help him a lot."

"True," Helen Louise said, "but I've sometimes sensed there is a part of Benjy that always holds back. He seems to observe most of the time, rather than to participate." She shook her head. "Pay no mind to me. It's probably just my imagination."

"No, I think you're right," I said after thinking about what she'd said for a moment. "Benjy's experiences have taught him to be cautious, I reckon, but I think Miss An'gel and Miss Dickce are doing a great job with him. Miss Dickce adores him, and he adores her."

"We strayed from the point a bit," Helen Louise said. "Zac

might be interested in Benjy—he's a handsome young man. But Benjy will have to sort that out himself. Right now I'm really curious about that scene we interrupted between Zac and Ellie Arnold. What was that all about?"

"She called him a little rat, didn't she?"

"When a woman calls a man a rat," Helen Louise said, one eyebrow arched, "that usually means he's done her wrong."

"Romantically?" I asked, interested.

Helen Louise nodded. "Usually. I don't know Ellie well, but given what I know of Zac, and given whom I've seen Zac with, I don't see a romantic connection at all. That's why it puzzles me."

"Maybe Ellie fell for Zac, not realizing he's probably not interested in women," I said.

"Possibly," Helen Louise said, "but that doesn't always deter a woman. There are still women around who think they can change men."

I chuckled, remembering a few of the stories Stewart Delacorte, who along with his partner, Haskell Bates, occupied a suite of rooms on the third floor of my house, had told me about his own experiences.

"What's so funny?" Helen Louise asked.

"Oh, thinking about Stewart. He told me a few stories about women who tried to change him," I said. "Back to Ellie and Zac, however. Do you really think that argument was about a relationship gone wrong?"

Helen Louise shrugged. "It could be all in her head, of course. I was simply explaining the context in which I think women usually call men a rat."

"Good to know," I said. "I hope that Ellie won't make difficulties this week over whatever the issue is between them."

"Ditto for Zac," Helen Louise said, a sharp note in her voice. "It isn't only women who make difficulties, you know."

"I do. I'm sorry," I said.

Diesel meowed loudly and began to stir. He squirmed around until he sat between us on the sofa. He yawned before he put a paw on my leg.

"What do you think he wants?" Helen Louise asked.

"I think he wants to go for a w-a-l-k," I replied.

Diesel chirped happily, and I shot Helen Louise a rueful grin.

"He even knows what it is when I spell it," I said. "He's used to going outside most days, so I should probably take him down to the garden and let him sniff around."

More warbling convinced me that was indeed the thing to do.

Helen Louise chuckled and stroked the cat's head while I retrieved his harness and leash. Diesel behaved well most of the time, but in strange surroundings I thought it best to make sure he was safely tethered to me. He was a beautiful animal, and I didn't want to take any chances that someone might try to steal him or hurt him.

"Let me visit the powder room," Helen Louise said as she rose from the sofa, "and I'll go with you. We can come back afterward and have a snooze."

"Sure." By the time she returned, I had Diesel harnessed and ready to go.

Instead of taking the elevator, we decided to walk down the stairs. Diesel looked about as we walked, occasionally pausing to sniff the carpet and often making the muttering sound that never failed to amuse me. He sounded like an elderly man grumbling about the state of the world.

As we neared the head of the stairs, ready to start down, I

could hear loud voices emanating from somewhere below us. Helen Louise and I exchanged startled glances. "What now?" I said.

"Heaven only knows," Helen Louise replied. "Maybe Cora has frightened yet another guest."

When we reached the bottom of the stairs, we could see that the source of the argument was a man in his late forties who faced Arthur across the reception desk. At the moment the stranger simply stood and glared at the clerk, and Arthur stared back at him.

"As I have informed you," Arthur said in the tone that signals the speaker is about to lose his temper, "every single room is booked this week by a group, even though we do have empty rooms. We can't possibly give you a room without the permission of the group leaders."

"I know about the group," the stranger replied, his tone a match for Arthur's. "That's what I keep telling you."

"And I keep telling you your name isn't on the list. There's no mention of a Denis Kilbride anywhere."

Denis Kilbride drew a deep breath himself. "Then that's my fiancée's fault. She's always careless about details. Get on that phone and call Ellie Arnold and let her know I'm here."

FIVE

So Ellie Arnold was engaged to be married. In the group's meetings she rarely shared anything personal, so this news came as a surprise, at least to me.

Helen Louise, Diesel, and I had paused at the foot of the stairs, not wanting to intrude, but now Kilbride caught sight of us. I didn't really know the man, but I recognized him as a prominent businessman in Athena who owned significant rental properties in town. I had also occasionally seen him in Helen Louise's bistro, and she had once or twice mentioned that he had hired her to cater a few meetings for him.

Seeing Helen Louise, he came forward with a smile and an outstretched hand. "Helen Louise, great to see you. Ellie didn't tell me you would be here." He glanced at me. "I know you must be Charlie Harris, and that is Diesel." After shaking my hand, he extended his fingers to the cat.

Diesel gave his fingers a cautious sniff, then meowed. "He's quite a cat," Kilbride said. "I don't envy you your cat food bill." He laughed, and I smiled politely.

"Mr. Kilbride." Arthur motioned for him to approach the desk again.

"Excuse me," Kilbride said as he turned away and walked back to the reception desk. "I need a room with a bathtub, too, not just a shower. I have a bad back, and I'll need to soak in the tub."

I led Helen Louise and Diesel out of the lobby and down the hall to the garden in back of the hotel. We stepped out into the mild afternoon sunshine with a temperature hovering somewhere around seventy-five degrees. The garden occupied about as much square footage as my backyard in Athena, a nice size but not huge.

We followed Diesel as he ambled around, investigating anything that took his fancy, like an herbaceous border around a circular bed of what appeared to be several types of wildflowers. I didn't recognize any of them, but I supposed they were native to the area.

After a few minutes we found a bench under a tree at the back of the garden where we could rest. Diesel stretched out in a patch of sunlight while Helen Louise and I enjoyed the shade. Asheville had an elevation above sea level of over two thousand feet, and the resulting summer climate made it a popular tourist destination. I leaned back against the bench and closed my eyes, enjoying the quiet and the pleasant scents wafting in the breeze. Helen Louise did the same, and, heads together, we both dozed off.

I awoke sometime later and felt a bit disoriented. I felt Diesel tug at his leash and realized he must have awakened me. As my brain cleared I remembered where we were. "What is it, boy?" I said softly. Helen Louise stirred beside me.

I heard voices and looked in the direction of the sound. At the back entrance to the hotel stood two people chatting. One of them was Melba Gilley, the other her new friend, Paul Bowen. From what I could hear, Melba sounded tense. Their voices were too low for me to make out their words, but the tone was plainly audible.

"Not right now, boy," I said softly. "I think Melba wouldn't want to be interrupted. Let's stay where we are."

Diesel stopped straining at the leash, but he uttered a couple of sad meows. I thought Melba might have heard him because I saw her head twitch briefly in our direction, but her focus snapped right back to Paul Bowen. He had placed his hands on her shoulders and had drawn her closer to him.

I glanced away, not wanting to invade their privacy any more than I already had.

"What do you think is going on over there?" Helen Louise asked, her lips against my ear.

"I don't know," I whispered back. "I think maybe they're having a disagreement."

"They haven't raised their voices," Helen Louise said. "That's a good sign."

I glanced toward the back door and found to my surprise that Paul Bowen had disappeared. Melba stood where he had left her, apparently staring into space. Had he gone to get something? Drinks, perhaps? There were several tables with chairs at one side of the garden.

Melba turned her back to the door and surveyed the garden. I decided it would be okay to let Diesel go to her, and I let go of his leash. "Go ahead, boy. Go see Melba." Diesel meowed before he trotted off in her direction.

I nudged Helen Louise. "I think we'd better follow him." She nodded and rose from the bench alongside me. We stepped out of the shade and headed toward Melba.

Diesel had reached her, and I heard her say, "Sweet boy, what on earth are you doing out here? You're not by yourself, surely." She glanced around and saw us approaching. "Well, thank goodness. I was going to read you the riot act, Charlie Harris, if you'd let this baby out in the garden by himself."

She didn't appear in the least self-conscious. She must have realized that we were in the garden while she was involved in her conversation with Paul Bowen, but she gave no sign that there was any kind of a problem.

Helen Louise and I both hugged her and asked her about her trip to Asheville.

"We spent the night in Atlanta, then drove on over to Asheville yesterday," Melba said. "Paul's car is the most comfortable thing I've ever ridden in, and thank the Lord, he doesn't drive like a speed demon." She scratched Diesel's head and received a happy purring sound in return.

"Sounds like a pleasant trip." Helen Louise shot me a sideways glance.

If Melba was upset with Paul over something, there was no indication of it in her demeanor now. Perhaps we had misread what we had seen a few minutes ago.

"We drove over from Gatlinburg this morning," I said. "Such a beautiful area. I'm so glad we came."

"I'm really looking forward to this." Melba gave the garden an appreciative glance. "I'm thinking it sure would be nice to have coffee out here in the morning, or a drink in the evening."

"As long as the weather stays like this, it would be," Helen Louise said.

"What is Paul up to?" I asked, unable to restrain my curiosity. "Didn't we see him with you a minute or two ago?"

Melba gazed at me with narrowed lids. "He had to make a business call. Why are you so interested?"

I shrugged. I should have been more subtle with my question. "Just wondering. I expect we'll see him later on."

Helen Louise surprised both Melba and me with a sudden question. "Do you know Denis Kilbride?"

"What on earth made you think of him?" Melba asked, obviously puzzled.

"He arrived earlier, before we came out to the garden," I said. "Maybe half an hour ago."

Melba looked thoughtful. "I know him. He's been bird-dogging Ellie for the past few months. I can't believe he followed her all the way here."

"He told the desk clerk, Arthur, that Ellie is his fiancée," Helen Louise said.

"That'll be news to Ellie, I expect." Melba snorted derisively. "She'll have a fit when she finds out he's here."

"Is he a stalker?" I asked bluntly.

"I don't know if I'd go that far." Melba seemed hesitant. "He's used to getting what he wants, and he wants Ellie."

"How well do you know her?" Helen Louise asked.

Diesel strained at the leash suddenly, catching me off guard. I dropped the leash, and the cat shot off toward a corner of the garden.

"Diesel, you come back here." I rarely raised my voice to the cat, but this kind of behavior frightened me. He had probably seen a bird or a squirrel.

When I caught up to him a few minutes later, he was rooting under a bush. I picked up the leash and admonished him. "Bad boy, Diesel. Bad boy." I flapped the leash lightly to get his attention.

"Everything okay?" Helen Louise spoke from behind me. I turned to see her steps away, Melba nowhere in sight.

Diesel removed himself from under the bush and chirped and warbled at me.

"No harm done, I guess," I replied. "He must have seen a critter and couldn't resist going after it."

Diesel now sat at my feet and gazed up at me, looking innocent and carefree, except for a smudge of dirt in his whiskers.

Helen Louise chuckled and reached down to brush the dirt away. Diesel's nose twitched, and he sneezed. "You were a bad boy to run off like that, sweetie," Helen Louise told him, her tone soft despite the words. "You'd better not do that again."

He warbled, managing somehow to look both sad and contrite.

I chuckled. "Rascal. That's what I should have named him." I gave the leash a gentle tug. "Come on, boy. Let's go back inside." I glanced at Helen Louise. "Is that okay with you?"

She nodded. "I could use a glass of water right about now."

"Same here. Let's go back to the room. I noticed complimentary bottles of spring water on the counter."

I waited until we were back in the room, our thirst quenched, before I queried Helen Louise about what I had missed when Diesel bolted. "What did Melba have to say about Ellie Arnold?" I removed Diesel's harness and leash as we talked.

"She's known her since she was a little girl." Helen Louise laughed. "You might have known. Evidently she used to babysit her. Ellie's family lived on the next street, or something like that."

"Where Melba is concerned, Athena is a small, small town," I said. "It never fails to amaze me how many people she knows, or at least has heard something about from somebody she knows well."

"She's better than the Internet," Helen Louise joked. "She knows things you won't ever find searching the net."

"Did she tell you anything more about Ellie and Denis Kilbride?" I drained my water bottle and set it on the coffee table.

"Kilbride isn't an Athena native," Helen Louise said. "He moved there about a dozen years ago, and Ellie was already working at the bank. Not as a loan officer, though. That came later. That's how they met, actually. A while after Ellie got promoted, Kilbride came into the bank to get financing for one of his business plans, and she handled it."

"Sounds like that was some years ago," I said. "Has he been carrying a torch for her ever since?"

"It was about four years ago," Helen Louise said. "I think that's what Melba told me. After he secured the loan, and everything was set, Kilbride asked Ellie out. He's an attractive man, and she went out with him. And they've been on-again, off-again ever since. Then Paul Bowen appeared, and Melba went off with him."

"I hope Kilbride's being here isn't going to disrupt the group," I said. "We don't need any emotional dramas going on to ruin everything."

"Don't be so pessimistic." Helen Louise reached over to give my hand a squeeze. "I know how open conflict affects you, but I'm betting everyone will behave. Now that Denis Kilbride is here, maybe Ellie will forget about whatever issue she has with Zac, or vice versa."

"I sure hope you're right," I said. Diesel meowed loudly as if in agreement.

"I think we've talked enough about all this," Helen Louise said. "I'm ready for a real nap. How about you?"

"Sounds fine to me." I looked at Diesel. "You stay here, boy, all right?"

The cat looked at me and meowed. He stretched out on the sofa once Helen Louise and I got up and headed for the bedroom. We closed the door behind us and left Diesel to his nap.

SIX

After dinner that evening, the mystery group assembled in the designated meeting room. Miss An'gel and Miss Dickce greeted us as we entered. I had retrieved Diesel from the bedroom and brought him down with us.

I shot Ellie Arnold a curious look. Denis Kilbride had joined her for dinner, and I wondered whether he planned to join the group for its first meeting. He disappeared upstairs after the meal, however, and Ellie came alone into the room. She avoided looking in Zac's direction, I noticed, and he paid her no attention, either.

Miss An'gel, I had little doubt, had the hotel arrange the seating in a loose circle. She and Miss Dickce took chairs side by side, and the rest of us found places on chairs and sofas. Helen Louise and I occupied one of the latter along with Johnny Ray Floyd. Celia Bernardi and Zac Ryan shared the other sofa with Burdine Gregory. Elmore, Benjy, Melba, and Paul Bowen occupied the remaining chairs. Diesel chose to stretch out on the floor beside me at one end of our sofa after greeting most of the group.

"Now that everyone is comfortable," Miss An'gel said, "we shall begin. Sister and I are pleased that so many of the group decided to join us on this little adventure. I believe we're going to have a lot of fun discussing mysteries and their writers, and the highlight might well be tomorrow when we visit Biltmore. Has anyone in the group ever been there before?"

Helen Louise and Celia raised their hands.

"I'm sure you won't mind having a second visit," Miss An'gel said, "especially with the group. I've arranged for Diesel to go along with us, thanks to a special dispensation."

Hearing his name, Diesel meowed, and Miss An'gel smiled. "I'm sure he'll be a perfect gentleman while we're there. We'll meet in the morning at eight for a small bus to take us to Biltmore. Now, for tonight, why don't we take turns talking a little about our favorite classic mystery writers, the ones we'll each be talking more about during the week. We can move on in a few days to more recent writers."

"Sister, you're forgetting something," Miss Dickce said, her tone pointed.

Miss An'gel turned to look at her. "And what, pray tell, is that?"

"Since Sister has forgotten, I'll tell you all about it." Miss Dickce smiled. "The hotel has a list of the best restaurants in town, with varying levels of prices, and all you have to do is ask Arthur at the front desk for a copy. They were supposed to put them in your rooms but that didn't happen. Those of you who have been wanting to try North Carolina barbecue will have several choices."

"Thank you, Sister," Miss An'gel said. "Now, who would like

to talk first?" She looked pointedly at me, and I knew I'd better not ignore the prompt.

"I'll go first," I said at the same moment Burdine Gregory raised her hand.

"Please do, Charlie," Miss An'gel said. "Burdine, you'll be next."

"I'm sure none of you will be surprised by my choice," I said, "because you've heard me mention Margery Allingham a few times before. She is my favorite Golden Age mystery writer."

Benjy's hand shot up. He wasn't a regular member of the group, though I knew he did enjoy reading mysteries. "Excuse me, Charlie, but what is the Golden Age?"

"Good question," I said. "It's the period between the two World Wars when the classic detective story flourished, roughly 1920 to 1940. Some push it a little later, to the end of World War II. It was a time when writers like Agatha Christie, Dorothy L. Sayers, and Margery Allingham flourished and thousands of detective stories were published. They were all chiefly what we would call 'fair play' stories, in which the authors lay out the clues to allow the reader to solve the mystery along with the detective in the book."

"Thanks," Benjy said. "I've read Agatha Christie, and Miss Dickce has some books by a writer named Anthony Gilbert I've read. I think he fits the period."

"Yes, Anthony Gilbert does, though she—and she was a woman named Lucy Malleson—continued writing until around 1970." I glanced around the room. No one was openly yawning, and I took that as a good sign.

"Back to Margery Allingham. She was the creator of Albert Campion, a private detective who lived under a pseudonym. We find out eventually that he's actually a member of the royal family, though not in the direct line of succession, as I recall. His family mostly turns a blind eye to his activities. His stock-in-trade is an air of genial idiocy. He also wears large horn-rimmed spectacles. The villains generally underrate him because he appears foolish to them, but he's actually really clever."

"What is it you admire so much about Allingham?" Paul Bowen asked. "I've seen the name, but I've never read any of her work."

"I love her writing and the creative mind behind it. If you read her books in chronological order of publication," I said, "I think you'll see the way she grew and changed as a writer. She published her first book at sixteen, and she was younger than the other Golden Age queens of crime like Christie and Sayers. You can see the effects of the two World Wars in her work, I believe, in ways that you don't in the others. Sayers, for example, stopped writing mysteries before World War II. Christie continued, but the war really doesn't make much impact in her books. At least not in the way it does in Allingham's work."

"Thank you, Charlie. You know I'm also an Allingham fan, and I think you've given us enough to intrigue those who haven't read her," Miss An'gel said. "Burdine, who's your favorite?"

Burdine leaned forward eagerly. "My favorite authors from this period are Richard and Frances Lockridge. They're Elmore's favorites, too." She glanced briefly at her husband, and he nodded. I had to wonder if they really were Elmore's favorites, or whether Burdine had decided they were. "They wrote the Pam and Jerry North books, about a sophisticated couple in New York who solved mysteries between rounds of cocktails." She laughed. "They also had cats. The best known ones are Martini and her kittens, Gin and Sherry. Pam was the one who actually solved the mysteries. Jerry was a publisher and was there in the background. Pam's logic is a bit screwy, but she always figures things out before Lieutenant Weigand, the New York City cop who's a friend of the Norths."

"Wasn't there a movie with Gracie Allen?" Melba asked, her brow wrinkled. "I'm pretty sure I saw it a few years ago on some old movie channel."

Elmore said, "Yes, she played Pam North in the movie. There was a stage play that was the source for the movie. A radio program and a television series, too. How many of you have read any of the books?"

I raised my hand, as did the Ducotes and Celia Bernardi. I let my gaze roam around the assembled company. Everyone seemed engaged in the meeting, although I did witness covert glances flashing back and forth between Ellie and Zac now, and Zac gazing at Benjy. The latter appeared oblivious to the attention paid to him by Zac.

Burdine took over again. "I love the husband-and-wife team, of course, but it's also that air of New York sophistication and glamor that appeals to me. The mysteries are good, too. Sadly, Frances died in 1963, and Richard stopped writing the series. He did write other mysteries afterward, and he remarried a couple of years after Frances's death. His second wife, Hildegarde Dolson, wrote a few mysteries of her own."

"I love the Lockridges," Celia said. "In fact, I was going to talk about them myself, but Burdine beat me to it." She sounded annoyed.

"Do you have another author you'd like to talk about?" Miss An'gel asked.

Celia shrugged. "I'll have to think about it. Go on to someone else."

Johnny Ray Floyd stuck up his hand. "I can go next, if that's okay."

"Certainly," Miss An'gel said.

"I love Agatha Christie, and I've read some of Ngaio Marsh, too, but my favorites from this period are Americans. Chiefly Rex Stout and Elizabeth Daly. Daly is at the tail end of the Golden Age. She didn't publish her first mystery until she was sixty-two, and that was in 1940. But Rex Stout fits the period. His character was Nero Wolfe, and Wolfe's sidekick was Archie Goodwin. They appeared in 1934 and continued on until Stout's death in 1975."

"I love Archie Goodwin," Ellie Arnold said, a touch of animation in her expression. "Did you see the TV series that Timothy Hutton did? I thought he was great as Archie."

"Yeah, he was good." Johnny Ray nodded. "Got it all on DVD, as well as the one with William Conrad and Lee Horsley. There's even an Italian series I've read about, but I haven't seen it."

"I've always thought it interesting that Nero Wolfe and Archie Goodwin are private detectives," Miss Dickce said. "Archie also functions like a private eye. Do you know what I mean?"

"I think I do," Helen Louise said. "When I think of a private detective, I think of Hercule Poirot, or Miss Maud Silver, Patricia Wentworth's series character. They operate in a more genteel world, while the private eye, like Philip Marlowe or Sam Spade, operates on the mean streets."

"Yeah, that's it," Johnny Ray said eagerly. "Wolfe is like Poirot, the eccentric genius, and Archie is more like Marlowe or

Spade. He gets out on the mean streets and leaves Wolfe in the brownstone where life is real civilized, with orchids and gourmet food."

"Great description, Johnny Ray," I said.

"Thanks, Charlie," he replied.

"Speaking of Patricia Wentworth," Miss Dickce said, "is anyone planning to talk about her and Miss Maud Silver?"

For a moment there was only silence. Then Celia responded in a grudging tone that she guessed she could, since Burdine had scooped her on the Lockridges.

"That's great," Miss Dickce said. "I was hoping someone would."

"If you'd rather talk about her yourself," Celia said, "I can come up with someone else."

I thought she sounded determined to be negative and hoped that we weren't going to be treated to this kind of behavior all week. I suspected that if she kept it up much longer, Miss An'gel would give her a good talking-to, as only she could. She wouldn't let Celia disrupt the meetings in this way.

"No, no, you go ahead," Miss Dickce said. "I'm eager to hear what you have to say about Wentworth. You probably know more about her than I do."

That last sentence was aimed at Celia's vanity, and it apparently hit its target. Celia brightened visibly.

"Patricia Wentworth was a pseudonym," Celia began, but got no further.

The door opened, and Denis Kilbride strode in, his expression stormy. He gazed around the room until his eyes settled on Zac. He advanced upon him, paying no heed to Miss An'gel's attempts to forestall him.

"I don't know what the hell kind of game you think you're playing, but if you don't stop, I'll put an end to it, and you won't like the way I do it." He brandished his right fist.

Zac stood and pushed back his chair. "I don't know what you're talking about, you raving baboon. But you come on at me, I'll have you crying for mercy in three seconds."

Johnny Ray surprised everyone in the room by jumping up from his chair, grabbing Kilbride by the shoulder, and spinning him around. Then, with a neat right hook, he put Kilbride on the floor.

SEVEN

"Looks like he's out cold," I said, shocked by what had occurred seconds before in the meeting room.

Johnny Ray Floyd rubbed his knuckles and appeared quite satisfied with himself. "I've been wanting to do that for six months. I'm glad the jackass gave me a good reason for it."

Zac Ryan laughed. "You saved me the trouble. Thanks." He extended a hand over the prone man, and Johnny Ray took it. They shook briefly, then both stepped back to let Ellie Arnold drop to her knees beside Kilbride.

She patted his cheek gently. "Denis, are you all right? Speak to me, Denis."

In the meantime, Miss An'gel had evidently called the front desk, because Arthur came sauntering in. I would have thought he'd gone off duty by now, but here he was.

"What is going on here?" Arthur looked to Miss An'gel for

an answer after he spotted Denis Kilbride on the floor. "What do you expect me to do about this?"

"This man burst in on the group and behaved in a rude, somewhat threatening manner," Miss An'gel said tartly. "I expect we might possibly need the services of a doctor or nurse. Do you have anyone on call for such things?"

Arthur goggled at her. "Yes, there is a doctor I can call, but wouldn't it be easier to call 911?"

"No need to call either." The shaky voice came from the man on the floor. "Get me some ice, wrapped in a towel, all right?" While shooting daggers at Johnny Ray and Zac, Kilbride endeavored to sit up with Ellie's assistance. "My back is killing me. I've got to get upstairs to my room."

Helen Louise had remained by my side during the altercation, but I suddenly noticed that Diesel was nowhere to be seen. My heart beat furiously at the realization. Had he bolted out the open door of the meeting room?

"Help me find Diesel," I said to Helen Louise. "You look in here, and I'm going to see if he's run out of the room. Please, Lord, let us find him quickly."

I had barely reached the door before Helen Louise called out to me. "Here he is," she said, the relief obvious in her tone. "Under the sofa."

I rushed back to her and got down on my hands and knees to coax my cat out from under the sofa. "It's okay, boy. Everything is all right. You can come on out."

Diesel didn't appear to believe me, but I kept talking to him while the conversation buzzed through the room. I tried to block it out. My sole concern at the moment was Diesel, and I didn't want to have to wait until everyone else had vacated the room to get him to come out.

After three rounds of my litany of reassurance, Diesel crawled out, his leash trailing. I hadn't realized I had let go of it, or he never would have been able to bolt. I sat back on my heels and gathered him closer. I stroked his head and murmured to him. Helen Louise got down on her knees on the other side and also spoke soothingly to him. By the time I thought Diesel was calm enough to release, the room around us had quieted considerably.

I resumed my seat on the sofa, alongside Helen Louise, and Diesel settled by my legs. Denis Kilbride had left the room, along with Ellie Arnold and Arthur the desk clerk supporting him. Everyone else now watched Diesel and me.

"Is Diesel doing okay now?" Miss An'gel's expression of concern touched me.

"He's fine, I think," I replied. "He was startled by the loud argument." I glanced over Helen Louise to Johnny Ray on her other side. "You sure seemed to enjoy that."

Johnny Ray laughed. "You bet I did." He shot a quick look at Miss An'gel. "That jackass did me dirty a few months ago, and I've been looking to pay him back."

"What did he do to you?" Burdine Gregory asked. "He doesn't own a plumbing company, does he?"

"No, he doesn't," Johnny Ray said. "He does go around buying up property, though. I was looking to expand my premises a few months ago, and the empty lot next to my place finally came up for sale. I agreed to the asking price and was all set to finalize it when that bas—um, that jerk came in and offered the seller about twenty percent more, if what I heard is true."

"That's terrible," Burdine said. "Is the property worth that much?"

"Nope," Johnny Ray said. "At least not as an empty lot. Can't figure out why he'd pay so much more than market value for it, unless he thinks there's oil on the property."

"Utterly absurd," Miss An'gel said. "I thought he was a sharp businessman." She frowned. "Did he have any reason to do it out of spite? I have heard he doesn't like being crossed."

Johnny Ray grimaced. "He doesn't like me, because he tried to bully me when I did extensive work on one of his properties. Tried to con me into doing the work at cost, telling me he'd make sure everyone knew I'd done the work. Free advertising, he called it."

"That's outrageous," Helen Louise said, angry on his behalf. "You don't need that kind of advertising. Your reputation is one of the best in Athena."

"That's what I told him, but he still acted like I owed him a favor," Johnny Ray said. "Finally had to threaten to sue him to get him to pay me what he owed me." He glanced at me and grinned. "I sicced my lawyer, Mr. Sean Harris, on him, and he paid up pretty quickly after that."

"I'm glad my son came through for you," I said. I remembered now that Sean had made brief mention of a case a month or so ago about a businessman refusing to pay a debt, but he hadn't told me the names of anyone involved. Sean had called the recalcitrant businessman worse names than jackass, as I suspect Johnny Ray would, too, except for the presence of women in the room.

"Aren't you concerned," I continued, "that he could bring charges against you for assault?"

Johnny Ray shrugged. "He came in behaving in a threatening manner, and I think I was within my rights to do something about that."

"He wasn't threatening you, though," Zac Ryan said. "He was threatening me."

"Don't matter," Johnny Ray said. "He threatened me a couple times back when I was trying to get the money he owed me. Idiot didn't realize I recorded him when he called me. I think all I'd have to do is bring up suing him, and that would be the end of it."

I thought he might be overly optimistic in that regard, but I wasn't going to argue with him.

Melba then put forth the question I thought several of us really wanted to ask. "Zac, why on earth was he threatening you? You're a professor, not a businessman."

Zac shrugged. "Beats me. He must have me confused with someone else."

His tone came off as a bit too nonchalant, I thought. I wasn't convinced by his words, and I imagined that no one else was, either. I fully expected Melba to laugh, but I saw Paul Bowen touch her lightly on the arm. The Ducote sisters eyed him speculatively, and Burdine looked ready to challenge him.

"Whatever the issue is," Miss An'gel said firmly, "I trust you will work it out privately. The group really cannot have this kind of interruption. We came here to enjoy ourselves and share our love of the genre with one another."

Even Burdine, who sometimes misread conversational cues, couldn't misread that one. Zac shot Miss An'gel a look of gratitude, and I wondered what it was he was so anxious to keep covered up.

I knew it was none of my business, but I had begun to get that uneasy feeling there were some potentially dangerous undercurrents in the group. Kilbride was an outsider, in that he wasn't a member of the group, but he obviously had connections with Ellie and Johnny Ray. Apparently with Zac as well. I had to wonder about Paul Bowen, since he was a banker, but I didn't know about Elmore and Burdine. As I recalled now, I'd heard them mention a son, Todd, their only child, who had died recently.

Perhaps there was some kind of triangular relationship, with Zac interested in either Ellie or Kilbride. That could explain the argument we had interrupted earlier today between Zac and Ellie. But maybe my imagination was running away with me, as it often did.

I tuned back in to hear Helen Louise say, "Are we going to wait for Ellie to come back?"

Miss An'gel and Miss Dickce exchanged glances. Then Miss An'gel responded. "No, I don't think so. Perhaps Celia would like to talk about Patricia Wentworth now, unless either Melba or Paul is ready."

Melba shook her head, and Paul deferred to Celia.

Celia offered a gracious smile. "Thank you, Paul. Patricia Wentworth was the pseudonym of Dora Amy Elles Turnbull. She was born in India during the time of the British Raj. I forget exactly where." She paused for a breath. "Her father was a general. She eventually returned to England and at some point started writing novels. Her contribution to the genre was a female professional investigator, Miss Maud Silver. Miss Silver spent many years as a governess, but she decided that she would turn her talents to solving mysteries. Thus she became a private inquiry agent, as she styled herself. She appeared two years before Christie's Miss Jane Marple. The books are about as English and cozy as you can get. Miss Silver knits frequently, usually making something for one of her niece Ethel's growing family. She is extremely sharp and often gets to the solution before the policemen in the case. They, naturally, are in awe of her, and one of her former pupils from her governessing days is one of the policemen she generally encounters."

"I think you've hit the nail right on the head," I said. "The Miss Silver books are as cozy as they come. If you want to retreat from the world, brew yourself a pot of tea and settle down with Wentworth."

Celia nodded approvingly. "Perfect escape reading. Though she's best known for the Silver books, she wrote just as many books, I believe, without her—all mystery or suspense stories."

"Thank you, Celia," Miss An'gel said.

Before she could continue, Ellie came back into the room. She went straight to Miss An'gel. "I'm so sorry about all this. I had no idea Denis was going to show up here." Her hands clenched. "I'm horribly embarrassed that he should have caused such a scene."

"Ellie, dear," Miss Dickce said, "it's not your fault. You are not to blame for Mr. Kilbride's poor behavior."

"Sister is right," Miss An'gel said. "It was an unfortunate scene, but it might have been far worse if Johnny Ray hadn't intervened." She cast a stern glance at Johnny Ray.

Ellie forged ahead. "If you'd like me to forgo our activities this week, I'm fully prepared to pack up and head home tomorrow morning."

A chorus of protests arose. I don't think any of us held Ellie to blame, but for my part, I did hope she, or someone, could persuade Denis Kilbride to behave more circumspectly. We couldn't have him barging into our meetings threatening violence.

"I don't think you need to do that," Miss An'gel said. "I will have a talk with Mr. Kilbride in the morning and make it plain that any further such behavior will not be tolerated."

Ellie, as well as everyone else in the room, had no doubt that Miss An'gel would put the fear of God into Denis Kilbride. She was the most formidable person I'd ever known, and if anyone could get through to Kilbride, Miss An'gel would.

If he didn't shape up, his goose was cooked.

EIGHT

Miss An'gel had instructed us at the end of our meeting last night that we had to be on our minibus and ready to go no later than seven-thirty this morning. Anyone who turned up late would miss the Biltmore tour. We were being admitted at eight a.m., an hour before tours for the general public began, and we must be on time.

This strict insistence on punctuality didn't bother me, nor did it irk Helen Louise. Unpunctuality has long been one of my pet peeves, and Helen Louise, as a successful business owner, was perfectly aware of the value of time. The two of us and Diesel were on the bus and settled by seven twenty-five, along with Melba and Paul. Miss An'gel, Miss Dickce, and Benjy greeted us when we came aboard.

I figured at least one person would miss the departure time, because in my experience of groups, there was always one person who had not the least regard for time. I have always considered it excessively ill-mannered to keep people waiting. I knew Miss An'gel felt the same and took it as a personal insult when she encountered what we both felt was rudeness. Naturally, there were times when persons were unavoidably detained, but when certain people invariably showed up late, the consistency of the behavior argued for a personality trait, not a constant state of emergency.

To my surprise, however, every member of the group made it onto the bus with a minute to spare. The last to arrive was Ellie Arnold, and her appearance shocked me. She looked like she had barely slept during the night, and she had been less than careful with her toilette this morning. I nudged Helen Louise, and she nodded. Leaning toward my ear, she said, "Rough night. I wonder if she had it out with Denis Kilbride."

If she and Kilbride had argued, they were too far away from our suite for us to have heard anything. "I wish he would go back to Athena and leave her, and the rest of us, alone. This is supposed to be fun."

Down at my feet, Diesel must have sensed my irritation. He shifted uneasily and meowed. Helen Louise rolled her eyes at me as she reached down to soothe the cat. "It's okay, boy," she said in a low tone. "Your daddy is a little grumpy, that's all."

I pulled out the small bag of treats I had brought along for Diesel and gave him one. The treats were insurance that he would behave well during the tour and on the bus rides. Once he knew there were treats available, he would be a good kitty and not act out. He knew that if he misbehaved, no more treats would be forthcoming. I rubbed his head after he finished the treat, and he pushed against my hand.

By this time the bus had started us on our short trip to the Biltmore estate. Miss An'gel informed us that we would be driven right up to the house itself, rather than being dropped off in the parking lot and having to wait for one of the estate buses to transfer us. Burdine thanked her profusely for arranging all this, saying that she particularly appreciated not having to deal with crowds of people touring the house at the same time we were there.

The day promised to be warm and sunny, and I too was grateful that we would be through the section of the house open to the public before the hordes arrived.

At five minutes to eight our minibus pulled up in front of the magnificent structure of Biltmore House, built in the style of a French Renaissance château between 1889 and 1895 by George W. Vanderbilt II. With an amazing footprint of nearly 179,000 square feet and 250 rooms, it was the largest house ever built in the United States. We would see only a small fraction of it, however. I imagined it would take a week of long tours to see everything the building held.

Our tour guide ran through the customary rules, looked askance at Diesel but seemed reassured by the presence of the cat's harness and the leash in my hand, and we were soon on our way to view the opulence of the Vanderbilt family home.

The old saying that the rich were different remained prominently in my mind as we made our way through the house with the guide. So many details to absorb, so much elegance and sheer opulence to see. We were allowed to take pictures with no flash, and in most sections we toured there was sufficient light for me to take pictures on my phone. I got several good photos of Helen Louise and Diesel in various places, particularly in the lovely winter garden that is actually inside the house. I would have called it an atrium, although it wasn't open roofed, merely vaulted. Whatever one might call it, I found it charming.

The banquet room, with its table capable of seating sixty-four persons, was the largest room in the house and had a seventy-foot vaulted barrel ceiling. The two-story library contained over ten thousand volumes in eight languages. Apparently George Vanderbilt had wide-ranging interests in classical literature and other subjects. I could happily have spent several hours, if not days, in that library, poring over volume after volume.

I had never visited a house with an indoor pool, a gym, and a bowling alley in its basement, but after visiting Biltmore I could say that I had. I imagined that one could live a rather full life at Biltmore without the necessity of ever leaving the grounds of the estate. Unless, of course, you desired to travel, and Vanderbilt obviously had, because he had brought bits and pieces of Europe home from his trips and had them installed in his magnificent house.

Before our visit I had only skimmed the history of Biltmore I found online. During the tour, I decided I would purchase a book in the gift shop. I was sure to find one that would tell me all I would ever want to know about the house, and I found exactly what I wanted. Once we finished the tour we had about an hour to visit the gift shops and food shops to refresh ourselves as needed before we reassembled at the meeting point to board the bus for our hotel. There were many items to tempt the souvenir shopper, and both Helen Louise and I succumbed to the lure of coffee mugs and T-shirts. I picked up a few things to take home for family members as well, and Helen Louise shopped for her staff at the bistro. We already had a small box in the trunk of the car with gifts from Gatlinburg and Cherokee. I have always had low resistance in souvenir shops, as my children could easily and willingly attest.

Helen Louise and I weren't the only members of the group laden with bags when we all met to board the bus back to our hotel. There were no stragglers, so the wait was brief. Once we were moving, Burdine said, "That was excellent. Gorgeous house, but I can't imagine living in a place like that."

Zac laughed. "I can't imagine being a servant in a place like that a hundred years ago. You'd spend most of your time walking from one task to another if you worked abovestairs." He shook his head. "You'd have to be really fit to work there."

"I couldn't get over how enormous it is, either," Melba said. "I knew it was the largest house in the country, but even knowing that, you're not really prepared for the sheer size and scale of it."

"If I'd been working there back then," Johnny Ray said, "I'd have been working on the farm or down in the basement somewhere. I don't expect they'd have black people working in the house."

"That's a good question," Helen Louise said. "I wish you'd asked the tour guide about it."

Johnny Ray shrugged. "Didn't think much about it at the time. I think I might bring the family back later in the week to see the farm and all the rest of it. Junior would love to see the library, but the twins would drive us crazy, trying to take them through the house."

"I can see that younger children might not be that interested.

Probably overwhelming to them," Paul Bowen said. "The guide said it was wired for electricity from the beginning. Can you imagine what the electric bill would be for that place?"

"At the time George Vanderbilt had the place built, he was pretty wealthy, though he didn't have as much money as some of the other Vanderbilts," Elmore said.

"Doesn't the family still own the house?" Celia asked.

"Yes, two of his great-great-grandchildren now run the estate," Miss An'gel said.

"While we were walking through, I couldn't help thinking about all the Golden Age English detective stories I've read," Celia remarked. "I've never been to England to see any of the stately homes there, but now I feel like I have more of a sense of what they must be like. Or were like in the twenties and thirties when Agatha Christie and others set their books in such places."

"I kept expecting a butler or an upstairs maid to pop up along the way." Burdine laughed. "Or someone running screaming down the hall claiming they'd found a body in one of the bedrooms."

"How about in the bowling alley?" Benjy grinned. "Or at the bottom of the swimming pool? Those would be great places for a corpse to turn up."

I couldn't suppress a grin. Get a bunch of mystery readers together, and they'd spot all kinds of opportunities for disposing of a body. I wondered whether mystery writers did the same thing. I figured they probably did.

"Or a body thrown to the ground from that beautiful loggia we saw," Melba said. "Wasn't that view of the Blue Ridge Mountains gorgeous? Imagine being able to sit out there and relax, enjoying the view, sipping a cocktail." She laughed. "I could get used to that kind of lifestyle in a hot minute."

Paul Bowen regarded her with amusement. "You'd like to be one of the idle rich?"

"Why not?" Melba said.

"I'll keep that in mind," Paul responded, and Melba flushed slightly.

I wondered how serious things were between Melba and this latest boyfriend. They hadn't been going out all that long, as far as I knew. Perhaps Melba would confide in me at some point. We were close, more like brother and sister in many ways than simply good friends.

Helen Louise broke the embarrassed silence after Paul's teasing remark. "I can't imagine that Vanderbilt had much of his inheritance left after Biltmore was finished."

"Not all of it was finished when he died in 1914," Elmore said. "Didn't the guide tell us the music room wasn't finished until the 1970s?"

"Yes, she did," Miss Dickce said.

We continued chatting about the wonders of Biltmore until we reached the hotel. As Helen Louise, Diesel, and I were waiting to get off the bus, I checked my watch. Ten thirty-two. An activity-packed few hours this morning, and we still had plenty of time to do other things like visit local bookstores, one of my favorite things to do whenever I traveled. Luckily for me, Helen Louise enjoyed bookstores also, so I didn't have to go by myself or negotiate for time to do it on my own.

We were now free until two this afternoon, when the group would reconvene to start with our more formal talks about our favorite Golden Age writers. I had offered to go first. I was used to doing talks with readers' groups from my days as a public librarian in Houston. I occasionally worked with groups at the Athena Public Library, where I volunteered once a week. Zac was my partner for the session, and he would be talking about Phoebe Atwood Taylor, an American author from his home state of Massachusetts.

We took our time getting off the bus, letting the rest of the group precede us into the hotel. When we stepped off, Miss An'gel stood waiting for us a few feet away.

"Diesel was such a good boy today," Miss An'gel said. "How on earth do you get him to behave so well?"

We headed for the hotel, but I paused right inside the door, pulled out the bag with one remaining treat, and showed it to her. "He loves these and doesn't get them often," I explained. "He knows that if he's a bad boy, he won't get any. He'd rather have these than not, so if he knows I have them, he's good as gold."

Miss An'gel laughed. "I wish that worked with humans."

"That reminds me," I said in an undertone. "Have you spoken to Denis Kilbride yet?"

"Not yet," Miss An'gel said. "Since we had such an early departure, I thought it better to wait until we returned from our excursion. I'm going to see if he's in and talk to him now."

I caught sight of Arthur as he bolted from behind the desk. He moved so quickly toward us I thought he would bowl Miss An'gel right over. Arthur stumbled to a halt a foot away from us. Now that he stood closer, I could see he was unnaturally pale and trembling.

"Young man, whatever is the matter?" Miss An'gel said.

"Oh, Miss Ducote, thank the Lord you're back. I didn't know who else to turn to," he gasped. "The most terrible thing. Moments ago. It's the first time." He paused to gulp down a breath.

"First time for what?" Miss An'gel asked tartly.

Arthur turned even whiter as he forced out a response. "Finding a dead guest."

NINE

"Who's dead?" I asked, praying that none of Johnny Ray's family had died unexpectedly. Then it hit me. The only other guest was Denis Kilbride.

"Mr. Kilbride," Arthur said. "Cora found him dead in his bed only about three minutes ago."

"What have you done about it?" Miss An'gel asked sharply.

"What should I do?" Arthur appeared to be on the point of collapse. "This has never happened to me before."

Helen Louise muttered something under her breath. I thought what she said was "about as useful as tits on a boar," but I could have been mistaken. I understood her sentiment. Arthur was an even dimmer bulb than I had reckoned.

"Go call 911 immediately," Miss An'gel said. When Arthur hesitated, she pointed to the desk. "Now."

The fierceness with which that one word was uttered galvanized Arthur. He hurried back to the desk, where he scooped up the phone.

Miss An'gel, Helen Louise, and I exchanged glances. Diesel meowed loudly, obviously aware of the sudden tension around him. Luckily the rest of our group, including Miss Dickce and Benjy, had made it upstairs before Arthur made his announcement to Miss An'gel. We didn't need more people downstairs milling around when the emergency response team arrived.

A thought struck me. "What about Cora? Where is she?"

"Certainly not here," Miss An'gel said, "unless she's fallen asleep in the office behind the reception desk."

I heard Helen Louise attempt to stifle a gurgle of laughter, and I understood how she felt. The thought of Cora, who had already frightened several guests who thought she was a corpse, had a certain black humor. Miss An'gel cast a swift glance at Helen Louise, and I would have sworn later that I'd seen the corners of Miss An'gel's mouth quirk.

Miss An'gel approached the desk and questioned Arthur further. Had he or Cora locked the door of Kilbride's room? Yes, he had. Where was Cora? In the office, as Miss An'gel had posited.

Now we could hear sirens approaching. Helen Louise and I, without speaking, made the same decision. We headed for the stairs. "We'll be in our room," I called over my shoulder to Miss An'gel, and she waved us on our way.

I felt a bit cowardly at leaving Miss An'gel downstairs to deal with Arthur and the emergency team, but I knew Miss An'gel wasn't fazed by this the way an ordinary mortal would have been. Where was the hotel manager? I wondered suddenly. Or the owner? Had Arthur even thought to alert his boss about the situation?

Probably not, I decided as we reached our room. Helen Louise unlocked it, and we shut the door behind us. I immediately released Diesel from his harness, and he trotted off to take care of business.

"I'm glad you wanted to get out of the way." Helen Louise dropped onto the sofa. "I was ready to drag you out of there if I had to." She grimaced.

"We haven't heard anything to suggest that Denis Kilbride was murdered," I responded, a bit on the defensive. "I'm not like an ambulance-chasing lawyer."

Helen Louise patted the spot next to her. "I know, love. I didn't mean to sound accusatory. Come sit down." She grinned suddenly. "It's only that when someone discovers a dead body and you're anywhere in the vicinity, some conclusions are difficult not to leap to."

"I'll ignore your tortured syntax and focus on what you mean." I smiled to remove any sting from my words. "Yes, I know. My first reaction was to think 'Oh no, not again.' Hopefully we'll find out it was a natural death. I bet he had a bad ticker."

"I'm pretty sure he smoked," Helen Louise said, "but I don't know how heavily. Whenever he came in the bistro, he usually ordered food that was guaranteed to clog his arteries."

"Sounds like he liked the same things I do," I said, somewhat morosely. Kilbride was about my age.

"True," Helen Louise said, easily reading my mood, "but you don't smoke. Never have, as far as I know."

"There were a few rebellious cigarettes back in junior high," I said, "but that was it. Decided pretty quickly it wasn't for me."

"Good for you," Helen Louise said. "My mother caught me sneaking a cigarette once when I was about fourteen, and she convinced me that was a mistake. I didn't do it again."

I knew that Annabelle Brady had been a tough disciplinarian, and I suspected that her method of convincing her daughter not to smoke involved corporal punishment and frequent verbal reminders. The latter probably went on for years, too.

I said nothing of this, however. My parents had been pretty strict also, but I rarely got spanked by either of them. I hadn't spanked my children, either, though there had been times when Sean tempted me during his teenage years.

Diesel returned from his business and spread himself over our laps on the sofa, his back legs and tail hanging over a bit. He stretched luxuriantly while Helen Louise stroked his belly.

"How about we pick a restaurant for lunch?" I said. "We'll have to leave His Majesty here, though, unless we can find a restaurant with outside seating that allows pets."

"There are probably several," Helen Louise said, "but you'll find that they allow dogs, not cats."

I pulled out my phone and did a quick search, and I found a total of nine. I looked them over. "You're right. Dogs are okay, but cats aren't mentioned. A few mention pets but I think that they mean dogs."

"You could call," Helen Louise said.

I shrugged. "As much as I'd like to take him with us, I think we'll have to leave him here when we eat out. We won't be gone that long. We have to be back here for our afternoon session anyway."

"True," Helen Louise said as she continued to stroke the nearly blissed-out feline.

"I think I'll look for pet sitters after the afternoon session," I said. "I'm sure we can find someone who will come and sit with him when we want to go out and explore Asheville."

"Excellent idea," Helen Louise said. "I hope he appreciates all this trouble."

Something about her tone gave me the idea she wasn't happy we had brought Diesel with us, even though we had discussed it thoroughly—or so I thought—before we decided to make this trip.

"Second thoughts?" I said lightly.

Helen Louise looked at me, her expression puzzled. The comprehension dawned. "About bringing Diesel with us? To be honest, maybe a few. Mostly because of feeling guilty."

"About what?"

"Leaving him alone for any length of time," she said. "He's used to having a human around pretty much every hour of the day, every day of his life since you rescued him."

"I feel guilty, too, sometimes," I said. "He came into my life when I needed a companion who didn't fuss, didn't judge, who accepted me the way I was. I can never forget that. He helped me enormously. He still does, whenever I'm worried about something." I felt a bit choked up by the time I finished.

Helen Louise laid a hand on my arm and gave it a squeeze. "I know, love. He was precisely the anodyne you needed at the time. I love him, too, and wouldn't for the world want you to neglect him. He is always a comfort and such a sweet boy."

I nodded. "But sometimes it's not always convenient to have him along. I understand. And I don't know that it's in his best interest to go out in public places where there can be a lot of strangers. It's best that he stays here, where it's quiet. We will leave the television on, and I think he'll be content with that for now."

"And put the Do Not Disturb sign on the door when we leave," Helen Louise said.

"Yes, of all things, that," I replied. "Now, where shall we eat lunch?"

We found a suitable place only a few blocks from the hotel, thanks to the list prepared for us. We left Diesel with a promise to return soon. He meowed and turned his back to us, a sure sign of feline disapproval. I hated leaving him like that but I knew he would forgive, if not forget.

Sign on the door, we headed out. We decided to go down the stairs at the end of the corridor rather than down the main staircase. We didn't want to walk into the middle of what might have been going on downstairs. I figured there hadn't been sufficient time for the investigation to be completed, so we avoided that area of the hotel.

On the way to the restaurant we talked about the sudden death of Denis Kilbride. I wanted to believe that it was natural, or accidental, and not the result of foul play, but I couldn't help feeling that this death would turn out to be deliberate. Both Zac Ryan and Johnny Ray Floyd had experienced difficulties with Kilbride. Johnny Ray had always come across as a hardworking, good-natured man devoted to his family. Zac was still mostly an unknown quantity. He hadn't revealed much personal information to the group, but he had been a member for only two months now.

"I'm praying that this isn't another murder," Helen Louise said. "But if it turns out to be, I know we'll be in the thick of it."

"Let's keep hoping it was something simple like a heart attack and not murder," I said.

"We can hope that all we want," Helen Louise replied, a trifle sharply, "but hoping won't make it so."

We reached the restaurant. I opened the door for Helen Louise to enter, and I followed her. *Pleasant ambience*, I thought immediately, and there were delicious scents already in the air, though the lunch hour hadn't officially begun.

Over the tasty meal we talked about anything but the death of Denis Kilbride. We discussed potential wedding dates and venues. Helen Louise preferred a church wedding since this was her first. I had no problem with that. I didn't see any need for a huge affair, although Helen Louise and I both had a wide acquaintance in town. I knew many people would expect to be invited, and I supposed I should resign myself to a large party. Basically, whatever Helen Louise wanted was fine with me. I wanted her to have the wedding she had always wanted.

A text message from Miss An'gel ended our discussion, and I signaled for the bill.

We need you here at the hotel. I'll explain when you get here.

TEN

I showed the text to Helen Louise, and she grimaced. “At least we were able to finish our meal,” I said.

“Thankfully.” She pushed back her chair. “I’m going to the powder room before we walk back.”

“I’ll meet you out front.” I responded to Miss An’gel’s message to let her know we would be there in less than ten minutes.

We didn’t talk on the way back to the hotel. Miss An’gel’s text had used ambiguous language. *We need you here at the hotel* could have meant many different things, none of which had to do with murder. I figured she must have called a group meeting to discuss whether we should continue with our planned schedule. Denis Kilbride hadn’t been a part of the group, but with everything that had happened involving him, would members still be in the mood to talk about murder mysteries?

I would have to think about that myself. I hadn’t known Kilbride, really, and I felt no personal loss at his death. I did feel shock, though, because it was always disconcerting when someone around one's own age died. Stark reminders of your own mortality could be extremely upsetting.

We found Miss An'gel awaiting us at the reception desk. Arthur, still looking shell-shocked by the experience of dealing with sudden death, stared mutely at us.

"I'm sorry I interrupted whatever you were doing," Miss An'gel said. "But I felt that we should talk about what has happened, and I can bring you up to date."

"Are we going to have the whole group together?" Helen Louise asked.

Miss An'gel shook her head. "No, I'd prefer to talk to the two of you at the moment."

"In that case," I replied, "let's go up to our suite. We left Diesel on his own, and I know he'll be happy to see you, Miss An'gel."

She smiled briefly. "That's fine."

We headed upstairs, and moments later we entered the suite. I called out to Diesel but spotted him under the sofa before he responded. He offered a plaintive warble before he crawled out to join us.

Miss An'gel greeted him, and he responded happily. For the moment he ignored Helen Louise and me. He remained beside Miss An'gel's chair during the ensuing conversation.

"Let me fill you in on what we know so far," Miss An'gel said, after refusing bottled water or any other refreshment. "You know already that Cora found Denis Kilbride only minutes before we returned from our visit to Biltmore."

Helen Louise and I nodded, and Miss An'gel continued. "I must say that Arthur is more of a twit than I expected. He's the owner's grandson and has trouble keeping a job, I've been told, so his grandfather decided to try him out here." She grimaced. "He's not much help in an emergency, I must say. But that's neither here nor there. The proper persons showed up, the emergency services people and a police officer. The EMS team said Kilbride was dead, but there was apparently no overt sign of what led to his death. They took the body away in the ambulance to the medical examiner's office, where the medical examiner will determine the cause of death."

"What do you think happened?" I asked. "Heart attack, maybe?"

Miss An'gel shrugged. "I didn't go into the room, so I couldn't say. The EMS team apparently didn't find anything suspicious. They simply followed procedure, since no one knew who his doctor is and how to get in touch with that person."

"Did they look for medications?" Helen Louise asked. "The doctor's name is usually on the bottle."

"I'm sure they would have done that," Miss An'gel said, looking slightly troubled. "Of course there's nothing to say that he was taking any kind of medication on a regular basis."

"Something to find out," I said. "Perhaps Ellie would know. She seems to be the only one of us to have a personal relationship with him." *That we knew of*, I thought.

"Possibly Zac," Helen Louise said. "Remember, he was threatening Zac last night before Johnny Ray decked him."

"I have to say that the obvious animosity between Johnny Ray and Mr. Kilbride worries me," Miss An'gel said. "I've known Johnny Ray for years. He does all our plumbing work, as his father did before him. He's a good man, but if the medical examiner finds any connection between the altercation last night and Mr. Kilbride's death, it could mean trouble for Johnny Ray."

I hadn't thought much about the incident since last night, but I well understood Miss An'gel's anxiety. I had no idea how the police and the medical examiner would treat Johnny Ray if the blow had led to Kilbride's death.

"We can't let ourselves anticipate problems because we simply don't know the full story," Helen Louise said. "We don't need to upset Johnny Ray by talking about what happened last night unless it's absolutely necessary."

"You're right," I said, "but I imagine Johnny Ray has already thought about it himself. He's a smart man, and he's read enough murder mysteries to be savvy to the potential sequelae of knocking another man out."

"Do you know what the issue was between Kilbride and Zac Ryan?" Miss An'gel asked.

Both Helen Louise and I shook our heads. Miss An'gel sighed. "Zac is such a personable, intelligent young man. I know his fellow faculty members and the students in the art department think highly of him. I'm wondering how he and Kilbride are connected. Surely not romantically."

"I wouldn't think so," Helen Louise said, "unless Kilbride also dated men."

Miss An'gel shot her a shrewd look. "Entirely possible, of course. I've known any number of men like that."

I had thought about that already, but I had been hesitant to mention it in front of Miss An'gel. She was the age, roughly, that my mother would have been were she still living. I had never discussed such things with my mother, and I couldn't bring myself to introduce the topic in front of Miss An'gel. Helen Louise wasn't squeamish about that kind of thing, however.

"We should probably ask Melba," I said. "If anyone knows about that, it's likely to be her."

Miss An'gel nodded. "She manages to hear all kinds of things about people in town, that's true."

"Everyone likes Melba, that's why," Helen Louise said. "I don't think she actively encourages people to gossip. It's just that she's the kind of person that people tend to confide in."

I chuckled. "She told me not long ago that whenever she's been on a plane, the person next to her invariably started telling her their life story."

"Thank goodness no one does that to me," Helen Louise said. "Miss An'gel, did anyone tell you how long it might be before they have any answers about Denis Kilbride's death?"

"I asked the police officer, and he told me it could be tomorrow, or it could take several days," Miss An'gel replied. "It depends on how busy the medical examiner is, and whether she has to send anything to the state crime lab for further analysis."

"What are we going to do about the group's plans for the week?" I asked.

"Sister and I talked it over briefly, and we think we should continue as planned. Mr. Kilbride wasn't a member of the group, after all." Miss An'gel paused, looking troubled again. "If any member feels unable to continue with our program, of course neither Sister nor I would insist that they stay the week."

"I don't think anyone will want to leave," Helen Louise said, "unless it's Ellie. I don't know how close she really was to Denis."

"I haven't seen her since we returned from Biltmore this

morning. I'm not even sure if she's aware of what happened. I had Arthur call her room once the EMS team and the police officer arrived, but there was no answer." Miss An'gel stroked Diesel's head, and he chirped happily. "She hadn't come back by the time you two returned, as far as I know."

I glanced at my watch and noticed that it was now nearly one o'clock. I mentioned this to Miss An'gel, and she rose immediately.

"Thank you, Charlie," she said as I got to my feet to see her out. "I've lost track of time somehow. I must go and check in with Sister. She might have talked to Ellie. If not, I'll find her and let her know right away. I'll see you downstairs at one-thirty."

"We'll be there." I closed the door, and Diesel, who had trailed behind her, turned and came back with me to the sofa. "I imagine everyone knows by now, don't you think?"

Helen Louise shrugged. "Probably. I'm sure Arthur would have made it his business to share the news with anyone he saw. I wonder whether they sent poor Cora home."

"I'm surprised someone more senior hasn't taken Arthur's place, frankly," I replied.

"Surely there's someone who could."

"You'd think so, wouldn't you?" I said. "I'm going to wash up before we head downstairs."

Diesel accompanied me, as he often did at home. One thing about having cats—and dogs, too—you rarely had to go to the bathroom by yourself. I had no idea whether Diesel considered himself to be supervising me, lest I get into trouble by myself, or if he simply wanted the comfort of being near me as much as possible. I preferred the latter explanation. I found comfort in his presence often enough.

I wondered how Ellie would take the news of Denis Kilbride's sudden death. Would she be devastated? How would the others react? Johnny Ray might well be upset, and I couldn't blame him. Kilbride's death so soon after the altercation between them would worry him, I was sure. I was still puzzled by Kilbride's animus toward Zac Ryan, though. What had caused it? And why had Ellie called Zac a rat? Were the two connected somehow?

All this speculation was probably moot, I told myself sharply, because Denis Kilbride's death would turn out to be from natural causes. I was going to stick with that theory unless there was significant evidence to prove one wrong.

I finished my ablutions, and Diesel and I found Helen Louise in the living room brushing her hair and touching up her makeup. She generally wore only a minimum of makeup most of the time. Her clear skin and vivid coloring—red full lips, black curly hair, and flashing blue eyes—served her better than anything artificial, I had always thought.

We left the room at one twenty-five, bringing Diesel, harnessed and leashed, with us. Arthur was absent from the reception desk, and we saw no one else until we entered the meeting room. There we found Miss Dickce, Benjy, and Zac Ryan. Not long after we arrived, the others trickled in, all except Miss An'gel and Ellie Arnold.

Once we finished exchanging greetings, Miss Dickce cleared her throat. "I'm sure Sister will be along any minute now, but I'm not sure whether Ellie will be joining us." She paused. "I don't know whether everyone has heard about this yet. You might have been present when the police and ambulance were here. I apologize for breaking the news to you so bluntly. Denis Kilbride was found dead in his bed this morning by the maid."

I was watching Johnny Ray Floyd while Miss Dickce made the announcement, and his shocked expression, rapidly replaced by one of fear, worried me. Burdine and Elmore apparently already knew, as did Celia Bernardi. Zac, Melba, and Paul were the only ones besides Johnny Ray who hadn't known.

The others pelted Miss Dickce with questions about Kilbride's death, talking over one another in their shock and eagerness for more information. Johnny, however, sat mute next to Helen Louise on the sofa.

I leaned across Helen Louise and grasped Johnny Ray's arm. "Are you okay?" I asked.

For a moment I thought he hadn't heard me, but then he turned to me, his eyes wide with apparent shock. "I didn't hit him that hard, did I? I didn't mean to kill him. I'm not a killer, I swear I'm not."

ELEVEN

"We don't know that what happened last night has anything to do with his death," I said to Johnny Ray, trying to reassure him. "He probably had a heart attack. He was a smoker, someone said, and he liked rich food. Don't get yourself worked up over what could very well be a natural death."

Helen Louise echoed my reassurance, and Johnny Ray began to look less sick at heart. "I hope to the Lord y'all are right," he said. "I couldn't live with myself if I was responsible for somebody dying like that." He shook his head. "How could I ever look Lou or my kids in the face again?"

"You're a good man," Helen Louise said as she slipped an arm around his shoulders. "Try not to worry about this and get yourself all agitated. Charlie's right, he probably had a heart attack or simply died quietly in his sleep. It happens."

Johnny Ray sighed. "Maybe so."

I hoped Helen Louise and I were telling Johnny Ray the truth.

I sent off a quick prayer on his behalf. I could only imagine the mental and emotional anguish he would be going through until the cause of Kilbride's death had been determined.

I glanced at Zac Ryan, sitting on one side of Miss Dickce, Benjy on the other. He appeared disconnected from the conversations going on around him. Was he concerned? I wondered. Did he know anything?

Miss An'gel entered the room then, one arm around Ellie Arnold's waist. Pale, disheveled, Ellie clung to Miss An'gel. All conversation in the room ceased at the sight of her. Miss An'gel led her to the chair that Zac hastily vacated at a nod. Miss Dickce and Benjy switched to other chairs so that Miss An'gel could sit next to Ellie.

The uneasy silence continued once they were seated. We all waited for Miss An'gel to speak. After a glance at Ellie's bent head, Miss An'gel faced us.

"I know this has come as a shock to all of us, but especially to those who knew Mr. Kilbride," Miss An'gel said. "I discovered that Ellie was unaware of what happened until half an hour ago, so she is understandably shaken by it. She insisted on coming with me, however, and I think it's good for her to be with all of us."

Ellie raised her head and nodded. I noticed with some surprise that there was no evidence of tears or crying. That struck me as a bit odd, but then people reacted to bad news differently. Ellie might have been one of those stoic types who suppressed emotion rather than letting it show. I didn't know her well enough to say.

"I know you all have many questions," Miss An'gel continued, "and I will answer all that I can. You must realize, however, that I know only what I've observed today and what the

EMS team and the police officer told me." She proceeded to tell the rest of the group what she had shared earlier with Helen Louise and me.

When Miss An'gel finished her summation, there was silence for a few seconds. Then Elmore Gregory said, "Heart attack. He smoked like a chimney for years."

Burdine Gregory nodded. "Yes, he sure did. Whenever I saw him around town, he was always smoking."

"It's sad, because he wasn't that old," Elmore continued. "I had a good twenty-five years on him, I'll reckon, but I quit smoking over forty years ago. It just don't do to smoke these days with everything we know about cancer and all that."

"Exactly," Burdine said.

Ellie Arnold broke her silence. "Yes, he did smoke, though he was really trying to quit. He told me before I left to come here that he hadn't had a cigarette in three weeks." She closed her eyes for a moment. They fluttered open, and she went on. "But I suspect he fell off the wagon. He started smoking when he was seventeen, he told me, so it was a habit for over thirty years." Her eyes welled with tears suddenly, and she wiped them away with a shaking hand. Perhaps the reality had finally begun to set in.

"That does take a toll," Miss An'gel said. "Was he on any kind of medication that you know of?"

"His cardiologist put him on a couple of meds. He had high blood pressure," Ellie said. "Because of smoking and all the rich food he insisted on eating. He didn't always take it like he was supposed to, though."

"Do you know the name of his cardiologist?" Miss An'gel asked.

"No, I don't think he ever mentioned a name to me," Ellie said. "I know the cardiologist was in Memphis, though. Not anyone in Athena because he went to Memphis a few weeks ago for an appointment with him."

Miss An'gel looked at me, and I nodded. Surely if Denis Kilbride had had his medications with him, the EMS team would have found them and been able to track down his doctor. Had Kilbride failed to bring them with him? Or had the EMS team somehow overlooked them? I knew Miss An'gel would follow this up with the proper authorities to find out the truth of the situation.

Ellie suddenly stood. "I'm sorry, I don't think I can do this after all. I'm going back up to my room for the rest of the afternoon." She rushed out of the room despite Miss An'gel's attempts to speak to her and offer assistance.

Miss Dickce said, "It's obvious that she's having a hard time over this. I think we should let her alone for now, and when she needs to talk to someone, we'll be available, either one-on-one or as a group." Her gaze swept the group, and everyone nodded. "Excellent. Either Sister or I will check in on her later around dinnertime, but until then I think we can let her be."

"Yes," Miss An'gel said. "Given the current situation, I must ask you whether you all wish to continue with the activities planned for the week. While Mr. Kilbride wasn't a member of the group, he was known to a number of us. You might feel that our discussion of murder mysteries is somewhat inappropriate now. We need to come to a consensus."

Zac Ryan responded without hesitation. "I don't see any problem with continuing our program as planned. I barely knew the man, and frankly I have no idea what had him so upset with me last night. Too bad for him that he checked out that way, but it's nothing to do with me."

That struck me as more than a bit cold-blooded, but it was, I decided, pragmatic. If Zac was telling us the truth, he truly had no idea why Kilbride had come storming in the door, wanting to confront him.

Paul Bowen said, "I knew Denis through business. He was a client of our bank, and I had occasion to work with him on several projects. We were not friends outside business, however, so I don't know much about his private life. I guess I agree with Zac; his death is unfortunate, but I don't see that it has anything to do with the group, despite Kilbride's bizarre behavior last night."

Burdine piped up next. "Elmore and I agree with Zac and Paul. We didn't know Kilbride personally, so I don't see that this thing should affect us getting on with our business."

"Heavens no," Celia Bernardi said. "I don't see why we should disrupt our plans for the death of a man who was mostly a stranger to us. I'm sorry for Ellie's sake if she was close to him, as I gather she might have been. I can understand if she wants to withdraw and go home, but I think the rest of us can go forward with a clear conscience." She threw a swift but obvious glance at Johnny Ray when she finished.

Johnny Ray cleared his throat. "I'm real sorry about what happened last night between me and Denis Kilbride. I shouldn't have done what I did, and I've been praying that me hitting him didn't have anything to do with his death." He paused for a moment, then rushed on to get out the next sentence. "If it turns out he died because of me, I'll take the consequences."

"I don't think it will come to that," Melba said. "Denis Kilbride was a heart attack or a stroke waiting to happen. On top of the smoking and his diet, he had a hair-trigger temper. You put all those together, and you get a dangerous combination. He was liable to drop dead any second, and you don't know what went on after y'all had your run-in last night. Most people didn't like him. Even Ellie didn't like him that much, I'd say."

"Melba's right," Helen Louise said. "Don't go borrowing trouble, as my mother used to say."

Johnny Ray responded with a weak smile. "Thank you, ladies. I appreciate it, but my heart's not going to be easy until I am one hundred and ten percent sure that I didn't cause his death."

"It's going to be rough for you until we hear something," Miss An'gel said. "Have faith, Johnny Ray. We'll stand behind you."

"Thank you, Miss An'gel," Johnny Ray said. "That means a lot."

I could feel the undercurrent of unease building in the room like a slowly rising tide. The longer we discussed the subject of Denis Kilbride's sudden death, the more the tension mounted. We all wanted answers, but I figured those answers would be pretty slow in coming. Here in Asheville, none of us had any connections with the local authorities the way we did back in Athena. Chief Deputy Kanesha Berry wasn't in charge of the investigation, natural death or not.

"Do you feel that you can continue to participate in the group's activities?" Miss Dickce asked Johnny Ray.

"I'd like to," Johnny Ray said. "I've been looking forward to this, and so have Lou and my kids." He shrugged. "Waiting to find out what happened is hard, though."

"Did you tell your wife about what happened last night?" Zac asked.

Johnny Ray nodded. "Yeah, I told her. She wasn't happy, but she understood why I was so angry with Kilbride. The kids don't know anything about it, though."

"We've heard from everyone now, I think, except Charlie and Helen Louise," Miss An'gel said after a glance at Benjy, who nodded.

"I'm fine with going on with our schedule," Helen Louise said.

"I am, too," I added, and Diesel meowed loudly. That elicited smiles or chuckles from the rest of the group, even Johnny Ray.

As the mirth quieted down, we all heard a knock at the door. "Come in," Miss An'gel called, and a man of about seventy, silver haired, fit, and distinguished in appearance, stepped in. I estimated that the suit he wore must have cost a couple of thousand dollars.

"Good afternoon, Howard," Miss An'gel said. "This is an unexpected surprise." She stood and proffered her hand as he approached. He accepted it, and then Miss An'gel introduced him to the group as the owner of the hotel, Howard Hindman.

Hindman stood beside Miss An'gel and glanced around at each of us. "I am regretful that you should all have this unpleasant experience here at my hotel, and I offer my most sincere condolences to any who were friends of the deceased. I can assure you that we are cooperating with the authorities to the fullest extent, and if you have any concerns about your stay, please feel free to let me know." He paused for a deep breath. "My grandson has been relieved of duty for the next few days to recover from the shock he suffered, and a replacement will be at the desk from this afternoon on during the day shift.

"Now I regret I must take Miss An'gel away from you for a few minutes," he continued. "A police officer will be here to speak with all of you soon."

TWELVE

I could feel this new ripple of anxiety that shot around the room as Miss An'gel left escorted by Mr. Hindman. A police officer wanted to speak to all of us. Was this connected to the results of the autopsy on Denis Kilbride?

No, I decided. That surely couldn't be. There hadn't been enough time to conduct an autopsy, even if the medical examiner had nothing else to do. The earliest we could expect to hear back about it was sometime tomorrow afternoon. The police probably wanted to find out more about Kilbride's background.

I stated this aloud, against the low buzz of conversation. Miss Dickce spoke up in agreement, sounding calm, and the tension seemed to dissipate. I felt myself relax, and I reached down to stroke Diesel's head, aware of his restlessness. He was sensitive to these moods, and I didn't want him to feel distressed by them.

The group fell silent as we awaited Miss An'gel's return and the advent of the policeman. Five minutes passed, then ten, then fifteen. I felt the unease of others around me. I knew that, like me, they all wanted to get this over with. What was holding up the policeman?

The door opened, and Miss An'gel walked in with an officer in uniform. She introduced her as Sergeant Bloesch and then introduced each member of the group in turn. The sergeant acknowledged each of us with a nod.

"Good afternoon, ladies and gentlemen," the sergeant said. "Sorry to keep y'all waiting while I talked with Miss Ducote and Mr. Hindman, but we have procedures that need to be followed. I have been gathering information on the deceased, Mr. Kilbride, and I need to talk to y'all to find out whether you have any further information before I report back to my boss and to the medical examiner.

"I'd like to talk to you one-on-one." Sergeant Bloesch pulled out a notebook, flipped it open, and found the page she wanted. "I'll start with Mr. Johnny Ray Floyd."

I heard Johnny Ray's sharp intake of breath. I felt for him, but he had to face up to this, whatever the outcome.

He stood. "I'm Johnny Ray Floyd."

"Thank you, Mr. Floyd. If you'll come with me, this won't take long." Sergeant Bloesch walked to the door and held it open.

Once the door closed behind them, we all looked to Miss An'gel to enlighten us.

"All I know is that the police department decided to send a more senior officer to talk to the group. Sergeant Bloesch doesn't know for sure when the medical examiner will perform the autopsy, but she said it could be done within a couple of days. They have no reason so far to treat it as a suspicious death, but in such cases they have to find out what they can about the deceased."

"What about his medications and his doctor?" Helen Louise asked. "Did the EMS team find any?"

Miss An'gel looked suddenly distressed. "No, they did not. That was the first thing I asked the sergeant. They looked for them but none turned up. I know Ellie said he wasn't always good about taking his medicine, but I'd be surprised if he left on a trip and forgot to bring them."

"I don't know about that," Burdine Gregory said. "If it weren't for me, Elmore would go off without his every time we go somewhere."

"That's because I know you'll make every step I do and some I don't, because you want to show you're better at packing for a trip than I am," Elmore replied.

"Point taken," Miss Dickce said. "If you're in a hurry to get going, sometimes you can forget to pack the simplest things. I've done that myself, and I daresay that most of you have done it, too."

I almost always forgot something when I packed, which I tended to postpone until the last minute. I said as much, and several people laughed.

"I shared with the sergeant what Ellie told us about Mr. Kilbride's cardiologist," Miss An'gel said, "but who knows how many cardiologists there are in Memphis. That could take them several days to track down. We don't even know which pharmacy he used."

"Do you think there's something sinister about the fact that they couldn't find any medications in his room?" Paul Bowen asked.

Miss An'gel frowned. "I think *sinister* is rather a strong word, Paul. It's certainly curious, but who's to say?"

"Did anyone here see him last night after he left this room?" Melba asked. "I saw him going into his room with a sack. I figured he'd been out to buy liquor."

"What time was that?" Paul asked.

"Around ten-thirty," Melba said. "Not long after you'd gone to your room for the night. I'd stuck my head out the door because I thought I heard someone talking in the hall."

"Did you see anyone besides Denis Kilbride?" Zac asked.

"No, I didn't," Melba said. "Maybe it was the television coming from next door that I heard."

Paul shook his head. "Not from my room. I didn't turn it on at all last night."

"I'm in the end room," Melba said, "so it must have been someone in the hall. Guess whoever it was ducked into their room before I looked out." She glanced around the room, but no one spoke.

I doubted Melba imagined it, so whoever it was—perhaps someone who had spoken to Kilbride?—didn't want to admit to it. That bothered me. Why not admit to it?

Maybe it was Johnny Ray, I thought. He might have tried to apologize to Kilbride and been ignored. I didn't think that was the case, however. As far as I knew, Johnny Ray hadn't felt any significant remorse about the altercation until he heard of Kilbride's death today.

"Did anyone else see him or speak to him?" Helen Louise asked. "I didn't, nor did Charlie."

"We saw him in a bar down the street," Burdine said. "We went for a walk before bedtime, and I spotted him through the window when we paused to have a look at the place. I wanted a nightcap, but when we saw him in there with Ellie, we walked on."

"Looked like they were arguing about something," Elmore said. Burdine nodded.

"What time was that?" Miss An'gel asked.

"Eleven, near's I can recall," Elmore said. Once again Burdine nodded.

That was odd, I thought. Melba had seen him around ten-thirty going into his room with a bag that might have contained liquor. But half an hour later, Burdine and Elmore saw him in a bar with Ellie.

"Did you come back the same way?" Zac asked.

"We did," Elmore said, "but it was only about five minutes later. Burdine started getting cold. I told her she ought to've brought a wrap, but she didn't pay any attention."

Burdine bridled at Elmore's words but to my surprise, for once she forbore to comment.

"Were Kilbride and Ellie still in the bar?" Miss Dickce asked.

"I didn't look," Elmore said. "Did you?"

Burdine shook her head.

"Has Sergeant Bloesch talked to Ellie yet?" Helen Louise asked.

"I don't think so," Miss An'gel said. "I'm sure she will before she finishes questioning the group."

Ellie, I reckoned, had most likely been the last to see Denis Kilbride last night. She hadn't mentioned anything about it when she was with the group a little while ago, but no one had thought to ask her.

"Zac, what about you?" I remembered that he'd asked Melba

whether she had seen anyone besides Kilbride when she looked out into the hall. Why had he asked her that? Simple curiosity? Or was he the one who had been talking to Kilbride and wanted to know if he had been seen?

"What do you mean?" Zac said, appearing startled. "Are you asking if I saw him last night?"

"Yes, that's what I'm asking," I said. "He seemed pretty determined to talk to you. I'm sure we're all wondering whether he found you last night to discuss whatever it was he wanted to discuss with you."

"Whatever it was, I'll never know," Zac said with a shrug. "I didn't see him again last night. After we finished here, I went straight to my room, locked the door, and stayed there until it was time to go to Biltmore."

He sounded convincing, yet I couldn't help but be a bit suspicious. His answer seemed a little too pat to me. After a moment's reflection, however, I chided myself. Was I trying to make more of this than it was? There was a mystery here, but whether it had anything to do with Kilbride's death, I didn't know. Probably none of my business. Simply my unbridled curiosity at work. That's what my son, Sean, would have said if he were here, and he would be right, I decided.

"Didn't you eat breakfast?" Burdine asked, sounding appalled.

Zac laughed. "I had some fruit and cheese in my room. I don't eat a heavy breakfast." He smirked at Burdine, and I could almost hear the additional words *like some people I could name.*

Burdine laughed. "You're welcome to your fruit and cheese, honey. I'll take my eggs and bacon and grits every time."

Zac didn't respond to this sally.

I glanced at my watch. Sergeant Bloesch seemed to be taking a long time with Johnny Ray. I hoped that wasn't a bad sign. The group fell silent as the minutes ticked by.

After nearly a quarter of an hour passed, Sergeant Bloesch came back. This time she wanted Zac. I was watching him, figuring he would be next, and I would have sworn that he paled when she called his name. Maybe the sergeant could get out of him the issue between him and Kilbride. If he was smart, he would tell the truth. I well knew, however, that in these situations even innocent people will prevaricate because the police make them nervous.

We watched Zac precede the sergeant from the room. I began to wonder who might be the next to go. Johnny Ray did not return, and that I had expected. The sergeant wouldn't want us talking among ourselves more than we already had, and no doubt Johnny Ray was ready to go back to his family once the sergeant finished with him.

So much for our schedule, I thought. We would simply have to adjust to the changes brought by Kilbride's unexpected death. For the first time, I was shocked to realize, I wondered whether he had any family to mourn him. Was there anyone besides Ellie who would feel the loss? No one in the group appeared to, other than the normal regret for a person who has died unexpectedly and at a relatively young age.

Melba startled me by moving from her seat next to Paul Bowen and inserting herself between Helen Louise and me on the sofa. Diesel greeted her with loud meows, and she patted his head.

"Sorry to push myself in the middle," she told Helen Louise and me in a low tone, her expression apologetic. "I wanted to talk to you, and I don't want to be overheard. I figured this was best, since we can't leave the room or go over in the corner without people getting suspicious."

Both Helen Louise and I assured her we didn't mind. "What is it you want to talk about?" I asked.

"Zac Ryan," Melba said, her voice barely above a whisper. "I think I know what was going on with him and Denis Kilbride."

THIRTEEN

Trust Melba to know what is going on when nobody else does, I thought. Aloud, I said, "Tell us what you know."

Melba glanced first at me, then at Helen Louise. Now, her head bowed slightly, she looked at her hands in her lap as she began to speak. "This is kind of embarrassing, and how I came to know about this isn't what you may think after I tell you. Just keep in mind that the person who told me about this knows what he's talking about usually, and I have no reason to doubt him."

More intrigued than ever, I said, "We understand, don't we?"

Helen Louise said, "Of course we do. Go ahead."

Melba expelled a pent-up breath. "All right. Here's the skinny. Apparently Denis Kilbride liked to walk down both sides of the street, if you get my drift."

Why couldn't she say it outright? I wondered.

"You mean he and Zac?"

Melba nodded, and Helen Louise and I exchanged glances.

"While he was dating Ellie?" Helen Louise asked, obviously perturbed by the information that Denis had been unfaithful to Ellie.

"I believe so," Melba said.

"Is this well known around town?" I asked. "That he was bisexual, that is."

"I don't think so," Melba said. "My source's information comes from Memphis, at one of the clubs there. And a hotel."

"Goodness me," Helen Louise said. "Do you think Ellie found out about it?"

Melba shrugged. "I'm not sure."

"I bet she did," I said. "That would explain the argument we overheard yesterday, when Ellie called Zac a rat."

"I think you're right, Charlie," Helen Louise said.

"Do you think I ought to tell the sergeant about this?" Melba asked. "Who knows what she might ask when she's interviewing us, and if she asks me what I know about Denis Kilbride, should I tell her this?"

"That's a tough one," I said. "Right now we don't have any reason to think that his death is anything other than natural. If we knew it was due to foul play, then I'd say go ahead and tell her everything you know. But unless she gives you some indication that his death wasn't natural, I wouldn't volunteer the information."

"I agree," Helen Louise said. "No point in bringing up sexual escapades that we don't really know much about."

"Thank you both," Melba said. "I feel better now. I'm praying that poor Denis died naturally, but I have this awful feeling it's going to turn out to be a lot more complicated."

Sergeant Bloesch came back and this time took Burdine and

Elmore with her. Melba went back to sit with Paul, and we chatted among ourselves about various topics, none of which had anything to do with Denis Kilbride. The room slowly emptied until only Helen Louise, Miss Dickce, and I remained. By now we were getting close to dinnertime, and Diesel had grown restive. I decided that the next time the sergeant came in, I would ask her if I could take Diesel upstairs to our room before she questioned Helen Louise and me.

As if she had read my mind, the sergeant walked into the room. Before she could speak I stood and asked permission to take Diesel upstairs to our suite. The sergeant shrugged and gave her permission. She asked Miss Dickce to accompany her, and I told Helen Louise I would return in a few minutes.

"Come on, boy," I said to the cat, and Diesel happily accompanied me upstairs. As we headed toward our room I glanced ahead at the door, and what I saw caused me to stop abruptly about thirty feet away. From this vantage point it looked to me like the door stood ever so slightly ajar. I proceeded toward it now with caution. Was there a burglar in our room?

When we reached the door, I held Diesel back from entering the room until I peered through the crack. I saw nothing amiss in that first glimpse of the room, but my area of vision was necessarily small. I slowly pushed the door open wider, and the scene that gradually revealed itself to me showed me that everything appeared to be the way we had left it. Puzzled, I pushed the door all the way open and advanced into the room.

Had we not closed the door properly when we went downstairs earlier? I thought about it for a moment before I concluded that we had closed the door completely. With pets in the house I had learned that doors had to be closed and locked to keep a certain feline from opening them and getting out. Diesel had learned early on how to manipulate doorknobs, and he often let himself out on the back screened-in porch at home.

Then a slight sound coming from the bedroom reached me, and I froze in place, Diesel by my side. He looked up at me and seemed about to meow, but I stuck a finger to my lips. He knew that gesture, and for once, he obeyed it. He must have sensed my disquiet. Usually nothing deterred him if he had a comment to make.

We moved as quietly as possible toward the bedroom door. It stood wide open, and when we reached it, a figure crouching by the bed stood, turned around, and screamed.

Cora. Only the maid. I felt relieved but also a bit annoyed.

Cora sank onto the bed, one hand clasped to her chest. She gasped out the words, "You frightened me."

"Sorry about that. You made me a bit nervous, too." I knew my tone was somewhat brusque, but that was my irritation coming through. "What are you doing here? I didn't see your cart. Are you looking for something?"

Cora nodded, still seated on the side of the bed. She took a couple of deep breaths to calm herself. Then she patted her head. I noticed that the dainty linen-and-lace cap she wore wasn't there.

"Did you lose your cap?" I asked.

"No," she said. "I lost my pin, and I thought it might have fallen out in here when I made your bed earlier."

"Was it there?"

"No," she said. Her eyes welled with tears. "I can't find it anywhere. My great aunt left it to me in her will a few years ago. It's an antique, the only really nice thing I have."

"I'm sorry to hear that," I said, full of sympathy for her.

Keepsakes from departed relatives were precious reminders of family, and losing a treasured one could be devastating.

"Thank you." She rubbed away the tears and got up from the bed. "I'm sorry if I startled you. I'm just beside myself over this."

"I promise we'll keep on the lookout for it," I said. "If we find it, we'll let you know immediately. I'm sure the other guests will be happy to do the same."

These words didn't seem to cheer Cora. "It's really valuable. If somebody finds it, they may decide to keep it for themselves. I'll never see it again."

"I don't think that's the case," I said in a hearty tone. "I know these people, and I don't think any one of them would do such a thing. I'll talk to them for you, don't worry."

She looked up, a dawning expression of hope in her eyes. "You'd do that?"

"Yes, I will. You go on about your work, and stop worrying. I'm sure your pin will turn up."

She sniffed. "Thank you, sir. I'll be on my way now." She hurried past Diesel and me and out of the room.

Diesel had remained at my side during my conversation with Cora, and now that I thought about it, I realized it was unusual. Normally if he's in the presence of someone who's sad, he wants to comfort the person. But he hadn't attempted that for Cora. Something about her had put him off, whereas it hadn't when he first met her. I couldn't figure out what it meant.

Surely she wasn't lying about the loss of her pin. Had it been an excuse for her to search our room? Had she been looking for some trifle to steal?

Suddenly I wasn't sure about leaving Diesel alone in the room. I didn't like the idea of someone coming into the room and leaving the door open. Diesel had more than his share of feline curiosity, and if he spotted an open door, he'd likely walk through it.

I knew I needed to get back downstairs soon, but I thought I could take long enough to let Diesel drink some water, eat a little kibble, and do anything else he found necessary before I took him back downstairs with me. The next time I saw Cora I would stress to her the importance of making sure the door was closed properly if she happened to find Diesel alone in our suite.

Helen Louise texted me a couple of minutes later, asking me why I was taking so long. I replied that we would be back in a couple of minutes.

"Come on, Diesel. Let's go," I said.

I heard a few more sounds of scratching in the litter box, and then the cat came loping toward me from the bathroom. I reattached the leash, and we headed downstairs to rejoin Helen Louise.

We found Sergeant Bloesch waiting for us at the door to the meeting room. "I'm sorry for the delay," I said.

"It's okay." She indicated that Diesel and I should precede her into the room. She closed the door firmly behind her and took a chair opposite the sofa where I sat with Helen Louise, Diesel at our feet. "Sorry this has taken so long," she said. "Miss An'gel assured me you're used to this kind of thing." She looked pointedly at me.

"Yes, I suppose I am."

Helen Louise chuckled.

The sergeant nodded. "What I'm looking for is any background you can give me on the deceased. We're still trying to find out about his doctors and any medication he might have been taking."

"We can't help you there," I said.

"No," Helen Louise said. "Neither of us knew him. More of a passing acquaintance than anything. He would sometimes eat at the French bistro I own, but I didn't know the man, except by reputation."

"Same for me," I said. "I couldn't tell you anything about his personal habits or his private life. I've heard more about him since we arrived in Asheville than I ever knew before."

"And what would that be?" Sergeant Bloesch asked.

"Apparently he was dating Ellie Arnold," I said. "Right, Helen Louise?"

She nodded. "Yes, though that's the extent of what I know about their relationship."

"Is there anything else, anything at all, that you can tell me about him?" Sergeant Bloesch looked hard at me for some reason. I had to wonder exactly what Miss An'gel had told her about me. Surely she hadn't regaled the sergeant with any of the murder investigations in which I was previously involved. I squirmed in my seat.

"Nothing that I imagine you haven't heard already from other members of the group," Helen Louise said.

I nodded. "He seemed to have a combative personality, if what we witnessed last night was any indication of his character."

"I'd like to hear your take on what happened," the sergeant said.

Helen Louise and I exchanged a glance, and I turned back to face the sergeant. "We—the group, that is—were in this room discussing Golden Age mystery writers, and Denis Kilbride suddenly swept in, making angry statements to Zac Ryan. That was when Johnny Ray Floyd stepped in and knocked Kilbride down. If he hadn't, I'm not sure what would have happened. Kilbride seemed really angry to me, and I suspect things would have turned violent between him and Zac Ryan."

"How did Ryan react to this?" the sergeant asked.

I tried to recall. "I can't remember. I don't think he had much time to react, because Johnny Ray stepped in so quickly."

"Do you agree with this description?" Sergeant Bloesch looked at Helen Louise.

"Yes, that's how I would describe it," she replied.

"You didn't observe anything that Mr. Harris didn't mention?"

"No," Helen Louise said. "Wait, there was something else. Zac and Johnny Ray shook hands after the punch."

"You're right." I felt annoyed with myself for forgetting that.

The sergeant scribbled something down before she resumed her questioning. I thought it odd that she didn't ask further about the handshake.

"Did you see Mr. Kilbride again that evening?"

"No," we said in unison.

"How about this morning?"

"No."

The sergeant considered us for a moment. Then she rose. "Thank you both. I appreciate your time." She nodded at Diesel. "Would it be okay if I rubbed your cat's head?"

"As long as he's okay with it. Hold out your hand toward him," I said.

Diesel sniffed the outstretched fingers. He evidently liked

whatever information he gleaned from his sniffing, for he rubbed his head against the sergeant's hand. She smiled and rubbed his head in return. Diesel purred for her.

"He sure is beautiful," she said. "I like cats, and I would love to have a Maine Coon."

"They're wonderful cats," I replied.

Sergeant Bloesch petted Diesel for a few seconds more. She straightened. "Thanks again."

After she exited the room, I leaned back and let myself relax. I hadn't realized I had been tense during our session with the police officer. Helen Louise seemed to relax also.

"What took you so long upstairs?" Helen Louise asked.

I told her about Cora and the lost pin.

"I noticed that pin," Helen Louise said thoughtfully. "It's quite beautiful, and I think it might be valuable as well."

"Do you think anyone in the group would keep it and not say anything if they found it?"

Helen Louise didn't respond right away. When she did, she surprised me. "Yes, I can think of one person."

FOURTEEN

"Is a member of the group a kleptomaniac?" I asked, astonished by Helen Louise's reply.

Helen Louise shrugged. "She could be a kleptomaniac, but I think she might do it deliberately because she likes beautiful things and can't afford them."

"Who?" I asked. "It has to be either Burdine, Celia, or Ellie."

"Celia," Helen Louise said.

"How on earth do you know this?" I asked, still trying to assimilate it.

Helen Louise stood suddenly. "Let's go back to our room and discuss this. I'm ready to get out of here for a while."

"Yes, of course," I said. "Come on, Diesel." We followed her out of the room and back up the stairs to the suite.

Helen Louise tucked her feet up under her in one corner of the sofa while I sat at the other end. Diesel curled into a large ball between us. "Okay," I said. "Now tell me how you know about Celia's sticky fingers."

Helen Louise gave a mirthless chuckle. "Sounds like the title of a melodrama. A few women from church have talked to me about this. We're all members of the Altar Guild, and Celia is, too. According to them, she has helped herself to trinkets from their purses at church and during visits to their homes."

"Has anyone confronted her about it?" I was trying hard to picture Celia as a thief and failing. She seemed so proper and ladylike most of the time.

"Usually people manage to get things back when they visit her house. She doesn't try to hide them, so it's easy to find them and reclaim them. Celia never says anything about it."

"That's bizarre," I said. "Has she ever taken anything of yours?"

Helen Louise laughed. "No, thankfully, because I never carry anything in my bag that would appeal to her. She hasn't been inside my house in years. I've rarely had time to host an Altar Guild meeting since business at the bistro really took off."

"I'm glad for your sake, then," I said. "Has anyone spoken to your priest about it?"

"No, because he can be a bit overbearing sometimes," Helen Louise said. "I imagine most of the women in our congregation are aware of it. I doubt Altar Guild members are the only women that Celia has taken things from. Things like this get around."

"What about the shops around town?" I asked, aghast at the potential scope of Celia's thievery.

"That I'm not sure," Helen Louise said. "I think Celia is aware enough not to shoplift from the stores in town. I believe she limits herself to private merchandise, if I can call it that."

"That's a small mercy," I said. "What do you think we should do about this? If Celia took that pin, we can't let her go back to Athena with it."

"If Celia runs true to form, the pin should be easy to find in her room," Helen Louise said. "Surely Cora will look in there. Did she tell you when she discovered she'd lost it?"

"No, she didn't, and I didn't think to ask," I said. "It must have been sometime today, don't you think? She would have noticed it if it had happened yesterday. She would have been looking then." I paused as I remembered something. "She did say she wondered if she'd lost it when she made our bed earlier. I didn't see Cora around the hotel this morning before we went to Biltmore, or after we got back. Did you?"

"No," Helen Louise said. "Do you think we could ask her more about it? I'm sure she'd appreciate help finding it, and maybe we could find some tactful way to hint to her that she should check Celia's room again."

I snorted with laughter. "If you can do that, then you ought to be a diplomat in Washington."

Helen Louise gave me a rueful grin. "You're right."

"We can ask her to tell us more about when she realized it was gone, and that might give us an opportunity to nudge her. She might even come up with the idea herself, if she hasn't already."

Helen Louise shifted on the sofa until she could reach the phone on the end table. She considered the menu on the phone, then punched a number. She identified herself and requested to have Cora come to our room when it was convenient. She listened for a moment, and her expression turned puzzled. "Thank you, I understand. Tomorrow, then."

She replaced the receiver and put the phone back on the end table. "Cora isn't working today, I was told. So I suppose she was here on her day off. Her bad luck that she found the body."

I frowned. "If that's the case, what was she doing in here earlier today making the bed? Wouldn't another maid have been doing it?"

"Maybe they're shorthanded today, and Cora was filling in," Helen Louise said. "The bed was unmade when we left for Biltmore, I do know that."

"And it was made when we returned," I finished.

"Is a puzzlement," Helen Louise said.

"Excuse me?" I said. That phrase sounded familiar, but I couldn't place it immediately.

"The king of Siam," Helen Louise said. "Don't you remember? *The King and I.* The king said it."

Recognition dawned, and I smiled. "Yes, I remember. Yul Brynner and Deborah Kerr. This situation definitely is a puzzlement."

"If Cora is still on the premises," Helen Louise said, "whoever I spoke to might mention that we want to talk to her. Otherwise, we'll have to wait until she's back on duty."

"Yes," I said. "In the meantime, we can do a little snooping on her behalf. What do you think?"

Helen Louise grimaced. "You mean, go to Celia's room for a visit, and while we're there, casually look around."

"Basically, yes," I said. "You said she doesn't hide things, so if that's the case, we should be able to spot it."

"Whoever spots it takes it and returns it to Cora, no questions asked or answered." Helen Louise sighed. "That's as good a plan as any, I suppose. Do you want to call her and invite ourselves to her room? Or simply go knock on her door without advance notice?"

I considered the issue briefly. "I think we go right now and knock on the door. She does like Diesel, and if he goes with us, she'll probably be willing to talk to us."

"You're being used as a pawn in your daddy's machinations." Helen Louise focused her attention on Diesel as she spoke. "How do you feel about that?"

Diesel responded with an interrogative-sounding trill. After a brief silence, he meowed.

"I think he's in," I said with a grin.

Helen Louise laughed. "Like Daddy, like kitty." She rose from the sofa and slipped her shoes back on. "All right. Let's go and do this."

Celia responded after the second round of knocking. She appeared fully alert when she opened the door. I was glad we hadn't wakened her from a nap. The moment she spotted Diesel, she smiled. "Y'all come on in. I was getting a little bored in here by myself."

Diesel padded after Celia and sat by her when she resumed her place in an overstuffed armchair in the small sitting area near the window. Helen Louise and I chose a sofa upholstered in the same fabric across from her. Celia had a room, rather than a suite, but it appeared to be every bit as comfortably appointed as our suite. The four-poster bed had to be an antique, I thought, but the bed linens and covering would be completely contemporary.

"The rooms here are certainly comfortable, aren't they?" Helen Louise said. "Your room is charming, don't you think?"

"I'm happy with it," Celia said. "What do y'all think about

this terrible business with Denis Kilbride? I didn't really know the man, but it's awful when someone that young dies suddenly."

"Yes, it is," I said. "I think he was close to my age, and that's a sobering thought."

"A few years younger than you, I would have said," Celia replied. "Though I thought he looked older from all that hard living he apparently did." She stroked the cat's head, and he purred for her. "Such a sweet boy."

"I didn't really know him," I said. "I sure was surprised by what happened last night." While I spoke I let my gaze travel slowly around the room. No sign of the pin from my vantage point.

"He did appear to be a man with a temper," Celia said. "And what on earth could that nice young man have done to make Kilbride upset with him? I've always found Zac to be pleasant and respectful."

"Yes, he does have nice manners," Helen Louise said. "I wasn't aware that the two of them knew each other myself."

"Me, either." I was trying to think of some reason to get up and roam around the room. I could see an assortment of things lying atop the bureau on the other side of the bed, but the light was a bit too dim for me to make out any details. I couldn't think of a plausible reason to get up and have a look over there.

Helen Louise got up from the sofa. "Pardon me, Celia, but I need to get up and move around a bit. My back stiffens up when I sit for very long, and we've been sitting almost the whole afternoon while we waited for the police officer to talk to us."

"Goodness, I certainly understand," Celia replied as Helen Louise began to move slowly around the room. "I suffer terribly from sciatica quite frequently, you know, and sitting too much only makes it worse. That's why I walk so much, especially around my neighborhood and to church."

I watched Helen Louise covertly as she moved around. "Walking is really good for you," I said. "I walk to work at Athena when the weather permits. Diesel likes to walk, too, because he always meets people who want to stop and pet him."

Hearing this, Diesel warbled and chirped, bringing a smile to Celia's face. At the moment Helen Louise was behind our hostess, and she looked at me, shaking her head slightly. No pin in sight, evidently.

"I talked to that maid, the one who's always falling asleep, you know," Celia said. "Cora, isn't it? Yes, that's her name. Anyway I told her walking ought to help her. Isn't that terrible, falling asleep like that all the time. She scared the dickens out of me yesterday, but when we talked earlier, she explained it all to me."

Helen Louise resumed her seat, and I said, trying not to sound too inquisitive, "Have you seen her today? We thought she had the day off."

Celia frowned. "Well, if she had the day off, why was she in her uniform when she came by my room to talk to me?"

I felt completely stupid. Cora had been wearing her uniform when I saw her as well. That detail had completely slipped my mind.

"Charlie saw her, too, this afternoon." Helen Louise gave me a sly wink. "He found her in our room. She said she was looking for a piece of jewelry she lost. Did she happen to mention it to you?"

FIFTEEN

I hadn't expected Helen Louise to ask Celia point-blank about the pin, but she knew more about the woman and her alleged kleptomania than I did.

Directness achieved results. Celia nodded. "Oh, my, yes, the poor thing was in such distress. She asked if I'd seen it. I mean, I had noticed her wearing it, of course, but I hadn't seen it elsewhere."

"Surely it will turn up soon," I said. "Someone could have picked it up and not thought anything about it."

"I suppose that's true," Celia said. "But if you have an eye for beautiful things, you'd spot that pin right away. Such a lovely thing. Quite old, too. My dear grandmama on my mother's side—her own mother, you know—had one she had been given by her mother. That pin was sadly lost in a house fire when I was a young girl. Grandmama's house burned down, you see."

I got a little lost trying to sort out the mothers and grandmothers, but that didn't really matter. Celia obviously knew the value of the pin, and this made me wonder whether she hadn't taken it after all. An object that held such sentimental associations would be too tempting to resist, perhaps. The only way to find out would be to conduct a thorough search of Celia's room. I wasn't prepared to do that, nor would Helen Louise be.

If anyone searched the room, it would have to be Cora herself, I decided. I wouldn't recommend that to her, however. She would have to figure that out for herself. I was sure that Helen Louise would agree with me.

Celia startled me with an exclamation. "Good heavens, is that the correct time?" She pointed to the digital clock on the bedside table. "Surely it can't already be almost five o'clock?"

I checked my watch. I had set it to the eastern time zone when we were in Gatlinburg, so I knew it was correct. "Yes, seven minutes to five."

Celia appeared agitated now. "Oh dear, I'm so sorry to cut your delightful visit short, but I have a dear friend here in Asheville, Betty Milton, and I promised to have dinner with her tonight. Oh, I really must get ready."

Helen Louise and I rose immediately. "We understand completely," Helen Louise said. "We'll be going now so that you have time to prepare for dinner with your friend."

"Yes, come along, Diesel. We're going back to our room."

We showed ourselves out and made our way back to our suite. When we were inside once again, I asked Helen Louise whether she thought Celia really had plans for dinner with a friend.

She shrugged. "I don't see why not. Why are you so suspicious of that? Do you think she got rattled and wanted to get rid of us?"

"Maybe." I explained my thoughts about the lure of an object with sentimental connotations.

Helen Louise pondered that for a moment. "That's possible, I suppose, but why would Celia get suspicious of us and want to get rid of us? We weren't pressing her for information about the pin that I recall."

"Maybe her guilty conscience," I suggested, although that sounded weak even to me.

"That's really stretching it," Helen Louise said with a chuckle. "You do get some wild ideas occasionally."

"I know," I said ruefully. "Maybe I'm determined to find a mystery where there really isn't one. I'm addicted, I guess."

"And this is a mystery week, after all," Helen Louise said.

Diesel chirped loudly then and caused us both to laugh.

"When the cat agrees, you know you have a problem," Helen Louise said.

"I suppose," I replied, and almost started laughing again.

"I propose to you, Mr. Harris," Helen Louise said, "that we forget about lost pins for the rest of the evening, perhaps even the rest of the week, and focus on enjoying ourselves. Since we have the evening free of group activities, what shall we do?"

"Miss Brady, I accept your proposal and will gladly forget about lost pins. I believe I can suggest a couple of things we can do to while away the time," I said.

"Do tell me of your ideas," Helen Louise said.

I did, and she agreed to them at once. We left Diesel on the sofa with the television on while we put the ideas into action elsewhere.

When we returned, sometime later, we found Diesel sound asleep on the sofa. He woke at my touch and meowed at me.

Then he yawned and twisted onto his back so that I could rub his belly. After about fifteen seconds of that, he twisted again and slid down to the floor and ambled toward the bathroom.

"What would you like to do about dinner?" Helen Louise asked.

"We can go out, if you like," I said. "I think Diesel will be okay. I never got around to calling about a pet sitter last night."

"Probably too late to get one now," Helen Louise said. "Where's that list we were given? Didn't it indicate some places nearby that would deliver? We can eat in if you like. I'm happy to stay in tonight."

That is what we did. We found a Chinese restaurant that delivered on the list, and after I inquired, they agreed to supply some boiled chicken for Diesel as part of the order. The food arrived, hot and delicious, forty minutes later. The three of us enjoyed our dinner in and retired to bed around eleven, looking forward to a good night's sleep free of drama of any kind.

Whether it was the Chinese food—which I adored but didn't have that often—or my devious subconscious, which seemed to love to plague me, I had a night filled with peculiar dreams.

In one I was a detective faced with sorting out a series of mysterious thefts, and Helen Louise and Miss Dickce turned out to be a pair of international jewel thieves who used cats to help them. Diesel was the leader of the feline cohort, and he could speak English perfectly well.

I woke briefly from that one, convinced that I had heard Diesel talking to me. I soon lapsed back into sleep and fell into another weird dream. This one involved an elaborate party game in which I was the only one who had no idea what was going on. Everyone else was dashing around solving crimes while I sat in the midst of all the activity, asking someone to explain things to me.

When morning came and the sun began to suffuse the room with light, I awoke with a headache and a cat lying across my legs. Groggily I shifted Diesel aside so I could get up. Helen Louise appeared to be still asleep, and I moved carefully so as not to wake her.

I figured my dreams were meant to tell me that I was too preoccupied with murder and mysteries, like missing hatpins. I had mystery on the brain, as my late mother would have said. I chuckled and finished my shower.

By the time I had dressed, Helen Louise was up and preparing to meet the day. We went downstairs at eight for the buffet-style breakfast in the dining room, bringing Diesel with us. I had decided that, since the hotel wasn't open to the public for breakfast—only lunch and dinner—I would be safe in bringing Diesel down with us. We were the first to arrive. I made sure to get extra bacon to share with my cat when I filled my plate. We chose a table against the wall to keep Diesel out of the way of the other diners.

Miss An'gel, Miss Dickce, and Benjy arrived next. After they selected what they wanted, they chose a table next to ours, and we shared greetings. I was amused to see that Benjy's plate was piled high. The appetites of youth, when one's metabolism burned through the calories, I thought ruefully. I had tried to be conservative with my portions, but breakfast was my favorite meal. Particularly a breakfast that featured freshly made biscuits, gravy, grits, sausage, and eggs scrambled to perfection, not to mention four kinds of jam—apricot, plum, blackberry, and grape. I could almost believe that my housekeeper, Azalea Berry, was in the hotel kitchen this morning.

The rest of the group, including Ellie Arnold, who chose a table to herself despite Melba's invitation to join her and Paul, arrived soon after. Johnny Ray, with his wife and three children, provided considerable interest. The eldest of the three, J. R., was so well behaved as to be almost invisible. The five-year-old twins, however, made up for that with their antics. Nothing malicious, simply high spirits. Johnny Ray rode herd on them and never allowed them to become obnoxious, for which the rest of us no doubt gave silent thanks.

Miss An'gel stood and called for silence as everyone appeared to be nearing completion of their meals. "Good morning, everyone. Yesterday was quite eventful in an unexpected way, and we are still awaiting further information on certain aspects of it." She surveyed the room, and I thought her gaze lingered on the younger Floyds during those last words. I knew she wouldn't want to say anything that could possibly frighten the twins.

"We will resume our activities this morning to catch up," she continued. "I propose that we simply skip the session we were unable to hold yesterday and not try to alter the rest of our schedule. I'm sure we would all like to take advantage of all that this lovely city has to offer this week and not spend extra time indoors." She paused for comment.

"That's fine with us," Burdine Gregory said. Elmore nodded.

"We're good," Johnny Ray said.

"Same here," Paul Bowen said after a glance at Melba.

Celia, Ellie, and Zac all nodded, and Helen Louise and I said that we agreed. Diesel added his own comment with a loud meow, and that caused the Floyd children to laugh.

"Excellent," Miss An'gel said. "Then we'll gather in the meeting room at nine-thirty as planned." She resumed her seat.

"Do you remember what this session is about?" Helen Louise asked me, her voice low.

"You mean you didn't commit the schedule to memory?" I said in mock dismay. "Shame on you."

Helen Louise kicked my shin under the table, but lightly.

"All right," I said. "You don't have to resort to violence." Before she could kick me again, I hurried on. "We're having a discussion of Golden Age conventions. Like snowed-in country houses, small village settings, the all-will-be-revealed scene at the end—that kind of thing."

"That should be fun," Helen Louise said.

We finished our meal and headed upstairs to freshen up, along with several of the others. I checked my watch when we left the dining room. Already nearly ten minutes after nine.

The three of us came back downstairs thirteen minutes later, and when I opened the door to the meeting room, I saw that we were the first to arrive. I had expected Miss An'gel to be there, at least.

As we moved farther into the room, I discovered that we weren't alone after all. A familiar figure lay sprawled on one of the sofas. Cora was evidently having another of her narcoleptic episodes.

I motioned for Helen Louise to go and wake her. I thought it might startle her less than if I did it.

Helen Louise moved forward and bent to tap Cora on the

shoulder. She stopped, then drew back abruptly. She motioned for me to join her.

When I reached Helen Louise, I looked down at Cora, supine on the sofa. She had found her pin, I noticed. Someone had thrust it into her heart.

SIXTEEN

"We checked for signs of life, naturally," I said to Sergeant Bloesch, who arrived within seconds of the EMS personnel. "There were none. No pulse, no discernible breath, although she was still warm."

Sergeant Bloesch nodded. "All right, Mr. Harris. You and Miss Brady can go back to the dining room with the others. Him, too." She pointed to Diesel, her lips twitching into a brief smile.

"Thank you." I felt drained, although we had been with the sergeant for only twenty minutes or so. I recalled the shock and horror when Helen Louise and I realized Cora was dead. Obviously murdered. She certainly wouldn't have stuck her pin into her own heart.

Who would have wanted to murder Cora? Why? Could it have had anything to do with Denis Kilbride's death? We still hadn't had word of the autopsy results. If Kilbride's death turned out not to be natural and was classed as a murder, then Cora's murder had to be linked to his.

I didn't have time to share any of this with Helen Louise before we returned to the dining room. We went to our table and resumed our seats. Diesel lay on the floor by my feet. He could sense the mood, I knew, and as a result was quiet.

"Any news?" Miss An'gel asked.

I shook my head. Glancing around the room, I saw pretty much the same expression everywhere I looked. Shock gradually turning into dismay and worry. Johnny Ray had asked permission, and been granted it, to allow his wife and children to return to their room. That had surprised me a bit, but I was grateful. I couldn't see any purpose being served by keeping the children and their mother here.

"I can't believe somebody would harm that poor girl," Elmore Gregory suddenly burst out. "Who on earth 'ud do such a thing?"

"A psychopath," Burdine said fervently. "Some psycho killer came in off the streets and murdered her."

Zac Ryan laughed, the sound harsh in the silence that followed Burdine's melodramatic remark. "You've got to be kidding me. Why would some random person wander into this hotel and kill a maid? Use your brain, woman."

Burdine flushed an angry red, but before she could form a retort, Miss An'gel spoke sharply. "Let's keep any discussion on this terrible matter civil, if you please. While I agree with Zac that the likelihood of Cora's being murdered by someone off the street is slim, we as yet really don't know anything about her murder. So let's not indulge in idle speculation."

"Quite right, An'gel," Celia Bernardi said with a surprised

glance at Zac. He did not appear at all abashed by Miss An'gel's words, nor by Celia's look.

I wished Zac had more tact, but I had observed that he could be blunt to the point of rudeness on occasion. I understood his response to Burdine's remark, but I would never have said anything like that to her face. My Southern grandmothers would rise from their graves and strike me down if I ever dared be that rude to an older person.

What chilled me to the core was the knowledge that someone in this room might have killed Cora—whose surname we didn't even know, I realized. Or perhaps Arthur had had a brainstorm and decided to do away with her, blaming her for his problems.

That was ludicrous, I thought. *Really stretching there, Charlie*, I jeered at myself. *Slow down and wait for more information.*

That was good advice I gave myself. I took a few deep breaths and tried to relax. I wasn't on home ground here. I was in another state, in a city larger than Athena, and I didn't know anyone in local law enforcement. I doubted my assistance would be encouraged here. I could end up in trouble myself if I tried to be too helpful.

I caught Helen Louise regarding me with a sympathetic expression. She knew me well. I smiled and patted her hand where it lay on the table.

Miss An'gel's directive to keep conversation civil seemed to have put a damper on speech. *Just as well*, I decided, eyeing the patrol officer standing by the door leading out of the dining room. Though everyone in this room had read many mystery novels, they would soon discover that being involved in a real murder investigation was not simply a matter of being entertained for a few hours by a good book.

Most of the group knew about my own experiences back in Athena, though I had always shied away from the limelight. Word leaked out occasionally, but when confronted, I always downplayed my role. I gave the credit to Chief Deputy Kanesha Berry, the professional, and she was truly a professional. Ethical, driven, determined, intelligent, and honest. Athena County was lucky to have her. Our police department was too small to have its own homicide team, so the county took over, unlike here. And, when necessary, the Mississippi Bureau of Investigation stepped in. Usually, though, Kanesha and her team were more than capable of handling homicide in Athena County.

There were no doubt competent homicide investigators in Asheville. I had no idea what the crime rate was—or the homicide rate, to be more precise—but they wouldn't be inexperienced here. I needed to mind my business and let the professionals do their jobs. I would have to remind myself of that until this investigation concluded.

A little part of me said, *Yeah right. You're way too nosy to sit back and let others do the work without you.*

I told that little part to shut up and go away, but I knew it wouldn't.

I was nosy. I was also angry about Cora's death. There could be no reason good enough for the poor woman to be killed like that, and I wanted the person responsible to pay the price for it. A person possibly in this room, right this minute. I automatically checked Helen Louise, the Ducote sisters, and Benjy off the list, but everyone else was a suspect.

"Relax," Helen Louise said. "Have some more juice or coffee, or maybe another buttered biscuit with jam."

I shook my head. "No, I'm jittery enough as it is. That poor woman."

"I know," Helen Louise said. "I'm so angry right now. Such an inoffensive person. What could she possibly have done, or have known, to make someone want to kill her?"

"Once the police can answer those questions, they'll know who the murderer is," I said.

"Could be someone in this room now," Helen Louise murmured.

I nodded. "Unless it was a member of the hotel staff, I should think."

"Maybe there's an estranged husband or boyfriend in the background," Helen Louise said.

"Definitely possible," I replied, "and though that's pretty awful, it would be a better answer than having one of our group be the killer."

Sergeant Bloesch entered the room and called for attention to end the low buzz of conversation. Everyone turned toward her.

"I have to inform you that we are treating Miss Apfel's death as a homicide," she said. "A lieutenant from homicide has arrived, and we will be questioning everyone in turn, along with the hotel staff. This is going to take some time, and we realize this is inconvenient for you. The room you have been using for your meetings is sealed off as a crime scene. We will release it as soon as we're done with it. In the meantime, we ask that you stay here until you are called."

Burdine raised her hand, and the sergeant nodded. "What about going to the ladies' room?" Burdine asked.

Sergeant Bloesch indicated the officer standing at the door. "Let this officer know, and he'll get someone to accompany you."

"Accompany me?" Burdine sounded shocked. "Into the ladies' room with me?"

I would have sworn that the sergeant started to laugh but quickly suppressed it. "No, ma'am, not into the room, just to the room. The officer will wait for you and then escort you back here."

"Oh, that's better," Burdine said.

"Now, if there are no other questions?" The sergeant paused, but receiving none, she said, "Mr. Harris and Miss Brady, if you would come with me please?"

Helen Louise and I stood to follow her. Sergeant Bloesch stared at Diesel for a moment, then nodded. I brought him with me, and we followed her out of the room.

The sergeant led us to a small lounge next to our meeting room. One wall held shelves of books and a fireplace and mantel, and a large desk stood in front of another. A tall, balding man stood behind the desk and watched, his expression relaxed, as we approached the desk.

"Please, take a seat." His gruff tone and deep voice belied his appearance, and Helen Louise and I did as requested. Diesel hunkered down between us, and I rubbed his head to reassure him that everything was fine.

"I'm Lieutenant Wesner," he said as he resumed his own seat behind the desk. He glanced at his notes. "You are Mr. Charles Harris and Miss Helen Louise Brady from Athena, Mississippi. Correct?"

"Yes," Helen Louise and I said in unison. I thought I detected an East Texas twang to the lieutenant's voice. He reminded me of people I'd known in my Houston days.

"And who is that with you?" Wesner pointed to Diesel.

"His name is Diesel," I said.

"I see," Wesner said. "Now, you found the body."

"We did," I said.

"Tell me how you came to find it and what you did when you discovered it."

The routine began. I had been through this several times in the past, and the process had many tedious aspects. I started with our leaving our suite to come downstairs and carried the story forward to the point when we entered the room and spotted the sleeping—or so we thought—maid, Cora.

Helen Louise took it from there. "We thought it might startle her less to have me wake her," she said. "I was about to touch her shoulder when I spotted the pin sticking out of her chest. I motioned for Charlie to join me. We checked for signs of life, but there weren't any."

"We left the room then and went to the reception desk," I said, "and told the clerk on duty that we had found Cora dead on the sofa. He called 911, and we waited there until Sergeant Bloesch and the EMS team arrived."

"That's quite clear," Wesner said. "Did either of you know the deceased before you came to this hotel?"

"No," I said. "This is my first trip to Asheville, and I don't know anyone here. Anyone who's not in our group, that is."

"I've been to Asheville before, some years ago," Helen Louise said, "but I never met Cora until this trip."

"Do you have any idea who might have wanted to harm Miss Apfel?" Wesner asked.

Helen Louise and I exchanged a quick glance; then I faced Lieutenant Wesner. I knew what I was going to say might sound more than a little odd.

"It might have been the person who stole her pin."

SEVENTEEN

I could see that Wesner was taken aback by what I said.

"Could you explain that?" he said.

"The pin embedded in her chest was a family heirloom, according to what Cora told me." I went on to relate the circumstances of our meetings with Cora and everything she had told us about the pin and its disappearance. I did not mention the visit that Helen Louise, Diesel, and I had paid to Celia Bernardi. We had no proof that Celia had taken it, and I didn't feel comfortable mentioning Celia's habit of thievery. That would have to come from Helen Louise, who knew more about it than I.

Wesner listened to me without interruption, his gaze piercing and more than a bit unnerving. When I finished, he did not comment right away. The silence lengthened, and I wondered what was going through the lieutenant's mind.

He stood and said, "Thank you. I think that will be all for

the moment. Sergeant." He indicated that Sergeant Bloesch should show us out.

She opened the door and ushered us out. "You can go to your room if you like, or back to the dining room with the others." She shut the door firmly behind us.

"Didn't that seem strange to you?" Helen Louise asked.

I nodded. "I wonder what's going on, frankly. I expected him to have more questions. It's his investigation, though. What would you rather do? Go up to the room, or wait with the others?" I was torn. I hated to miss anything, which we would of course do by going to the room. On the other hand, sitting in the dining room for perhaps a couple of hours would be tedious.

"How about this," Helen Louise said with a faint grin. "I'll take Diesel up to the room and keep him company, and you can go back to the dining room so you don't miss anything."

I had to laugh. This woman read me all too easily. I couldn't hide anything from her.

"That sounds fine." I pulled her close for a kiss. When I released her, Diesel meowed loudly and rubbed against my legs. I scratched his head and told him what a good boy he was. I watched Helen Louise lead him up the stairs and waited until I could no longer see them before I went back into the dining room.

I felt the tension right away. All heads turned in my direction when I came into the room. Everyone looked expectant, but of course I had nothing to tell them.

Miss An'gel beckoned me to her table, and I approached her. "Please join us." She indicated an empty chair beside her, and I took it. "I presume Helen Louise has gone upstairs with Diesel."

"Yes, the sergeant said we could go upstairs or wait in here," I said, loud enough for the others in the room to hear.

"What's going on?" Elmore demanded. "How long are they going to keep us sitting here?"

"Don't ask me," I said. "You'll have to ask the sergeant or her boss that."

I thought for a moment that Elmore, or his wife, was going to argue the point, but Melba spoke up sharply. "Charlie's right. They'll get to us when they get to us. That poor woman was murdered."

"Yes, she was," Celia said. "That poor young woman, she couldn't have been more than forty, I'd say—still in the prime of life."

"Don't let's get maudlin," Zac said, a trace of impatience in his voice. "I'm sorry she died, but don't pretend that any of us knew her well enough to grieve for her."

Zac was right, in that tactless way he sometimes had, but his words came across as more than a bit brutal. Perhaps it was the fact that he was so much younger than everyone in the group except for Benjy. I noticed, however, that Benjy was regarding Zac with a frown.

"How did she die?" Burdine asked. "Was she stabbed or strangled? Or beaten to death?" The eagerness in her posture and in her tone disgusted me. I had never realized she had such a love of the sensational.

I saw the officer at the door step forward, but I forestalled him. "You ought to know by now, Burdine, that I can't share any details of what I've seen. You've read enough police procedurals to understand why."

She had the grace to look abashed, and I felt slightly remorseful for the chiding tone in which I had spoken. Only slightly, however. I could see Elmore smirking at his wife.

That put an end to attempts at conversation for the next few minutes. The silence lengthened until it became unnerving. Why didn't the lieutenant call someone else in for questioning? Was he talking to hotel staff first? That made sense, now that I thought of it. They could give him more background on Cora, her duties and her life, than could any of us.

Finally Sergeant Bloesch came back and asked for Ellie Arnold. Ellie had been so quiet all this time that I had forgotten she was here. She seemed to have withdrawn from everyone at the news of Cora's death, a frozen figure locked in silent misery, sitting in the corner.

The sergeant had to call Ellie's name twice before the woman responded. Then she got to her feet and slowly followed the sergeant from the room.

"What's up with her?" Burdine asked. "She's like a zombie this morning."

"The poor woman is in shock, I would say," Celia said. "And I think she's afraid of something."

"Afraid she'll be next?" Elmore said. "Could be any one of us. Whoever murdered that poor girl might want to kill somebody else now. You know what they say—once they kill they get the taste for it and don't stop."

Miss An'gel fixed Elmore with her glacial gaze, and he shut up immediately. "I don't think it behooves us to engage in conversation of that kind, do you?"

Elmore reddened but evidently could find no reply, not that Miss An'gel expected one. She continued to regard him, and he wilted further. Then she turned away from him to me. I knew she was frustrated by the need for silence on the details of Cora's death, but I didn't think now was the time for me to try to share them, even covertly.

The officer at the door kept a watchful eye on us. I thought about trying to text Miss An'gel the barest details of our discovery of Cora's body, but if I were caught, I might get in trouble. Miss An'gel would have to wait to satisfy her curiosity, as would everyone else.

Johnny Ray seemed to have withdrawn also. I regarded him for a moment. His gaze had turned inward, I felt sure. Until he found out the truth about Denis Kilbride's death and whether he'd had any role in it, he would remain unsettled and guilt ridden. I wished heartily I could have eased his mind, but I knew that didn't lie within my power. I did say a quick prayer on his behalf, however, and hoped for the best for him.

Ellie did not return to the dining room when the sergeant came back to ask for Burdine and Elmore. Johnny Ray was the next called, and then Zac Ryan. Melba and Paul were called separately, and finally I was left with only Miss An'gel in the room with me. I checked my watch, and nearly two hours had passed.

Miss An'gel looked at me. "I simply can't believe all this has happened, Charlie. This was meant to be a fun, carefree week, and instead we've stumbled into yet another murder, perhaps two." Her tone was not in the least accusatory, simply matter-of-fact. After a moment she continued briskly. "It has happened, and we must do our duty as called upon by those in charge."

"Yes, ma'am." I knew she was itching to solve this mystery as much as I was. I wasn't the only amateur sleuth in Athena. Miss An'gel and Miss Dickce had had their own adventures in detection. We both well knew that it was up to the official investigators to solve the case, but we also knew that there were times when amateurs could pick up facts that might elude the police. When that happened, we would share what we knew with them. The goal was to bring the murderer to justice, not to find personal glory. Neither the Ducote sisters nor I had ever sought the spotlight.

I wished I could tell her what Helen Louise and I knew about Cora's murder, but under the still-watchful eye of the officer at the door, I didn't try. Before much longer we would be able to discuss the case. I also hoped we would soon know what had killed Denis Kilbride. If, as I suspected, Kilbride's death was not from natural causes, then it must be connected to Cora's murder. The coincidence of a natural death and a murder so close together in the same hotel was too great.

I knew Miss An'gel well enough to be sure that she thought the same. With her awareness of business dealings in Athena, she might have facts about Kilbride pertinent to his death. Throw Melba into the mix, with her uncanny knowledge of goings-on in Athena, and we ought to be able to come up with plausible motives for murder. Helen Louise, with her legal training and orderly mind, could spot flaws in logic that I, in my enthusiasm, might overlook.

Helen Louise and Diesel must have been wondering what was taking so long, I thought. I probably should have joined them upstairs an hour ago, but my insatiable curiosity kept me here. I hoped Helen Louise wouldn't be annoyed with me, though I really couldn't have blamed her if she was. I hesitated briefly, but then rose from my chair.

"Miss An'gel, I think I'd better get upstairs and check on Helen Louise and Diesel," I said.

Sergeant Bloesch's return forestalled any reply Miss An'gel planned to make. "Miss Ducote, Mr. Harris, would you come with me please? Lieutenant Wesner wants to see you both."

Miss An'gel rose immediately, and I followed her to the door. The sergeant ushered us to where Wesner waited, and he gestured to the two chairs that Helen Louise and I had occupied a couple of hours ago.

Once Miss An'gel was seated, Wesner picked up a small stack of paper and waved it at us. "We've been doing some checking on you with the authorities in Mississippi. Specifically, with the chief of police and the sheriff's department in Athena."

I wondered if he himself had actually talked to Kanesha. No doubt she would have had a few things to say about my helpfulness.

"According to my intel," Wesner continued, "you're both upstanding citizens who've assisted in the past with murder investigations in Athena and elsewhere. While I will not tolerate any interference in the work of myself and my staff, I am aware that we're working at a bit of a disadvantage in this situation. You know the people involved in this, whereas I do not. I am not officially clearing either of you from suspicion in this case yet, but I am willing to listen to what you have to say."

"Thank you," Miss An'gel said. "We both are happy to assist in any way we can."

I nodded. "Of course."

"If we are going to be able to assist you," Miss An'gel said, her tone not in the least placatory, "there is one thing we must know."

"You want to know about Denis Kilbride's death," Wesner said, his expression passive.

"Yes," Miss An'gel and I said together.

"Fair enough, I suppose," Wesner replied. "Denis Kilbride was murdered, probably with the same hatpin that killed Cora Apfel."

EIGHTEEN

Even though I had expected to learn that Denis Kilbride had been murdered, I couldn't help feeling shocked at hearing it actually stated, especially the method.

"In fact, Mr. Harris, it wasn't until you and Miss Brady told me earlier about Miss Apfel's search for the hatpin that I connected it with Mr. Kilbride's death," Wesner said.

"Do you mean that you thought his death was natural before that?" I asked, puzzled.

"Not exactly," Wesner replied. "The medical examiner found the spot on the back of Kilbride's head where a thin sharp object had been inserted, but we didn't know what it was. I think now it was most likely that same hatpin. The killer must have found it when Miss Apfel lost it, and then used it again on Miss Apfel. The question is, why?"

"I think she probably found it in the killer's room," Miss

An'gel said. "Naturally she wouldn't have had any idea that it had been used to murder Kilbride."

"Why would the killer want to kill her, though?" I asked.

"Once the results of the autopsy became known," Miss An'gel replied, "Cora might have figured out that it had been used to commit murder. I would think that you and your team would question everyone about the pin and be on the lookout for such an object, Lieutenant."

Wesner nodded. "Yes, we would. I believe you are correct, Miss Ducote. The killer might have planned to drop it somewhere in the hotel where Miss Apfel or one of the staff would find it, but if Miss Apfel forestalled that by finding it in the killer's room, that put the killer at risk."

I nodded. "That is probably what happened. The poor woman."

"Have you told the rest of the group yet that Kilbride was definitely murdered?" Miss An'gel said.

"No, only the two of you," Wesner said. "I realize it would be difficult for you not to share the news, however. I want you to keep it to yourselves until I have had a chance to question all the members of the group a second time. I plan to do that after lunch."

"I'm sure we can manage to keep it from the others until then," I said.

"Certainly," Miss An'gel said. "Is there anything more you wish to ask us?"

Wesner shook his head. "No, you can go. I've told everyone I'd like them to be in the dining room at two. I'll expect to see you both there." With that, we were dismissed.

Miss An'gel and I rose and left the room. We walked up the stairs together, speaking in undertones on the way.

"I will find it hard not to confide in Sister," Miss An'gel said. "We have rarely kept secrets from each other."

"Same here, with Helen Louise," I said. "Frankly, I can't see that it will hurt to tell them. I would trust them both with my life."

"As would I," Miss An'gel said. "Then I take it you'll be telling Helen Louise and I will tell Sister."

I laughed. "Yes."

"What are you and Helen Louise planning to do for lunch?" Miss An'gel asked.

"We had planned to go out," I said, "but now, I'm not sure. Frankly, I'm a bit anxious leaving Diesel alone in our room. He would be too easy a target if someone wanted to get at me."

"That's true." Miss An'gel paused at the top of the stairs. "Have you thought about engaging a pet sitter?"

"I have," I said, "but I haven't done it yet. I found a listing online, but for some reason, I'm reluctant to follow through with it."

"Sister and I have several friends in the area," Miss An'gel said. "Let us make a few calls, and I believe we might be able to find someone trustworthy. I wouldn't want anything to happen to that sweet kitty, either."

"Thank you." I appreciated Miss An'gel's thoughtfulness, but I wouldn't stop worrying. I hoped Helen Louise would understand.

We parted then, and I headed for our suite. I knocked on the door to alert Helen Louise, then unlocked it and walked in, shutting the door quickly behind me and making sure it was locked.

Helen Louise looked up from the book she was reading and smiled. Diesel ambled toward me, uttering warbles and trills of greeting. I rubbed his back several times before I went to kiss Helen Louise. She laid aside her book, the latest by Ellery Adams.

I was anxious to read it, but I had given it to her first because I knew how much she loved Adams's writing.

"How is it?" I asked after we kissed.

She laughed. "The kiss is nice, as always."

I grinned. "Thanks for the review, but I meant the book."

"Terrific, what else?" she said, patting the sofa beside her. "Sit down and tell me everything, and then let's get something to eat. Or shall we get something to eat and you can tell me while we're eating?"

"Whichever you would like," I said, sinking onto the sofa, "but I'm afraid I'm more nervous than before about leaving Diesel alone in the room." Diesel climbed up onto the sofa with us and stretched out.

"What's happened?"

I hadn't intended to alarm her, but from her tone I knew I had done that. "Lieutenant Wesner told me and Miss An'gel that Denis Kilbride was murdered, and he thinks the murder weapon was Cora Apfel's hatpin. You're not supposed to know that, however, so be surprised this afternoon when he tells everyone."

Helen Louise didn't look all that surprised by my news, and I hadn't thought she would be. "As we both expected. That Denis was murdered, that is. After we found Cora this morning, I did wonder about the hatpin, of course."

I shared the rest of the conversation that Miss An'gel and I'd had with the lieutenant, and Helen Louise listened without interrupting me. Then I told her about Miss An'gel's offer to call around to find a reliable pet sitter for us.

"That's kind of her," Helen Louise said, "but with a killer in the hotel, I don't think we can in all good faith ask someone to look after Diesel."

"I'm sure Miss An'gel will realize that," I said, feeling a bit guilty that I hadn't thought of this point myself. "Unless she finds us a retired police officer, that is."

"I wouldn't be at all surprised." Helen Louise chuckled. "In that case, I suppose it would be all right."

"We'll see. In the meantime, what should we do about lunch?"

"I don't imagine they'll be serving downstairs," Helen Louise said. "I'm sure the staff is too upset to focus on providing the usual lunch here."

"Probably so, but I guess it can't hurt to call."

Helen Louise reached for the phone beside her on the end table and punched in a number. "Yes, this is Miss Brady. We're wondering whether lunch will be served today as usual." She paused. "I see. Thank you." She replaced the receiver and turned back to me.

"That's one problem solved," she said. "They're serving. I keep forgetting they're open to the public, and that this is a popular place in the area to eat lunch and dinner. The dining room is opening a few minutes late, but if we go down now we shouldn't have a problem getting a table."

"When word gets out about a double murder in the hotel, the restaurant will be crammed with thrill seekers," I said gloomily.

"I doubt they've found out yet," Helen Louise said, "although that depends on the local media. I suppose we should turn on the local news at some point to find out what they're saying."

"Not now," I said. "I'm hungry. I need to wash my hands, and then I'll be ready to go."

"We'll be ready," Helen Louise said. Diesel meowed.

We walked downstairs with Diesel between us, his leash in my left hand. I wasn't about to leave him alone, and if anyone complained, I would take Diesel back upstairs and stay with him. I heard the murmur of voices before we reached the foot of the stairs, but the volume grew louder the closer we got. I estimated that about thirty people stood outside the dining room, waiting for it to open.

I didn't spot any of our group among them. I wondered whether these were the usual customers or the first wave of thrill seekers, anxious to say they had dined in the hotel where there had been two murders. I would have turned back if Helen Louise hadn't urged me forward.

"Everything will be fine," Helen Louise said. "Look, the doors are opening. These are probably the regulars."

I hoped she was right. As the last to arrive, we waited for everyone else to precede us into the dining room. We found our usual table against a wall unoccupied, and we took it. Diesel hunkered down under the table. I knew he was uncomfortable, but he would be safe as long as he was with us. I made sure I kept the leash looped around my left wrist.

We had to wait several minutes before a server appeared, but that was understandable, given the sudden onslaught of so many customers at one time. I eavesdropped on conversations at nearby tables. The little I managed to glean assured me that no one near us was aware of the murders yet.

"Thank goodness," I murmured as I examined today's menu.

Helen Louise shot me an interrogative glance, and I leaned forward to whisper to her. She nodded when I finished. "One meal in peace anyway," she said.

Mr. Hindman appeared in the dining room and began to make his way slowly around the room, chatting with customers. Evidently this was a usual practice of his based on my observation that he was greeted with a smile wherever he stopped. He didn't reach our table, some of his chats being extended, until Helen Louise and I were finishing our entrées. Diesel had been content beneath the table, and I slipped him a few bites of grilled chicken after I ascertained it had been cooked without anything harmful to cats.

"Good afternoon," Mr. Hindman said as he came to our table. "I trust everything is to your satisfaction."

"The food is delicious," Helen Louise said. "My compliments to your staff, especially after this morning's events."

Hindman stiffened briefly and glanced around as if to see whether anyone else had heard Helen Louise's remarks. He seemed satisfied that no one had when he faced us again. His expression had relaxed.

"I'm glad to hear it. Yes, they had quite a shock, as did I," he said. "You're part of the group from Athena, aren't you?"

"Yes, we are," I said.

"You're the couple with the Maine Coon," Hindman said. "Now I remember." He glanced down at my feet. "There he is. Such a handsome animal. I don't normally allow pets in the dining room, but An'gel insisted that I make an exception for this gentleman." He grinned suddenly. "And as I'm sure you're well aware, what An'gel wants, she never fails to get."

"Oh yes," I said. "I must tell you I appreciate your letting us bring him in here. I don't like leaving him in the room for extended periods of time. He's not destructive, but given the events of the past couple of days, I'm a little leery. I'm sure you can understand."

Hindman nodded. "Unfortunately, I do understand." He stepped closer and dropped his voice. "So far this hasn't hit the papers, but I suspect it will break in tomorrow's edition. Probably the newspaper website this evening."

"I hope you won't be overrun with ghouls," Helen Louise said.

"That's a risk I can't avoid," Hindman said. "If it weren't for the police, I would already have asked you all to leave."

NINETEEN

I didn't take in the full import of Hindman's words right away. Then what he said penetrated.

Before either Helen Louise or I could respond, he continued. "I'm sure you understand. A small boutique hotel like this can't afford adverse publicity."

"It's a bit late for that," Helen Louise said flatly.

"I suppose the police want to keep us all in one place because it's easier for them," I said.

Hindman shrugged. "That's what they said. Look, it's nothing personal. I'm sure most of your group are perfectly nice folks, but it seems pretty obvious that one of you isn't. Until the police figure out which one of you it is, I don't like the idea of any of my staff being put in danger any more than I relish the notion of having more of my guests murdered."

His voice had risen enough so that people nearby picked up on his words. Gradually the buzz of conversation ceased, and

Hindman realized what he had done. Chagrined, he turned around to face the dining room. Helen Louise and I took that as our signal to depart, and we did so while Hindman attempted to explain to the remaining customers.

"I understand his concerns as a business owner," Helen Louise said, "but it's still disconcerting to hear that someone wants to kick you out of a hotel."

"I understand it, too, but he set himself up by not paying more attention to his decibel level." I unlocked the door and ushered Helen Louise and Diesel inside. I bolted the door and followed Helen Louise and Diesel to the couch. I removed Diesel's halter and leash, and he stretched and rolled on the carpet in celebration.

"Naturally the police want us to remain here," Helen Louise said. "They don't want any of their suspects slipping away from them." All at once she uttered a bark of laughter. "This is the first time I've been one of the suspects. I don't think I care for it."

"Not a particularly pleasant experience," I agreed. "We have the advantage over the police here, however. We know we can immediately rule out five of the suspects."

Helen Louise thought about that for a moment. "Well, I'd say six, because you have to include Melba on that list, along with Miss An'gel, Miss Dickce, Benjy, you, and me."

"Good grief, yes," I said. "Don't ever tell her I'd forgotten her, even for a moment."

"The problem is, I have trouble seeing any of the remaining members of the group as a murderer," Helen Louise said. "The two most obvious suspects are Ellie and Zac, because of their relationships to Denis Kilbride."

"When you think about how it was done," I said, "I can't see how someone not intimately acquainted with Kilbride could have managed it."

Helen Louise looked startled. "I hadn't thought about that, but you're right. Unless he was asleep, I suppose."

"That could be," I said, "but then there's the problem of getting into his room. How would the killer do that unless he or she was already inside it?"

"Good point," Helen Louise said. "That makes it look bad for Ellie."

"I'm sure they know already about Ellie and Kilbride," I said. "I wonder if Melba has told the lieutenant what she knows about Kilbride's sexuality."

"Next time we see her, let's ask," Helen Louise said.

A knock on the door ended that conversation. I went to see who the caller was. To my surprise, Ellie Arnold stood there. "Ellie, do come in. What can I do for you?"

Ellie, pale and still disheveled, said, "Thank you, Charlie. I'd like to talk to you." The poor woman seemed to have forgotten her normally careful habits of dress and hygiene, thanks to the stress of the past couple of days.

"Come on in," I repeated.

She entered the room and sank into a chair. Then she seemed to register that Helen Louise and Diesel were present. "Hi, Helen Louise." Diesel chirped at her, and she smiled briefly.

"Ellie, how are you doing?" Helen Louise asked. "I know this has all been a terrible strain on you."

"It's a nightmare," Ellie said. "I keep hoping I'll wake up, safe at home in my bed, but instead I'm here, frightened and feeling so alone."

"You're not alone," I said. "You're with friends, remember

that." I felt sorry for her because she did seem to be in genuine distress. Whether any component of that distress was remorse, I had no idea.

"Do you know what caused Denis's death?" she asked, looking to me for the answer.

"I believe the lieutenant is probably going to tell us the results of the autopsy this afternoon," I said.

Ellie shuddered. "How horrible. I hate to think of anyone being cut up like that. It gives me nightmares."

Helen Louise reached over and took one of Ellie's hands in hers. "It is terrible to think about, I know. Try to focus on the good things."

"I've tried that," Ellie said, "but with Denis, there weren't always good things."

I wasn't quite sure how to respond to that.

"Would it help for you to talk to us about it?" Helen Louise said.

Ellie hesitated; then it all seemed to flood out of her. "Denis could be incredibly sweet, you know. He was flirtatious from the moment I met him at the bank, and he made it obvious he was interested in me. I thought at first it was because he badly needed a loan, but it wasn't long before he asked Paul Bowen to take over. He said he didn't want me to have any doubts about him, and I thought that was sweet. I knew he had a reputation as a ladies' man, but it wasn't till later that I found out he liked men, too."

"What did you do when you discovered that?" Helen Louise asked.

"I told him I never wanted to see him again," Ellie said, her expression hardening. "He was cheating on me. It didn't matter with whom, only the fact that he was unfaithful. My father cheated on my mother and made her life miserable. I wasn't going to go through all that because I saw what it did to my mother. She started drinking and never stopped until it killed her."

Helen Louise and I exchanged appalled glances. What a terrible burden this obviously had been for Ellie, and, I thought, what fuel for the anger that could lead someone to commit murder.

"Ellie, I'm so sorry," Helen Louise said. "That's terrible. No wonder you were upset with Denis."

"That's why the police will probably think I'm responsible for his death," Ellie said. "I think I hated him once I found out. But he wouldn't leave me alone. He kept pestering me, telling me he would stop running around if only I would agree to marry him." She laughed suddenly, a bitter, harsh sound. "There were times when I wished he would die and leave me alone, but I didn't really want him dead."

"Of course not," Helen Louise said.

Diesel went to Ellie and put his head on her knee. She put out a trembling hand and stroked his head. "He's so sweet," she whispered. Diesel meowed softly.

"When did you find out that Denis was cheating on you with a man?" I hated to be blunt, but if Ellie wanted our assistance, we needed to know.

"About six weeks ago," Ellie said. "I went by his place after work one day—his office, I mean—to confront him about it, and I walked in on him and that rat, in the middle of . . ." Her voice trailed off and she closed her eyes.

"We understand," Helen Louise said. "Was it Zac you found with Denis?"

Ellie nodded. "I wanted to blame him at first. Thought he was responsible, but then I learned more about Denis's past escapades. I wondered why he spent so many nights in Memphis, and then it all fell into place. That's where he met Zac, in a bar up there."

"How did you find out about Denis's past?" I asked.

Ellie shrugged. "Doesn't matter, I just did. I told Denis several times I would never take him back, but he wouldn't give up. I couldn't believe he followed me here. He wasn't supposed to know I was coming on this trip. Why wouldn't he leave me alone?" She sank back in the chair as if suddenly exhausted.

Neither Helen Louise nor I had a ready answer for that. Perhaps Denis really did love Ellie. Perhaps he had meant what he said about staying faithful to her. I rather doubted the latter, because in my experience, men who cheated didn't change their behavior that easily or permanently.

"I'm so sorry you've been through such a terrible experience," Helen Louise said. "It sounds to me as if Denis genuinely cared for you. Otherwise I don't think he would have been so persistent. No one could blame you for the way you felt after you discovered his betrayal, least of all Denis himself."

"Helen Louise is right," I said. "Everything we do in life has a consequence, and Denis was completely responsible for his own behavior. Not you, not anyone else, only Denis."

"Thank you," Ellie said. "You're right, and I know that. I did care for him, you know."

Helen Louise nodded.

I hesitated, but there was another question I wanted to ask. "Ellie, you said Denis wasn't supposed to know you were coming with the group to Asheville."

Ellie nodded. "I thought I could get away from Athena for a few days without him finding out about it. I told Miss An'gel that I wanted to come, but I didn't want anyone else to know until I got here."

"I was surprised to see you," I said. "I didn't think you were coming with us this week." I glanced at Helen Louise, and she shook her head to indicate that she hadn't known, either.

"Did he tell you how he found out?" Helen Louise asked.

"I demanded to know who had told him," Ellie said, "but he refused to tell me. My guess is that Zac somehow found out and told him."

"I'm not sure how Zac would have found out," I said. "Miss An'gel certainly wouldn't have told him. She wouldn't betray your confidence."

Ellie sighed. "No, I'm sure she wouldn't. I told my boss at the last minute that I needed some time off to take care of my aunt in Mobile who'd had a stroke." She raised her eyes to meet mine. "I do have an aunt in Mobile, but she's perfectly healthy as far as I know."

"Was Denis possessive of you?" Helen Louise asked. "Did he frequently ask you what you were doing, where you had been, things like that?"

"At the beginning, no," Ellie said. "Later on, though, he began to be. I thought at first it was simply a sign that he was getting serious about me, but toward the end I realized it was more than that."

If Denis Kilbride had such possessive tendencies, he might have used technology to keep track of Ellie. Perhaps a program on her phone, or a tracking device on her car.

"Ellie, did you drive here?" I asked.

The question surprised her, I could see.

"Yes, I did. Why do you ask?" she said.

"This is simply a guess on my part," I replied. "Maybe Denis put a tracking device on your car in order to know where you were going at any given time."

Ellie looked aghast. "That's horrible."

"It is," Helen Louise said. "In cases where one of the partners in a relationship is overly possessive, though, I don't think it's uncommon. From what you've told us, I can't say I'd be surprised if you find such a device on or in your car."

"That would also explain," Ellie said slowly, "why Denis wouldn't tell me who revealed my plans to him. He wouldn't need information from anyone else if I gave it to him myself without even knowing it."

TWENTY

"That's the simplest explanation," I said. "Do you know whether Denis drove here, or did he perhaps fly?"

"He drove," Ellie said. "He told me he had appointments he had to keep so he couldn't follow me immediately; otherwise he would have turned up sooner." Suddenly she got up, startling Diesel, and began to pace. "You know about these things, Charlie. What do you think? Did someone kill Denis? If he wasn't murdered, then why would someone kill that poor woman?"

Helen Louise shrugged when I looked to her for advice. I knew what that shrug meant: *Your guess is as good as mine on what to do in this situation.*

"Ellie, I can't speak for the police," I said, "but I have to say I do think it's likely that Denis was murdered and that Cora's murder is connected to his. The questions are these: Who had the motives? And who had the opportunities to kill them?"

"Those are questions we can't answer," Helen Louise said.

"The police will have to answer them, and they'll be doing it by asking us questions, probably over and over, until they find a pattern of some sort."

"Yes, you're right, I suppose." Ellie had stopped pacing and now leaned against the back of the chair she had formerly occupied. "I have to sit tight and let the police do their work. I'm sure I'll be their chief suspect once they know more about my relationship with Denis."

"That may be," Helen Louise said gently. "All you have to do is tell them the truth, though. They won't arrest you for a crime you didn't commit."

I hoped Helen Louise was right. Frankly, I thought Ellie had the strongest motive for murder. With Denis's death, she was rid of a possessive man who had stalked her and who had violated her trust. This wouldn't be the first time a woman had killed her lover for such reasons. Either one might suffice for a strong enough motive to kill.

I checked my watch. We had about twenty minutes before we were to meet with the lieutenant again in the dining room. I wondered what he would do if there were any straggling diners. That wasn't my problem, though. I mentioned the time to Ellie and Helen Louise.

"I look a mess, I know," Ellie said. "I guess I'd better go and do something about my face and hair. Thank you both for listening to me. I feel better somehow, getting all that out."

Helen Louise went with her to the door and gave her a quick hug. "Go wash your face and put on a little war paint. You'll feel better."

Ellie gave her a faint smile and was gone. Helen Louise shut the door and turned back to me, obviously troubled.

"Do you think she did it?" I asked.

She sighed. "I can't see that anyone else has a stronger motive, can you?"

"Other than Zac, no," I said. "But if she did kill both Denis and Cora, she's one hell of an actress."

"Yes," Helen Louise said. "That's what I can't get past. I don't think she is acting. I think that was all genuine. I can't be completely sure, though."

"Same here," I said. "There could be more going on that we don't know about, that even Ellie didn't know about. Denis was a businessman, and a successful one. Was he completely honest in all his dealings? I don't have a clue. We already know he treated Johnny Ray Floyd badly. Johnny Ray could have borne a bigger grudge against him than we know."

"I can't see Johnny Ray as a killer," Helen Louise said.

"I can't, either. I don't want to," I said. "But we both know that how we feel about a person's potential to be a killer isn't worth anything."

"No, it isn't," Helen Louise said. "The problem is, I can't see anyone in this group as a killer, even Zac."

I laughed at that. "Because he's the only Yankee in the group?"

"Don't be absurd," Helen Louise said, but there was no sting in her tone. "He is an outsider in a number of ways, but I can't see him as a killer, even if he was having an affair with Kilbride. I suppose we can't rule him out, though."

"No, we can't," I said. "From past experience, I'm aware that any person has secrets, depths to their character, that we can't possibly know about."

"That's unsettling," Helen Louise said. "Do you think that of me?"

"I guess I think that of everyone, even myself," I said. "We even have secrets we hide from ourselves, truths about ourselves, our motives, our emotions that we can't admit because it would be too painful."

"I don't know that I like the way this conversation is going," Helen Louise said, and I could tell I was making her uncomfortable. I made myself uncomfortable when I got into one of these moods of introspection.

"Sorry," I said. "I'm overstating the point. Other than Melba, the Ducotes, and Benjy, we don't consider any of the rest of the people in the group close friends. We know little about their inner lives and what really drives them. We can make guesses, based on externals, but that's only the surface of their characters."

"Now you've got me truly terrified," Helen Louise said. "I'm not used to thinking about other people in these terms. That's why reading writers like Ruth Rendell and Patricia Highsmith scare me, frankly. Their people are so damaged, so alien to my everyday experience, and you're starting to make me think our current situation is like one of their books."

"I'm sorry, honey," I said, taking her in my arms while Diesel chirped anxiously. She laid her head on my shoulder. "I didn't mean to get so dark and grim. I'm letting all this get to me. We're in a strange place, involved with a group in which we don't know half the people as well as we might have thought we did. Now we have two murders and a killer amongst us."

"I don't want to let you or Diesel out of my sight until we're safely home again," Helen Louise said, her voice muffled.

"We'll stick together, I promise."

Helen Louise drew back. "I promise, too."

Diesel meowed loudly, and Helen Louise and I chuckled.

"Yes, we're going to keep you close, too," I said. "We're not going to let anything happen to you, either."

"We'd probably better head downstairs now," Helen Louise said. "It won't do to keep the lieutenant waiting."

"No, it won't. Come on, boy. Back in your harness and leash," I said. Diesel grumbled but he behaved while I got him kitted out again.

When we reached the dining room we found a police officer standing at the door. Seeing us, he waved us in. Most of the group was there, except for Ellie and Johnny Ray. Two diners were paying for their meals, and once they were gone, we would have the dining room to ourselves.

Ellie came in on the dot of two, and Johnny Ray about two minutes after. The diners had left, and now only our group occupied the room.

We all waited quietly for about five minutes, and I felt everyone begin to grow restive around me. I wondered what was keeping Lieutenant Wesner and Sergeant Bloesch. I was about to step outside to query the officer at the door when I saw Wesner and Bloesch approaching from the direction of the small salon. I went back to my seat.

"Sorry to keep you all waiting," Wesner said. Sergeant Bloesch took up position in front of the door, now closed. "I know you've all been curious about the death of Denis Kilbride, and I can now reveal some of the results of the autopsy to you. His death was not accidental or natural. He was murdered."

"How?" Johnny Ray shot out the word. "How was he murdered?"

"The blow you gave Denis Kilbride was not connected to his death, Mr. Floyd," Wesner said.

"Thank the Lord." Johnny Ray dropped his head in his hands and began to sob in what I thought must have been relief. I was sure the suspense had been horrible for him.

Miss An'gel went to him and patted him on the back. "I know we're all happy for your sake that your punch didn't cause his death." She stayed by him, patting his back, until he regained control of himself. He pulled out a handkerchief and wiped his face. "Thank you, Miss An'gel, everybody."

I gave him a thumbs-up gesture, as did several other members of the group.

Wesner had waited, his expression impassive, until this interlude concluded. Then he nodded and began talking.

"After the examination of both victims, we are reasonably certain that they were killed by the same person. We are continuing our inquiries, and we appreciate your cooperation. It is my understanding that you were planning to stay here in Asheville until the coming weekend. I have spoken with the owner of the hotel to inform him that the police prefer that you all remain here. I also must insist that you not leave the city until our investigation is complete, or until such time as we conclude that you may safely return home. Is that clear?"

"Perfectly clear, and perfectly understandable," Miss An'gel said. "I don't believe any of us has any problems with your request, Lieutenant Wesner. I'm sure everyone will cooperate with your investigation to the fullest extent of their abilities."

Once Miss An'gel had spoken, no one in the group dared to question the lieutenant's directive. She had used that no-nonsense tone before which brave men and women quailed.

"Thank you, Miss Ducote, for your assurances on behalf of the group," Wesner replied.

"Can you tell us, Lieutenant, whether Miss Apfel had any family?" Miss An'gel said. "I'm sure we would all like to express our condolences to them."

Wesner said, "We have not found any kin yet, but I will let you know when and if we do."

"How sad," Helen Louise murmured. "The poor woman."

"Yes," I whispered back. "If they can't find any family, I'm sure Miss An'gel will insist on taking care of her burial expenses if there isn't any money."

"She lives up to her name, doesn't she?" Helen Louise said.

Diesel meowed loudly, causing several heads to turn in our direction. Wesner frowned. I gazed blandly back at him.

"My staff and I will be going through your statements, and we will be asking you many of the same questions we asked before," Wesner said. "We realize this is repetitious, but we have to make sure we are getting the fullest picture of the past couple of days here in this hotel. Any incident, anything you might have heard or seen, anything you might know about either of the victims, we want to hear about it. Nothing is too trivial. I want you all to keep that in mind."

Burdine Gregory raised her hand. "Can I ask a question, sir?"

Wesner nodded. "Of course, ma'am."

"Thank you," she said. "Are we allowed to leave the hotel at all? It's really nice here, of course, great hotel, but we really had hoped to see more of Asheville."

"You may leave the hotel," Wesner said. "There will be an officer on duty, and all we ask is that you let that officer know where you plan to go and for approximately how long. We have all your contact information if we need to get in touch with you. As I said earlier, our only requirement is that you do not leave the city."

"Thank you," Burdine said.

"You're welcome," Wesner replied. "Are there any other questions at this time?" He glanced around the room.

No one responded to this, and Wesner said, "Thank you for your attention. I know you might have had some plans for this afternoon, but I must ask you to stay close at hand, within no more than a few minutes' drive or walk from the hotel. We are going to start our next round of questioning. I don't know how long this will take, I'm afraid, but we will do our best not to inconvenience you more than we have to."

"Who's first?" Zac Ryan said, his tone slightly arch.

"You are, actually," Wesner replied smoothly. "Would you please come with us, Mr. Ryan?"

Zac, his face a bit red, got up and walked to the door being held open by Sergeant Bloesch. She held the door for the lieutenant, then followed him out and closed it behind her.

The door had barely closed before Burdine spoke. "That's the killer right there."

TWENTY-ONE

"What makes you say that?" I asked, shocked by Burdine's accusation. "What kind of evidence do you have that points to Zac's being the murderer?"

"I don't need evidence. That's for the police to dig up," Burdine said hotly. "I know he's the killer. Trust me, you'll find out I'm right when the police have finished investigating."

"It's a little strange to me," Johnny Ray said, "you making this kind of accusation, Burdine, because whenever we discuss the plot of a Golden Age detective story, you're always the one harping on how you have to look at the evidence before saying who the killer is."

"Yes, you do that, you certainly do, Burdine," Celia said. "That's right, Johnny Ray."

"So what if I do," Burdine retorted. "This isn't a plot out of Agatha Christie or Dorothy Sayers, is it? Get real. Of course he's the killer."

"Because he's a Yankee?" Miss Dickce said with a perfectly straight face. I recognized that twinkle in her eyes.

"That's part of it," Burdine said in a grudging tone.

"Well, I know the Yankees can be mighty dangerous sometimes," Miss Dickce said. "But this particular Yankee has never struck me as being dangerous. Dangerously attractive maybe, but that's about it."

Melba and Benjy erupted into laughter, and Burdine's face reddened to the point that I feared she might be about to have an attack of some sort.

"They're right, Burdine," Elmore said. "Stop being ridiculous. You don't know Zac killed anyone any more than you know what the Pope has for breakfast."

Burdine didn't respond to her husband. She got up and stormed out of the room, and I can't say that I was sorry she left. I doubted anyone else was, either, even her husband.

"I don't know what's got into her lately," Elmore said—mostly to himself, I thought. "Maybe she's going crazy." He looked at Miss An'gel and Miss Dickce. "What do y'all think is wrong with her?"

I could see that Miss Dickce had a ready answer, probably along the lines that Burdine had turned crazy as a Betsy Bug. Miss An'gel laid a hand on her sister's knee, however, and Miss Dickce kept silent, though I suspected it was a struggle.

"We are all feeling the stress of the situation," Miss An'gel said. "I think Burdine is simply overwrought, and the stress pushed her to the edge. If I were you, Elmore, I'd go to her and see that she does something to relax. Perhaps a nice long soak in a hot tub. That always helps me."

Elmore stood, looking grateful. "I think you're right, Miss

An'gel. I'll go find her, and I hope for her sake that cop don't want to talk to her for a while yet. Leastways till I can get her calmed down again." He left the room with a little wave to us.

"I don't know what to think about that," Celia said the moment the door closed behind Elmore.

"I think Miss An'gel is right about the stress getting to Burdine," Melba said. "I know it's getting to me. This is a new experience, being locked up in a hotel with a killer roaming the halls."

"We're not exactly locked up," Paul said. "That would be bad, but at least we can come and go, within reason."

"That's the point, that 'within reason,'" Melba said. "I don't know about the rest of you, but I don't like anybody restricting my movements." She held up a hand to ward off protests. "Yes, I understand why it's necessary, but I don't like it."

"I don't think any of us likes it," I said, my tone mild. I knew Melba in this mood. She was frightened, and she didn't like to admit that to anyone. I couldn't blame her for being frightened. I was frightened myself, not only for my personal safety, but for Helen Louise and Diesel as well. Not to mention Melba, the Ducotes, and Benjy, all dear friends.

"I know that," Melba said irritably. "Being told I can't do something makes me want to do it in the worst way."

Paul regarded her with a knowing smile. "So that's the key I've been missing. Good to know."

When the import of that remark finally hit Melba—the rest of us were grinning—she did something I hadn't seen her do since I couldn't remember when. She blushed. Then she flapped a hand at Paul and said, "I can't believe you said that. You're terrible."

Perhaps he was, from Melba's point of view, but Paul's witticism broke the mood of steadily rising fear and unease in the room. I noticed that even Ellie had smiled, albeit briefly. She did look better than she had a little while ago in our room. She had taken some trouble with her appearance. She had brushed her hair and applied some makeup. She was no longer pale as a snowball, for one thing, with a little healthy-looking color in her face.

Miss An'gel rose and motioned for Miss Dickce and Benjy to come with her. "I don't think we all have to sit in this room and wait to be summoned. The lieutenant or his sergeant can locate us when they want us. We can discuss our group activities later. I'm going to my room to relax and read a book. I hope you will all consider doing something to relax yourselves as well. Try to keep your stress levels down." She smiled at us as she headed for the door. Miss Dickce and Benjy followed. Miss Dickce rolled her eyes at me before she left their table. I could just hear her say, "Sister, or Her Majesty as she likes to be called, has spoken, and I must obey."

I had actually heard her say that once before, in an undertone, of course, because it would never have done for Miss An'gel to have heard her. Especially since we had been sitting in a busy restaurant at the time. I had struggled not to guffaw and spew iced tea all over the table, because Miss Dickce had caught me with a mouthful at the time.

"I'm going to spend some time with my wife and kids," Johnny Ray said, "and tell Lou the good news." He sped out after the Ducotes and Benjy.

Celia was the next to head for the door, but when she opened it to exit the room, Sergeant Bloesch stood there. Startled, Celia stepped back.

"Miss Bernardi," the sergeant said. "The lieutenant would like to speak with you now."

Celia appeared far from pleased at this news, but she made no demur and followed the sergeant.

"I'm going out into the garden," Melba announced. "I need some fresh air and sunlight. Ellie, Helen Louise, would you care to go with me?"

Paul Bowen had started to rise, but Melba's words made it clear that she was not interested in male company for her interlude in the garden. Was she punishing Paul for his joke? Melba wasn't generally spiteful. Maybe she simply wanted some time with her female friends.

Helen Louise glanced my way, saw my why-not shrug, and rose to accompany Melba. Diesel started to follow Helen Louise, and after a brief hesitation, I handed over the leash to her. It would do the cat good to get some of that same fresh air and sunshine, I decided.

Ellie elected to go with them, a bit to my surprise. She must have been coming out of the funk that she'd been in earlier, and I thought that was a good thing. I tried not to think about her having ulterior motives, if she were the killer.

That left me alone with Paul Bowen. I debated whether to go up to the room to read. I knew Paul only through the group, and his reading interests tended to be rather different from mine. His favorite genre was thrillers, writers like Lee Child and Michael Connelly. The only thriller writer I had read with any consistency was Dick Francis, the master of them all, as far as I was concerned.

Paul did like a couple of older writers, however, and one of them, to my surprise, was Josephine Tey. We had once had a spirited discussion about Tey's *The Daughter of Time*. I thought it a fascinating book, but based on shaky history. Paul, however, was rabidly pro–Richard III and thought it exculpated him completely from the murder of his nephews in the Tower of London. I tried to get him to read *The Murders of Richard III* by Elizabeth Peters, but he flatly refused. We had to agree to disagree at the end of our discussion if we were to remain civil to each other.

"Would you mind staying here a few minutes and talking to me?" Paul asked.

"Sure," I said. "What's on your mind?"

Paul came over and took the seat recently vacated by Helen Louise. He stared at the tablecloth for a moment before he raised his gaze to meet mine. "You've known Melba a long time, haven't you?"

"Yes, since about the third grade, I think." I hoped he wasn't going to share any intimate details about his relationship with Melba. I didn't want to know those things, and they were certainly none of my business. I loved Melba like a sister, but there are some things you don't want to know about a sister.

"Were y'all in the same year in school?" he asked.

"Yes, we were," I replied, curious to find out what he wanted to know.

"Do you mind telling me what year you graduated?"

I almost laughed. He was trying to discover Melba's age. She would threaten to kill me if she ever found out about this.

"No, I don't mind." I named the year, and I could see him doing the calculations. He smiled.

"I'd like to ask you a question, Paul," I said.

"I'll be forty-seven in a couple of months," he said promptly. "If that's what you want to know."

"It is," I replied. "Thank you."

"Not much of a difference," Paul said. "She's an amazing woman."

"She is that," I said. There were other things I wanted to say to him, things a protective brother might have said, but I kept my mouth shut. Melba would have skinned me alive.

"Actually, there is something else I'd like to ask you," I said.

"Sure, go ahead." Paul leaned back in his chair, evidently more relaxed now that he had the answer to what might have been a burning question.

"Denis Kilbride was one of your clients at the bank, wasn't he? What did you think of him?"

Paul's eyes narrowed, and I thought he might not answer.

"Yes, he was my client," Paul said. "He was a good businessman. The bank didn't lose any money with his projects." He shrugged. "As for what I thought of him, he was a client. I didn't socialize with him. He ran with a different crowd in town, people who were higher fliers than I'll ever be. I'm not meant to be part of the country club set, if you know what I mean."

"I do," I said. "I'm not, either. Did you think Kilbride was an honest man?"

"How should I know?" Paul sounded irritable now, and I wondered if I had managed to strike a nerve. I didn't think the question was all that personal. "As honest as the next wealthy businessman, I suppose."

That was a politician's answer if ever I'd heard one. Either Paul knew something about Kilbride's business dealings that didn't redound to Kilbride's credit, or there was something else. I wasn't sure I'd be able to get Paul to tell me, though.

"What about in his personal dealings?" I asked. "For example, with your coworker Ellie."

"Strictly none of my business." Paul stood and pushed his chair back. "I think I'll go upstairs and take a nap." He walked out of the room, leaving me on my own.

I had struck a nerve somewhere. The question was, why?

TWENTY-TWO

After thinking about Paul Bowen's abrupt departure from our conversation, I wondered whether I was putting too much weight on his actions. We were all under the strain of a double homicide investigation now, and there was no reason he had to talk to me or answer my questions. I was way too nosy, I knew that, and perhaps Paul simply didn't want to get entangled in a situation that was none of his doing, or of his business.

I didn't feel that I could ask Melba about Paul. I didn't want to put her in that position or to make her think I was suspicious of him. At least, not at this time. I would have to ask Miss An'gel or Miss Dickce about him. I figured they would know something since they did business with his bank.

As I glanced around me, I realized that I sat alone in the dining room. Helen Louise and Diesel were probably still in the garden with Melba and Ellie. I didn't think Melba would welcome my presence, so I decided to go back to the suite.

I glanced at the reception desk, surprised to find it unattended. I did hear voices coming from the office behind it, and I paused near the foot of the stairs to see if anyone came out. I thought I recognized Arthur's as one of the voices, and he sounded testy. The other came across as more placatory in tone.

My nosiness earned its reward. Arthur strode out of the office to take up position behind the desk, and Zac Ryan followed him. I couldn't linger where I stood, because I was in clear view of the desk. They would spot me if they happened to glance in my direction. I hurried up the stairs to get out of sight, then slowed my pace. Still, I arrived a bit breathless at the top and paused to catch my breath.

Arthur was a handsome young man, perhaps a couple of years older than Benjy. Had Zac set his sights on a more mature target? I wondered. I had no clue about Arthur's sexuality, and I didn't want to assume.

Was that all it was, though? Zac making time with Arthur?

Or was Zac questioning Arthur about the murders?

I stopped in front of the door to our suite to think about the implications of this. Zac, in addition to his interest in Golden Age detective fiction, was also a huge fan of Jessica Fletcher and *Murder, She Wrote*. Maybe he fancied himself as an amateur sleuth. No reason he shouldn't, I reckoned. If I could do it, so could he, or so I imagined he might have reasoned it.

After I unlocked the door and stepped inside, however, another, more sinister thought struck me. If Zac was the killer, as Burdine had so boldly stated, was he questioning Arthur in order to find out what Arthur knew? If Arthur knew anything incriminating, would it mean that he would have to be killed as well?

I leaned against the door after I shut it to consider what I should do about this, if anything. If Kanesha had been here and in charge of the case, I wouldn't have hesitated—well, at least not too long—in telling her my concerns about the situation. I didn't want anyone else to be murdered, but with Lieutenant Wesner in charge of the case, I didn't feel all that comfortable sharing my crazy ideas. I should probably try to talk to Arthur and Zac, separately, to see if I could get anything out of them.

Helen Louise's voice called out, startling me. "Charlie, is that you?"

Diesel trotted out of the bedroom and made a beeline for me. "Yes, love, it's me." I scratched the cat's head for a moment before I walked into the bedroom to find Helen Louise.

She sat, legs crossed in a near-lotus position, against the pillows and the headboard, a book in her lap. She smiled as I came forward into the room and bent to kiss her.

"I thought you'd be in the garden with Melba and Ellie." I sat on the bed near her.

"That's what I thought, too." She smiled. "But it seemed pretty clear to me that Ellie really wanted to talk to Melba, but not to me, so I made an excuse about finishing this book and came upstairs with Diesel."

"How is the book?"

"Excellent." She laid it aside. "Only about twenty pages to go, and then it's yours."

"Even better," I said. "Did you get any idea what Ellie was so anxious to talk to Melba about?"

Helen Louise shook her head. "No, she didn't give any real

indication. I'm sure, though, it had to be about Denis and his murder. What else could be worrying her so?"

"If she murdered Denis and Cora both, she might be a little concerned," I said in a vain attempt at humor.

Helen Louise shot me a look. "Ellie could be the killer, of course. I'm not going to rule her out. But do you really think that if she killed two people she's going to confess it all to Melba in the hotel garden?"

Diesel, who had jumped onto the bed with us when I sat on it, suddenly meowed.

"Yes, I know it sounds goofy," I said, looking at the cat.

"But stranger things have happened," Helen Louise said.

I nodded.

"Did anything interesting happen downstairs," she said, "when I left the room with Diesel and the other women?"

I shared my conversation with Paul Bowen with her, and she chuckled over his way of finding out Melba's age. "Why are men so obsessed with women's ages?" she said.

"Why do women like to pretend they're younger than they are?" I responded with a grin.

"Did Paul have anything else to say?" Helen Louise replied.

"Not really, but I did try to quiz him about his relationship with Denis Kilbride," I said. "He acknowledged the business connection but said that it ended there. He said Denis ran with a wealthy crowd, people Paul indicated were above his touch socially and financially."

Helen Louise nodded. "I've seen Denis in the bistro with some of the highfliers in the past. I doubt a bank employee like Paul could afford their company."

"That makes sense," I said. "Then he said he was tired and was going upstairs to take a nap."

"Are you trying to make some other connection between Denis and Paul?"

I shrugged. "Not really, but I don't know much about him. Melba hasn't been too forthcoming about him. He does seem really interested in her. Don't you agree?"

"Yes, I do," Helen Louise said. "I don't know much about him myself, and Melba hasn't talked to me about him either. I guess she's gun-shy after that dentist she dated briefly. And she may feel funny because Paul is about six or seven years younger than she is."

"I hadn't thought about that," I said. "Does that really bother her?"

Helen Louise considered the question for a moment before she responded. "I'm not really sure. I think it's simply that she doesn't want anyone to call her a cougar. It's a horrible epithet."

"It is," I said. "I wouldn't want to be the person to use that term to Melba's face, I can tell you that."

"I will try to get her to open up with me about him, though," Helen Louise said. "I hope it's only the age gap that's troubling her."

"Me, too. Speaking of age gaps, wouldn't you say Arthur Hindman is about twenty-two?" I waited for her nod to continue. "And Zac Ryan is about thirty." Again she nodded. "I heard them having what sounded like a mild argument when I was on my way upstairs."

"Explain, please," Helen Louise said.

Diesel butted his head against my side to let me know that he was tired of waiting for attention. He sprawled on his side on the bed near me to allow me to stroke him while I continued my conversation with Helen Louise.

I shared with her what I had observed, and Helen Louise's expression turned thoughtful. "Arthur is quite a handsome young man, you know, a bit more mature looking than Benjy," she said. "Zac could be interested in him."

"Do you think Denis's murder has anything to do with his past relationships with both men and women?" I asked.

"Either that, or related to his business dealings," Helen Louise said. "I'm inclined to think it's more the latter myself. Money is an awfully powerful motive for murder."

"Yes, it is. Or maybe it's a combination of the two somehow," I said. "That reminds me. I thought about asking Miss An'gel what she and Miss Dickce know about Paul Bowen. They do business with his bank."

"I think Paul and Stewart are about the same age," Helen Louise said. "You could try asking Stewart as well."

Stewart Delacorte and I had become close, and I thought of him like a younger brother. He was in his mid-forties, though perhaps a couple of years younger than Paul. If they had gone to school together, Stewart might have known him.

"Good idea," I said. "I'll text Stewart to ask him, but if he knows anything, he'll want to talk, and that means at least an hour on the phone."

Helen Louise grinned. "Yes, but you'll enjoy it."

"True." I pulled out my phone, opened the texting app, and found Stewart. I did not have the deftness with texting that my children did, being mostly a one-finger texter. I managed to compose a message with no errors, but only by going slowly. I asked

Stewart if he knew Paul Bowen, and if he did, to call me at his convenience.

I laid the phone aside, and barely had it left my hand before it started ringing. I looked at the caller ID.

"Stewart."

Helen Louise grinned.

I picked up the phone and answered the call. Before I could say anything, Stewart said, "Okay, who's dead?"

TWENTY-THREE

"Hello to you, too," I said. "And how are you?"

"I'm fine, Charlie," Stewart said. "Hello. Now tell me, who's dead? Is it Paul Bowen? Whom I don't know, by the way."

"Why do you assume that someone is dead simply because I texted you?"

"This is Charlie Harris, isn't it?" Stewart's tone had a sarcastic bite. "Why else would you be texting me and asking me to call you if you hadn't stumbled into another murder?"

Through my laughter, I managed to say, "All right. I give. There have been two murders."

"Two?" Stewart almost shrieked into my ear. "You haven't been in Asheville more than a couple of days. What's going on?"

"Give me a chance, and I'll explain, okay?"

"Go ahead," Stewart replied.

I gave him a quick summary of the two deaths and a list of the group members who were involved.

"Denis Kilbride," Stewart said. "I've been wondering for years when his antics would finally get him in big trouble. He tried to be discreet, but he managed to hurt a number of people."

"You didn't like him," I said.

"No, I didn't," Stewart replied. "I never got involved with anyone who was married, unlike Kilbride. I think he preferred that, actually, because he never had to make a commitment."

"Helen Louise and I have been discussing motives for his murder," I said. "Ellie Arnold is perhaps the chief suspect, since Denis was apparently pursuing her to the point of stalking. But she caught him with Zac Ryan, in flagrante delicto, and that was that."

Stewart laughed. "Zac Ryan, eh? From what I've heard through the campus grapevine, he's been busy in the short time he's been at the college. Working his way through a good bit of the local talent, so to speak."

I repeated this to Helen Louise, who shook her head. "Who has that much energy?"

I laughed and shared this remark with Stewart. He laughed, too. "Oh, to be thirty again," he said. "Seriously, though, I can't see Zac as much of a suspect. Unless he was desperately in love with Kilbride—which I seriously doubt—he has no stake in this game."

"You're probably right," I said. "It's looking more and more like Ellie to me."

"I know her," Stewart said. "Not from school, though, because she was several years behind me. Melba knows her. I've run across the two of them lunching together, or out at night, a few times. You'd best talk to her."

"Will do," I said. "Look, if you manage to find out anything about Paul Bowen or anything about any other of Kilbride's affairs, let me know, okay?"

"Sure will," Stewart said.

"Whatever you do," I said, after we had chatted about family matters for a few minutes, "do not let Sean and Laura know about this. Otherwise Sean will be calling me and fussing at me." They took rather a dim view of my sleuthing activities, even though Laura had been right in the middle of my most recent adventure in detecting.

"I'll try," Stewart said before he ended the call.

Again I laid my phone aside.

"I managed to hear most of what Stewart had to say," Helen Louise informed me. "I gather he thinks Zac had no motive for killing Denis Kilbride."

I nodded. "I tend to agree with him. If Zac has as much of a roving eye as Stewart claims, then I can't see him turning killer over Denis Kilbride."

"We've already noted his interest in Benjy and possibly Arthur," Helen Louise said. "I think that bears out what Stewart told you."

"What was it Auntie Mame said?" I asked. "Life is a banquet, and most poor suckers are starving to death!"

Helen Louise laughed. "That's it. It doesn't seem that Zac is starving by any means."

"So, Ellie remains our number one suspect," I said. "I think it's time to have another chat with Melba."

I texted Melba, but this time there was no quick reply. Helen Louise and I waited in silence for at least two minutes, but Melba didn't respond.

"Why don't you try calling her room?" Helen Louise said. "Or call her phone and leave a message?"

I decided on the latter option. She didn't answer the call, and so I left a brief message, asking her to call me at her earliest opportunity.

I got up from the bed and wandered over to the window. Our view looked out on the hotel garden. The afternoon sun rode high in the sky, and the leaves of the trees moved gently in the breeze. I felt suddenly that I had to get outside, into the sunshine. I turned to Helen Louise to find that she had picked up her book again.

"How would you like to go out into the garden with me?" I asked.

Helen Louise shook her head. "I'm going to read these last few pages, and then I think I'll nap for a bit, if you don't mind."

"Of course not," I said. "I just feel like going outside for some reason."

Helen Louise smiled and returned to her book. Diesel chirped at me. He understood the word *outside*.

"Come on, boy. You can go with me," I said.

Diesel jumped off the bed and ran toward the door to the hall. I fetched his leash and harness, and got him fitted into the latter, and we headed for the garden.

We met no one on the way down, and when we walked out into the garden, I couldn't see anyone out there, though there were several spots obscured from view by trees or shrubs. The sun felt warm on my face, and the breeze provided relief from the heat. We began to stroll. I followed Diesel's lead, letting him sniff and roam where he chose.

We—the mystery group, that is—had come to Asheville to get

to know one another better and have fun discussing mysteries. We had also come to see the sights of Asheville. So far we had seen Biltmore and the hotel, but not much else, other than a couple of restaurants. The irony of the situation was not lost on me. We had planned to discuss Golden Age literary conventions, one of which was the enclosed community beloved by the authors of the time. The stately home in the winter, sealed off by a blizzard. A remote island cut off from the mainland. A house during a terrible storm that left everyone inside vulnerable to a killer.

We were not involved in one of those scenarios, precisely, but we might have been. Two people in the hotel had been murdered, and the police wanted us to stay put to make their task of solving the crimes easier. I wasn't particularly frightened, I had to admit after I considered the notion for a moment. I couldn't see myself as a target for the killer. I hadn't been running around pestering everyone with questions, nor had Helen Louise.

The group did know about my penchant for solving mysteries, however, so perhaps it behooved me to be more careful about what I did and said. I could easily imagine what my son, Sean, the lawyer, would say to me, if he found out about the situation.

Dad, you need to keep out of this, he would say. *You don't have Kanesha here to keep you out of harm's way. If the killer thinks you're getting too close, he or she could attack you. Or even Helen Louise or Diesel. You shouldn't put yourself or them at risk.*

Yes, son, I would say, and I would mean it. But I wouldn't be able to help myself if I managed to stumble over any information that could be pertinent to the case. It would be my civic duty to share it with the authorities, right?

Of course it would be, I reassured myself. I had to resist the temptation to go too far in carrying out my so-called duty, however.

Diesel soon tired of wandering and sniffing, and I followed him to the bench where we had sat in the shade and dozed. Was that only yesterday? I wondered.

I made myself comfortable, and Diesel stretched out beside me. I leaned back and closed my eyes, taking in the scents and the solitude, finding them soothing.

I probably drifted off within minutes of getting settled on the bench, but I woke abruptly to a hand shaking my arm and a voice calling my name. I blinked and saw Melba bent over me.

"You were snoring," she said, standing back. Diesel stood against her legs, softly chirping.

"Sorry," I muttered. "I didn't know there was anyone around to hear me." I covered a yawn, then sat up straighter on the bench. "What's going on?"

"Helen Louise said you wanted to talk to me." Melba took the space on the bench vacated by Diesel, and the cat sat with his head on her knee, gazing up at her while she stroked his head.

"That's right, I do," I said, trying to pull my scattered thoughts together.

"About Ellie," Melba said in a helpful tone.

"Yes," I said. "You've known her since she was a child, right?"

"Yes, they lived a couple of streets over. My mother knew her mother, but I was several years older than Ellie. I used to babysit her when I was about fifteen," Melba said.

"Ellie said her mother was an alcoholic," I said.

Melba nodded. "Yeah, and a bad one. Started because her

husband was a rat, ran around after anything in a skirt, according to my mother. She said he was a handsome devil. Some men are too good-looking for their own good."

"I'm sorry for Ellie. Sounds like a miserable childhood."

"It was," Melba said, "but her aunt in Mobile took her in when her mother died. Her father had disappeared by then."

"Why did Ellie come back to Athena?" I asked. "There couldn't have been much for her there after her mother died. Unless she had other family in Athena."

"She had her grandmother, her dad's mother," Melba said. "Sweet old lady, and she loved Ellie, who was her only grandchild. She got to where she couldn't do for herself, and by then Ellie had finished college. She came back to look after her grandmother. Got a job at the bank and has been there ever since."

"What about her grandmother?" I asked.

"Mrs. Arnold died about six years ago," Melba replied. "Her aunt, her mother's sister, is still living in Mobile. I think she was quite a bit younger than Ellie's mother."

"I'm glad to hear she still has some family left," I said. "I don't suppose she ever hears from her father, if he's still living."

"He died about fifteen years ago," Melba said. "At least, that's what I heard." She looked me straight in the eye. "Okay, enough of the background stuff. I don't imagine that's what you really wanted to know."

"The background is important," I said. "Sounds like Ellie had a hard time with her parents, but thankfully her grandmother and her aunt were there for her."

"They were," Melba said. "Get to the point."

I could tell that Melba's temper was frayed, and I didn't want to set her off. I needed to be careful about how I got to the point.

"The point is, Ellie grew up being betrayed by the two most important people in her life, her mother and her father. That has to affect a person pretty deeply. Then she is betrayed, and betrayed badly, by the man she most likely was in love with. That betrayal could have pushed her too far."

"So she murdered Denis Kilbride for betraying her," Melba said flatly.

I shrugged.

"I wish I could tell you that you're wrong about Ellie, but I can't. I just can't."

TWENTY-FOUR

"She was a sweet child," Melba continued. "Not much self-esteem, would lie sometimes when she didn't need to, was really hard on herself but anxious to have your approval." She sighed. "I learned later on that these were typical traits for children of alcoholics, and I think some of these characteristics have caused her problems, particularly with relationships."

"Parents really can inflict a lot of damage on their children," I said, thankful as always that my parents had not been drinkers.

"They can," Melba said. "I think they're responsible for a lot. Ellie's parents, I mean. I think maybe that's why Ellie was drawn to Denis Kilbride. I'm not saying he was an alcoholic, but he did enjoy drinking. Maybe Ellie thought she could fix him. That's another thing about adult children of alcoholics. They sometimes have a need to fix someone who's damaged."

"Would you say that Denis Kilbride was damaged?" I asked. "Do you know anything about his background?"

"No, he didn't grow up in Athena," Melba reminded me. "Based on what I observed, though, I'd say his parents weren't much to brag about either."

"Getting back to the main point," I said. "You believe that Ellie could have killed Denis Kilbride."

Melba looked troubled, but she nodded. "I hate to say it, but I do. The thing I can't understand, though, is why she would kill that poor maid, Cora."

"What if Cora had evidence that pointed to Ellie as the killer?" I said. "Could she have panicked and decided she had to get Cora out of the way?"

"That's the only thing that makes sense," Melba said. "Maybe Cora tried to blackmail her, I don't know." She sighed. "I don't want it to be her, Charlie, I just don't. I look at her and see that poor sad little girl who only wanted to be loved."

I patted her hand. I understood how she felt, but at the same time I knew Ellie couldn't be absolved of killing two people simply because of her sad childhood. If Ellie really did kill two people. I didn't know why, but even after talking to Melba, I wasn't completely sold on Ellie as a murderer.

"We don't have any firm evidence that Ellie killed either of them," I said in an attempt to comfort Melba.

"No, we don't," Melba said. "But we don't have any idea what the police know, do we? They could have evidence that we won't know about until there's a trial."

"True," I said. "All that forensic stuff that we don't have any access to. I think, though, if they had found clear evidence, they'd have arrested someone by now. Right?"

Melba brightened at that thought. "You're right. So maybe I can still hope that Ellie's innocent after all." She got up from the bench. "Thank you, Charlie. That makes me feel better. Paul is expecting me, so I'd better get moving. We're going out for dinner."

"Enjoy," I said.

She paused long enough to say goodbye to Diesel; then she hurried off.

I watched her go, hoping that I hadn't misled her, that Ellie would turn out to be innocent. If Ellie hadn't killed Denis Kilbride and Cora Apfel, however, someone else had. But who among our number was a murderer?

I remained where I was, Diesel back on the bench stretched out beside me, mulling this over. A male voice called out my name and interrupted my reverie.

"Over here," I said in a loud voice. I thought I had recognized the voice, but it was not until Zac Ryan came into sight that I knew for sure.

Zac sauntered toward Diesel and me. I smiled. "You're looking for me?" I said.

Zac stopped about two feet away and regarded me with a serious expression. "Yes, I am. I want to talk to you about these murders."

"Sure," I said. "Diesel, get down and let Zac have a seat." Diesel glared at me and meowed loudly, but after a momentary hesitation, he did as I asked.

Zac laughed. "That's one smart cat. He really seems to understand what you say to him." He sat down beside me and leaned forward, elbows on his legs.

"Over time they get to understand what certain words mean," I said. "Maybe twenty-five or thirty. They go more by inflection and cadence, however, according to research I've read."

Zac held out his right hand for Diesel to sniff. The cat sniffed delicately, then meowed. Zac touched his head, and Diesel allowed himself to be stroked.

"I've never been around cats all that much," Zac said. "My mom was allergic, but I've actually been thinking about getting one to keep me company at home."

"They're excellent companions, although they aren't like dogs," I said. "Each one has its own personality, and a lot of them like their own space. It depends on the breed, too. Maine Coons are affectionate and loyal. I'd recommend a Maine Coon, if you want those qualities in a pet."

"Thanks for the advice," Zac said. "I'll keep it in mind. Now, about why I wanted to talk to you. These murders. First thing, I want you to know that I didn't kill either Denis or that poor maid, Cora."

"All right," I said. "Do you have any idea who did?"

"My chief suspect is Ellie," Zac said.

"Why Ellie?" I decided to be as noncommittal as I could so that Zac might tell me more than he intended.

"Because, well . . ." He paused and looked off into the distance. "Okay, here's the thing." He turned to face me. "I had a brief fling with Denis. Didn't last long, didn't mean anything to either of us." He stopped.

"You don't seem surprised," he continued. "Why is that?"

"Word gets around," I said.

"God save me from small towns," Zac said. "I should have figured something like that. Anyway, that's what it was. Ellie came by Denis's office after work one day and walked in on us."

"I don't imagine she took it well," I said.

Zac laughed harshly. "Like hell she didn't. She started screaming at Denis. I got my clothes on as fast as I could and got out of there. I wasn't even sure until later that she knew who I was or even paid any attention to me."

"That was before you joined our mystery group," I said.

"Yes," Zac said. "The moment I walked into the room at the library for that first meeting and spotted her, I almost turned around and walked right out. But I was really looking forward to the group and decided I wasn't going to walk out because of her." He paused. "At first, I didn't think she recognized me. I mean, it all happened so fast, and she seemed so focused on Denis."

"At some point, she realized who you were," I said when he fell silent.

"I think she recognized me right away," Zac said, "although she pretended not to. I kept wondering whether she would say something in front of the group, but then I realized she probably wouldn't. It would be too embarrassing for her. Me, too, I guess. She cornered me after the second meeting and told me she knew who I was and what she thought of me. How disgusting I was, all that kind of crap.

"I had no idea Denis was involved with her," Zac said, sounding slightly indignant. "For all I knew, he was strictly gay. That's when I found out the truth myself. I left him alone after that, told him to bug off when he texted me."

"How did you meet him?"

"A bar in Memphis," Zac said. "He was obviously on the prowl, and I was in the mood. I wasn't looking for a relationship, and he wasn't, either. We met a few more times because it was easy, nothing more than that. I had other things going, if you get my meaning." He cut a sideways glance at me.

"Yes, I do," I said.

"I'll be thirty in a couple months," Zac said. "I always said I wouldn't settle down until I turned thirty. After what's happened here, I'm beginning to see that would have some advantages. But who knows?"

"You're telling me that you had no motive for murdering Denis Kilbride," I said.

"Yes, absolutely," Zac replied. "He was a casual fling, nothing more. Nothing emotional invested in it. Everyone at the college knows I'm gay, so he couldn't have blackmailed me by threatening to out me."

"What you've told me sounds reasonable," I said. "I'm not the one who's in charge of the investigation, though."

"I know that," Zac said, a touch of impatience in his tone. "I've already told all this to Wesner."

A thought struck me. "Why did you react the way you did when Kilbride barged into our meeting and threatened you?"

Zac looked pained. "Dude, do you like having your dirty laundry thrown in your face in public? I sure as hell don't." He grinned. "Especially not in front of Miss An'gel and Miss Dickce. Miss An'gel scares me to death, and Miss Dickce's almost as bad. They remind me too much of my grandma Ryan, and she's a holy terror."

I laughed. "I see your point."

"I think you know I'm a big fan of Jessica Fletcher and *Murder, She Wrote*," Zac said. "I've always wondered what it would be like to be an amateur detective, and here's the perfect opportunity. A lot of amateurs are suspects in their first cases, aren't they? Weren't you?"

Startled by the last question, I answered without thinking, "Yes."

Zac nodded. "Thought so. Anyway, what do you say? Want to work on this together?"

I hadn't suspected that he would ask me this. How was I going to answer him? Despite what he told me, I had to consider him a suspect because he easily could have lied about his relationship with Denis Kilbride. What if he had fallen in love with Kilbride and felt every bit as betrayed by him when he found out about Ellie?

"I don't usually work, as you call it, with a partner," I said. "Other than the authorities in Athena, that is. I'm not some hard-boiled private eye who gets beat up by the police."

"I didn't think you were," Zac said with a hearty laugh. "You're not the Phil Marlowe or Spenser type."

"No, I'm not," I said. "Though I can't remember whether either Marlowe or Spenser ever got beaten by the cops. But that's beside the point."

"What is the point?" Zac said. "You still haven't answered my question about working with me."

That quote from one of the *Godfather* movies flitted into my brain. Keep your friends close and your enemies closer. I had no clue yet which category Zac fell into, but I figured it was good advice.

"Yes, I'll work with you," I said.

TWENTY-FIVE

"That's awesome," Zac said to my acceptance of his offer to work with him. "What should we do first?"

"First, keep in mind that Lieutenant Wesner and Sergeant Bloesch won't be happy with either of us if they get wind of this," I said.

Zac nodded briskly. "Yeah, I know that. Come on, Charlie. I'm not a complete beginner here."

"No, you're not." During the group meetings thus far we had all discovered that Zac was well read in mystery fiction for his age. He told us that, during his summers off from school, he might read two or three books a day, sometimes even four. He zipped through a lot of authors' complete works that way.

"One thing I don't know but that I think is important is everyone's movements," I said, thinking if I could get him onto this task it might keep him busy for a while and out of my hair.

"A timetable, you mean," Zac said, looking thoughtful.

"Yeah, I can work on that, starting with myself. You can fill in for you and Helen Louise, and we can go from there. I have my laptop in my room. I think I'll create a spreadsheet." He jumped up from the bench, startling both me and Diesel. The cat meowed in protest, but Zac didn't appear to notice.

"Sounds good," I said. "I'll make notes about our movements, and add in what I know of the other members of the group outside of our meetings."

"Great," Zac said, obviously eager to be off. "Anything else?"

"No, go to it," I said.

Zac sprinted away from us and soon disappeared from sight. I envied his energy, but I might find myself worn out trying to keep up with him. "Come on, Diesel. Let's go back to Helen Louise." The cat chirped happily, and we headed back into the hotel.

We found Helen Louise asleep, lying on her side, in the bedroom. I touched her gently on the shoulder, and Diesel, who had jumped on the bed before I could stop him, sniffed at her exposed ear. Helen Louise put a hand up to her ear and encountered feline. Her eyes opened, and she smiled up at me.

"Good nap?" I asked.

Helen Louise rolled on her back and yawned. "Yes, it was," she said. "But I'm glad you woke me. I didn't want to sleep too long." She rubbed Diesel's head as he pushed it against her hand. "Did you have a good time out in the garden, sweet boy?"

Diesel purred loudly in response.

"We certainly had an interesting time," I said, perching on the bed beside her. "Zac sought me out to discuss an idea he had."

"What was it?" Helen Louise said.

"He wants to work with me, as one amateur sleuth to another, to solve these murders," I said.

"What?" Helen Louise pushed herself up into a sitting position and leaned against the headboard. "He actually came to you and said that?"

"He did," I replied. "I was pretty taken aback, but we did discuss his relationship—if you could call it that—with Denis Kilbride. According to him, it was nothing special, certainly not on his part."

"Scratching an itch, basically," Helen Louise said sardonically.

I grinned. "Basically. I have to say he came across as sincere. He's young, not ready to settle down, and so on. He's turning thirty soon, he said, and that's the age he thought he would start settling down."

"If he truly had no motive to kill Denis Kilbride," Helen Louise said, "then he would have had no reason to kill Cora Apfel, either. So, if he's being completely honest, that leaves us with Ellie as the most likely suspect, since she's the only other one who had a personal relationship with Denis." She sounded disheartened by her own conclusion.

"Yes," I said. "I know it's rough, because you know Ellie, though you're not close. Sometimes the simplest answer is the right one."

"Why haven't the police arrested her by now?" Helen Louise said. "I thought they'd have jumped on her at the get-go, but they don't seem to have. Are they being overly cautious, or do they simply not have any evidence?"

I shook my head. "I don't know. It's puzzling me, too, but I'd guess that they don't have evidence that will stand up in court. They have to have more than hunches to make an arrest."

"What was your answer to Zac?" Helen Louise said. Diesel

nudged her hand because she had stopped paying him attention. She smiled and resumed scratching his head.

"I told him I would work with him." I held up a hand to forestall a protest. "I know it's a crazy idea, but you know that quote about keeping your enemies closer than your friends. If Zac lied about the nature of his relationship with Denis Kilbride and felt as betrayed by him as Ellie did, then he might let something slip."

"I can only imagine what Sean would be saying to you right now," Helen Louise said, her expression grim. "If Zac killed two people, he's set it up so that he can keep an eye on you, and if you figure out he did it, he'll kill you before you can do anything about it."

That idea had been resting uncomfortably in the back of my mind this whole time, and hearing Helen Louise say it aloud made my skin crawl.

"I know," I said weakly, "but what should I have done? Said no?"

Helen Louise thought about that for a moment. "I don't know. If you'd refused him, he might have thought that meant you suspected him. That could have been worse. This is crazy."

"I sent Zac off to make a timetable of everyone's movements," I said. "That ought to keep him occupied and out of the way for a while. And who knows? It might turn up some bit of information that could lead us to the answer."

"I suppose so." Helen Louise laughed suddenly. "I feel like I woke up in a Golden Age mystery. We're staying in an old house, cut off from civilization, and there's a killer among us. How many books have you read just like this?"

"Many," I said. "I know how you feel. I wonder if any other

members of the group fancy themselves as amateur sleuths? Wouldn't that be wild?"

"Please, don't even think that," Helen Louise said with a grimace.

I had a sudden vision of Burdine Gregory, on her knees, magnifying glass in hand, examining ashes on the carpet, trying to determine exactly what kind of cigar the killer had smoked before he struck. I snorted with laughter, and I caught Helen Louise eyeing me with concern.

I told her what I had been thinking, and she laughed. "That would be quite a sight," she said.

"She seems convinced that Zac is the killer." I frowned. "Now that I think about it, she seemed pretty spiteful when she said it."

"How does she treat him in the group get-togethers?" Helen Louise asked. "Is she rude to him? Does she ignore him?"

I thought about that for a moment. "I don't remember her being out-and-out rude to him, but I also don't remember her having any extended interactions with him. A few times she's disagreed with points he's made about the book or the author we were discussing, and she got testy when he challenged her to back up her points with examples."

"Maybe she doesn't like people telling her she's wrong about anything. It might be interesting to find out what she's got against him," Helen Louise said. "And whether she has told Lieutenant Wesner."

"She doesn't like being told she's wrong," I said. "But then I don't think any of us cares for that. It depends on how it's done, and in Zac's case, he's not particularly tactful."

"No, he isn't," Helen Louise said. "That's not enough to

claim he's a murderer, though. Surely there must be something more behind Burdine's accusation than lack of tact."

"I wonder if we can get her to tell us what it is," I said.

"You can certainly try," Helen Louise said, "but I don't think you'd get very far with her. She can be awfully stubborn when she wants to be."

"She can," I said. "If I ask her, all she can do is tell me it's none of my business." I paused, thinking about it. "Elmore, however, might be easier to talk to. If I can get him alone, that is. He might let something slip."

"That could work," Helen Louise said.

I glanced at my watch. Nearly five o'clock. A little early for dinner, but it wouldn't hurt to go downstairs and see whether anyone was hanging about. I was surprised Lieutenant Wesner hadn't sent for either Helen Louise or me for more questioning this afternoon, but he was probably concentrating his efforts on other suspects. I wasn't sure how seriously he considered me and Helen Louise as suspects, or Miss An'gel, Miss Dickce, or Benjy. Perhaps the testimonials to our sterling characters he received from the authorities in Athena had allayed his suspicions of us.

I heard a knock at the door and went to answer it. Diesel came with me, always curious to find out who had knocked.

I told him to stay back before I opened the door. He usually wouldn't go out unless he knew the person on the other side. I swung the door open to find a woman around my age in a maid's uniform, towels in hand. She had bleached blond hair, dark roots showing, and work-roughened hands. Her name tag identified her as Doris.

"Good afternoon, sir," she said, her voice husky. "Do y'all need any fresh towels?"

I started to answer that I didn't think we did, but an idea occurred to me. Instead, I said, "Please come in. I don't want my cat to get out. I'll go check."

Startled, Doris glanced down at Diesel, but then her face broke into a wide smile. "Hello there, beautiful. Boy or girl?"

"Boy. His name is Diesel." I shut the door behind her. "I'll be right back."

Helen Louise was in the bathroom. I knocked on the door, and it opened a crack. "Do we need any fresh towels?" I asked.

"Yes, we do. Is that the maid?" she said, opening the door wider.

"Yes, I'm going to try to get her to talk to me about Cora. I'll tell her you'll be out in a minute, okay?"

"Fine." The door closed.

Back in the sitting room I found Doris, now free of towels, bent over Diesel, rubbing and scratching him. I could see that the cat had no objections to this treatment. In fact, he was purring loudly. Doris was his kind of human.

"My partner is using the bathroom at the moment," I said. "I hope you won't mind waiting a minute or so."

Doris straightened, much to Diesel's disappointment. He warbled loudly, no doubt adjuring her to continue. She left off petting Diesel and picked up the towels. "I'll come back in a bit then, sir, if it's all the same to you."

"No, please don't go," I said. "I'd like to talk to you for a minute." I reached into my pocket for my wallet, thinking I might offer her a tip, but she saw what I was doing.

"Now, sir, that ain't necessary," she said. "I got a few minutes if you want to talk."

"Then, please, sit down." I indicated a chair across from where I stood.

Doris set the towels down on the coffee table and took her seat. She looked at me expectantly.

"I guess the staff here is upset about what's happened," I said.

Doris nodded vigorously. "Sure are. First time as I know of that we had a guest murdered in his bed. And then that Cora." She sniffed. "Well, all I can say about her is that I'm only surprised she didn't get herself murdered sooner."

TWENTY-SIX

"Really?" I said, taken aback by Doris's blunt proclamation about her former coworker. "Why do you think she was murdered?"

Doris sniffed again as Diesel rubbed himself against his new friend's legs. The maid patted his head for a moment before she answered me. "Well, it's like this. Cora was just hard-down nosy. Nosiest woman I ever did know. Had to find out everything she could about everybody. Asked questions like you wouldn't believe. Course, she didn't dare do that too much with the guests, because Mr. Hindman, he don't like us pestering guests at all. So Cora snooped around in their rooms." Suddenly she let out a cackle of laughter.

"Did you see her narcoplexy routine?" Doris asked.

"I did. We found her on the sofa in here when we first came into the room," I said. "Why do you call it a routine?"

"'Cause that's exactly what it was. Cora wasn't narcoplexic

any more than I am." Doris laughed again. "That's how she covered up her snooping. She'd hear the lock click and down she'd go and pretend to be asleep. I reckon what happened is that she tried it on the wrong person, and that's the person that killed her." She frowned. "She wasn't even supposed to be in your room. This isn't her floor."

"I didn't realize this wasn't her floor," I said. "I did find her in our room again. She was in the bedroom, but she was awake. She said she was looking for her pin, the one she used to keep her little cap on. Was that part of the routine?"

Doris shook her head. "No, I don't think so. First I heard of it. Course with Cora, you never could tell. She could be slick as eel snot when she wanted to be."

I would have to remember Doris's colorful image and repeat it to Helen Louise. In the meantime I tried not to visualize it.

"When we found Cora on our sofa, supposedly asleep," I said, "we were with Arthur Hindman. He seemed to think Cora's condition was genuine."

"Now, that Arthur is a nice boy, and he sure is something good to look at," Doris said, "but he don't have the brains the good Lord gave a goose. I figured he'd done told his grandpa about it, but Cora must've begged him not to. He's kindhearted, I'll say that for him."

"I'm surprised that Mr. Hindman hasn't found out for himself," I said. "Surely guests have complained about it."

"Cora's only been working here for about nine months," Doris said. "I reckon nobody's said anything—none of the guests, I mean—and the other staff don't care. Ain't their business."

"How many maids are there usually on duty at a given time?"

I asked. "This isn't a large hotel, but there's still a lot of work, I imagine."

"There sure is," Doris said. "And we stay booked for most of the year, too. People love coming to Asheville. There's usually two of us on duty, and there's one on call during the night, in case of emergencies."

"Surely you don't work seven days a week," I said.

"Lord, honey, we sure don't. There's a couple girls who do weekends and fill-ins when either me or Cora was sick. One of 'em is working Cora's shifts now. She's got taken on full-time, and she's happy about that. She has a family to feed."

I wondered why Helen Louise hadn't joined us. Surely she had finished in the bathroom. I found out later that she hadn't wanted to break the flow of the conversation, thinking that Doris's fountain of information might dry up if she came into the room.

I had one question more that I wanted to put to Doris. "You said Cora was really nosy and liked to find out things about people. Did she try to do anything with what she found out?"

Doris looked hard at me a minute. "You mean like blackmail?"

I nodded.

"Don't really know about that for sure," Doris said after a pause.

"Did she ever show signs of having more money than she could have earned working here?" I asked.

"Not so much money," Doris said slowly. "More like things."

"What kind of things?"

"Jewelry, sometimes, like that hatpin of hers, the one she claimed was a family heirloom." Doris gave a derisive snort.

"Family heirloom, yeah, but not her family. Some older woman stayed here about a month ago with her nephew in the biggest suite. I saw her wearing that hatpin, and from things Cora let drop, that wasn't no nephew with the woman."

I coughed to hide a laugh that I couldn't quite suppress. "Cora managed to talk the woman out of the hatpin somehow."

"Sure did," Doris replied. "And wouldn't you know, the killer used that hatpin on poor ole Cora." There was a note of grim satisfaction in her voice.

Cora had obviously seen or heard something connected to Denis Kilbride's murder, I figured. Had she tried to get some trinket, or perhaps even money, from the killer in return for silence? Or had she even attempted blackmail?

"Have you told the police about this?" I asked.

Doris looked pained. "I talked to that Sergeant Bloesch, but all she wanted to know about was my schedule, and how often I saw that man that was murdered. Which was once, by the way. He was in Cora's section, not mine, thank the Lord. After the sergeant found that out, she wasn't too interested in anything else I had to say. You reckon I ought to tell her this stuff anyway, I guess." Doris shrugged. "I don't mind doing it. Ain't no skin off my teeth, like my old granny used to say. Problem will be getting her to listen."

"I think you should talk to Lieutenant Wesner, her boss," I said. "He seems like a pretty good guy. I bet he'll listen to you. I'll even talk to him first, if that will help, to make sure he listens."

"Well, aren't you Mr. Big Shot?" Doris didn't appear impressed, despite her words. "Suppose I can talk to the cop on my own, but if I need help, I'll tell him about you wanting me to talk to him." Suddenly she picked up the fresh towels and rose. "How about these towels? You need 'em, or don't you?"

Helen Louise entered the room. "Good evening. Oh, fresh towels, how lovely. Yes, we could use them. Thank you."

Doris nodded and headed for the bathroom. She soon emerged with the used towels and marched to the door. She paused after opening it, turned back, and nodded at me. "I'll go talk to the cop." Then she was out of the room, the door swiftly pulled shut behind her.

"Goodness, what a character." Helen Louise took the chair Doris had vacated, and Diesel meowed loudly, as if in agreement.

"She certainly is. Did you hear everything?" I asked.

"Yes, I think so," she replied. "Based on what she told you, I can understand why Cora was murdered. She must have blundered into the murderer's path at some point."

"And if we knew when, we'd probably know who. Zac is working on it," I said. "I really ought to put together my own timetable of everyone's movements, to figure out who was where when and why."

"I'll work that out later, after I've had a glass or two of wine," Helen Louise said, smiling.

I laughed. "Speaking of wine, what would you like to do about dinner?"

"I would love to get out of the hotel for dinner," Helen Louise said, "but I don't think that's going to happen. We might as well have dinner in the restaurant here. There are a couple of items on the menu I haven't tried yet."

Diesel meowed and chirped as if he were trying to communicate urgently with us, and I wondered what it was he wanted to tell us. I also wondered if he knew that he was the reason we felt compelled to remain in the hotel.

"Let me call Miss An'gel," I said. "Remember, she said she'd ask her friends about pet sitters. Who knows, she might have found someone for us."

"At this hotel? With two murders?" Helen Louise sounded impatient. "It's highly unlikely anyone would care to."

"We'll never know if we don't ask." I resisted the urge to use the same tone with her. This situation was wearing on all of us. I picked up my phone and called Miss An'gel.

"Hello, Charlie, what's up?" she said.

"I was wondering whether you had asked your friends about pet sitters, by any chance. Helen Louise and I would really like to leave the hotel for dinner. A change of scenery, you know."

"I do," Miss An'gel said. "As a matter of fact, Sister and I are going out to meet friends tonight, but Benjy is staying in. I think he would be happy to watch Diesel for you."

"Are you sure it wouldn't be an imposition?" I asked.

"Not at all. I know he's been missing Peanut and Endora dreadfully," Miss An'gel said. "Spending time with Diesel will perk him up. I'll arrange for dinner to be sent up to your suite for him. He has his laptop with him and several of his favorite DVDs, so he'll be fine."

"That would be great," I said. "If six o'clock is agreeable to him, we'd appreciate it."

"I'll let you know if it's not. Otherwise you can expect him at six," Miss An'gel said.

I put my phone down and smiled at Helen Louise. "Benjy will come watch Diesel while we go out."

"I'm not going to question how you got this to happen," Helen Louise said. "I'm simply going to give you a big kiss and go get ready." She put her words into action so heartily that she left me a little breathless.

By the time Benjy knocked on our door, precisely at six, we were ready. "That's Benjy at the door," I told Diesel. "He's going to stay with you. Isn't that great?" Diesel scampered to the door and meowed.

Laughing, I opened the door to admit young Mr. Stephens, a laptop carrying case slung over one shoulder.

"Come on in. I told Diesel it was you, and he's really happy."

Benjy smiled as he scratched the cat's head. "I'm happy to see you, too, boy." He advanced into the room with the cat rubbing against him every step.

"Diesel, be careful, you'll trip Benjy," I said, but Benjy laughed.

"It's okay, Charlie. At home I'm used to having two of them doing it." Benjy set his laptop case on the coffee table. He seated himself on the sofa, and Diesel immediately jumped up and climbed into Benjy's lap. He butted his head against Benjy's chin, and the young man laughed again.

I left the two of them enjoying each other's company and went to the bedroom to see if Helen Louise was ready.

A couple of minutes later we left the room after having made sure that Benjy had our phone numbers. We walked slowly down the stairs. "You look lovely tonight," I said. "I'm not sure I'm dressed well enough to be escorting you."

Helen Louise laughed. "You look fine, but thank you for the compliment."

We reached the reception area, and I spotted the policeman

on duty, one elbow propped on the reception desk while he surveyed the area. "I'll just let him know where we're going," I told Helen Louise. I stepped away to talk to the officer.

He listened politely and made a note of our destination and approximate time of return. "Thank you, sir."

I went back to Helen Louise, struck by her odd expression. "You look like you've seen a ghost," I said in a joking tone.

"Not a ghost," she said. "I think I just saw Kanesha Berry."

TWENTY-SEVEN

"Where?" I said. "Why would Kanesha be here, of all places?"

"Going into that meeting room," Helen Louise said. "I don't know why she would be here. I'm telling you the woman looked like her."

"Did you get a good look at her?" I asked, still incredulous.

"No, not really," Helen Louise said. "I saw her out of the corner of my eye, a flash of movement. When I looked all I saw was her back as she disappeared into that room. The door shut, and that was that."

"If all you saw was her back," I said, "then it was obviously someone else."

"Probably," Helen Louise said. "But sometimes you do recognize people from behind. I do."

"I do, too." I took her arm and led her toward the street door. "In this case, you probably saw someone with a similar build and so on. Let's forget about it and focus on enjoying ourselves during our escape from the hotel." The taxi I had called was waiting for us, and we hurried toward it.

We thoroughly enjoyed our time away from the hotel. With Benjy looking after Diesel, I relaxed and was able to focus on dinner. We talked of personal things, ideas for the wedding and the honeymoon, nothing to do with the two murders at all. After an excellent meal, superb wine, and a dessert that was heaven on the tongue, we made our way back via another taxi.

By the time we reached our room, the time was nearly eight-thirty. I knocked on the door to alert Benjy that we had returned; then I unlocked the door. As the door opened I caught the sound of two voices, both of which I recognized. I swung the door wide open and let Helen Louise precede me into the room.

"I didn't imagine it," Helen Louise cried. "It was Kanesha."

Sure enough, Chief Deputy Kanesha Berry of the Athena County Sheriff's Department occupied one of the chairs in our suite. Benjy, seated in one corner of the sofa, had Diesel's head in his lap while the rest of the cat stretched out almost to the other end.

"This is a pleasant surprise," I said, advancing to shake Kanesha's hand.

While I greeted Kanesha, Helen Louise gave Benjy the dessert we had brought back for him. He loved sweets, and since I knew he wouldn't accept money for taking care of Diesel, we decided to bring him a piece of the chocolate turtle cheesecake that I had sampled at the restaurant.

Amidst thanks and greetings, Benjy extricated himself from Diesel, and Helen Louise took his place. I walked with Benjy to the door and saw him out.

"Thanks again for the dessert, Charlie." Benjy flashed a grin. "You know I have a big sweet tooth, but it wasn't really necessary. You know I love spending time with Diesel." With that he headed on his way, and I turned to our new guest.

"It's nice to see you," I said to Kanesha, "but of course I have to ask what brought you here."

"You'd do better to ask who, rather than what," Kanesha said with a mischievous smile.

"In that case, I don't need to ask." I chuckled. "That force of nature otherwise known as Miss An'gel Ducote."

"Exactly," Kanesha said. "Miss An'gel called me last night and told me what was going on. Of course, I'd already responded to queries from Lieutenant Wesner here, but Miss An'gel asked if I would come and assist, as she put it, since I know some of the people involved."

"Are you using up personal time to do this?" I asked.

"No, the sheriff agreed to let me come as a personal favor to Miss An'gel." Kanesha laughed. "I'm not sure how I feel about being a personal favor, but given the situation, I thought it might be a good idea. Someone has to keep you out of trouble with the police here, Charlie, and it might as well be me. I have the experience, after all."

I decided not to dignify those jesting remarks with a response.

"Have you met Wesner yet?" Helen Louise asked after a quick glance at me.

Kanesha nodded. "Yes, not long after I arrived from the airport. Talked to him until about fifteen minutes ago, when I came up here to wait for the two of you to return from dinner."

"How did he react to your presence?" I asked.

"Guardedly," Kanesha said. "As I would have if the situation was reversed. It is what it is, and he's a pragmatist like me. Basically, he wants this case solved, and I might have information and contacts in Mississippi that can help him do that more quickly than if he was working on his own."

"I really am glad to see you," I said. "The Mississippi connection is important, because the roots of Denis Kilbride's murder surely must be there, not here in North Carolina."

"I agree," Kanesha said.

Diesel meowed loudly, and the chief deputy shot an amused glance at him.

"Apparently the cat agrees, too," she said.

"He likes to contribute to the conversation every once in a while," Helen Louise said, "so we don't forget he's here."

"You probably can't tell us anything that Wesner shared with you in confidence," I said, "but Helen Louise and I have been wondering whether the lieutenant is planning to arrest someone anytime soon."

"You're right, I can't share much with you," Kanesha said, "although Wesner agreed I could use my discretion about that. I told him, face-to-face, how useful you have been in the past. He's not totally convinced, but at least he's taken you off the suspect list, unofficially."

"Meaning that officially I'm still on the list, along with Helen Louise," I said, and Kanesha nodded.

"Did he tell you whether one of the hotel maids, a woman named Doris, had been to see him?" I asked.

"He mentioned interviewing her," Kanesha said. "Does she have pertinent information?"

"She's full of it," Helen Louise said wryly. "She told Charlie a lot about the other murder victim, Cora Apfel, and it could have a bearing on the case. In fact, we think it probably explains why she was murdered."

Kanesha shook her head. "You do have a knack for getting people to talk to you, Charlie. Care to fill me in on what this Doris had to say?"

"I will, and I'll attempt to do it in less time." I launched into a résumé of the facts from Doris's revelations. When I finished about ten minutes later, slowed down by a couple of additions provided by Helen Louise, Kanesha looked pensive.

"I think you're right," she said. "Cora Apfel must have, knowingly or not, found out something the murderer thought would give the game away. Otherwise I can't see any reason to kill her."

"Has Wesner worked up any kind of timetable yet of where everyone was at particular times?" I asked. "For example, when Kilbride was killed? We haven't heard anything about that."

"I suppose it can't hurt to share that with you," Kanesha said. "The medical examiner thought he had died sometime between eleven p.m. and one a.m. He had been dead for some hours when the maid found him."

"Can you tell us how she found him?" I said, then realized how odd that sounded. "I mean, was he in bed, clothed, undressed, in a chair, for example?"

"I knew what you meant," Kanesha said. "She found him lying prone on the bed, wearing shorts and a sleeveless T-shirt. At first she thought he was asleep and started to back out of the room, because they're not supposed to enter the room when the guest is in residence, so to speak. Then she noticed that he wasn't breathing."

"If he was in that state of undress," Helen Louise said, "don't you think that points to someone on intimate terms with him being the murderer?"

"Generally, I'd agree with you, but there's another factor," Kanesha said. "He'd had a substantial amount of alcohol to drink, so in that state, he might have admitted anyone to the room, regardless of his attire."

"I see your point," Helen Louise said. "So that opens up the list of suspects again."

"It sure does," I said. "If he was drunk, he could have collapsed on the bed in a stupor, and the killer saw his chance and took it. Whoever it was didn't reckon on the medical examiner spotting the entry point of that hatpin."

"That's curious to me," Kanesha said. "The killer most likely is a member of your group, right?"

Helen Louise and I nodded. Diesel added his comment as well, in the form of a loud trill.

Kanesha shot a pained glance at the cat before she continued. "Surely the members of your group are well read enough to know that an autopsy would turn up something like that."

I hadn't thought about that point before. "You're right," I said slowly. "Most everyone in the group reads across the genres of mysteries, and most of them watch various crime shows on television, too. They should have sufficient knowledge to realize a careful medical examiner would find the entry point of the wound that killed Denis Kilbride."

"Maybe the killer didn't think it through completely," Helen Louise said, "or was simply overconfident."

"Or trying to blame someone else," Kanesha said.

"Is there any helpful forensic evidence?" I asked. "DNA left behind, that sort of thing?"

"There almost always is," Kanesha said. "Especially in cases like this. There couldn't have been much premeditation, because no one knew Kilbride would be here. That means it was an opportunistic murder, and it happened within a few hours of Kilbride's arrival at the hotel. The killer wouldn't have had much time to plan the murder."

Kanesha had answered my question without really answering it. I knew I wouldn't get anything more specific out of her. The killer had left evidence, but Kanesha wasn't going to tell Helen Louise and me what it was. This was the typical modus operandi for Kanesha, and it wasn't even her case. She wouldn't violate Lieutenant Wesner's trust and let slip anything he didn't want us to know, I was sure.

"How well do you know the rest of our group?" Helen Louise said. "Other than Melba, Benjy, and the Ducote sisters, that is."

"I've known Johnny Ray Floyd all my life," Kanesha said.

"Right, I'd forgotten that," Helen Louise said.

"I haven't met Zac Ryan," Kanesha said, "but I know the others, at least to speak to. The only other one I know well is Celia Bernardi."

I exchanged a glance with Helen Louise. I wondered if the reason Kanesha knew Celia well was because of Celia's little habit of taking things from her friends and acquaintances. I wondered if Celia had ever been arrested for her thefts.

I didn't feel that I could ask Kanesha point-blank about Celia. Perhaps Helen Louise could. I looked at her hopefully. She nodded.

"If you know Celia well," Helen Louise said, "then you are probably aware of her little quirk."

"I am," Kanesha said. "But I don't think that has anything to do with the present case."

"Thank goodness," Helen Louise said.

"I think that's about all that I can tell you without compromising Lieutenant Wesner's investigation," Kanesha said. "I've done what I can to assist him, and I'll be on hand the next few days. I'm confident that he'll wrap the case up before the week is out."

"That's good," I said, though I wished she would tell us more. I understood, however, that she couldn't.

Kanesha rose to go, but Helen Louise stopped her with a question.

"Kanesha, do you think it likely that the killer might kill again before he's caught?"

"Yes, I do." Kanesha looked straight at me, and I felt a chill on the back of my neck.

TWENTY-EIGHT

Helen Louise and Diesel walked to the door with Kanesha and bade her good night. I was still trying to process Kanesha's response to the question Helen Louise posed. The way she had looked at me when she said, "Yes, I do," spooked me. There were times in other murder investigations when I became frightened—or at the very least, nervous—but this really got to me.

Maybe that was why Kanesha did it, I reasoned. She was warning me to back off, not to blunder on and put myself in danger. She hadn't been happy with me the one time I had taken a serious risk with a killer. I hoped I had learned my lesson with that one, but she probably didn't think I had.

"That was pointed, wasn't it?" Helen Louise said as she and Diesel returned to the sofa.

"Yes, it was." I rubbed the back of my neck.

"Good," Helen Louise said. "In her way, I think she has become fond of you, Charlie, and she has your safety and wellbeing in mind."

"Maybe," I said. "I think you're right about her having my safety in mind, but I wouldn't go so far as to say that she's become fond of me, even in her cold, non-expressive way."

Helen Louise chuckled. "She's so much like her mother."

"Don't tell her that," I said.

Kanesha's mother—my housekeeper, Azalea Berry—had tolerated me when I first inherited my aunt Dottie's house in Athena. The house that Azalea swore Aunt Dottie entrusted to her care, even though I owned it. Over the years Azalea and I had developed a warmer relationship, though frankly I was still a little afraid of her. I was a little afraid of her daughter, too. They were both strong, independent women who did not suffer fools gladly. I no longer felt like a complete fool around them, only an occasional one.

"Did you bolt the door when Kanesha left?" I asked.

"Yes," Helen Louise replied. "After what she said, I was almost tempted to put a chair under the door handle as well."

"I doubt anyone will break in," I said. "We'd have to let the killer in ourselves, and we're not going to do that."

"No, we surely are not," Helen Louise said. "At this point, I don't want any of the group coming in here except our good friends. Not until Wesner is certain he's got the killer and is on the way to jail with him or her."

"Agreed," I said. "How about we forget all about the murders for the rest of the night, cuddle on the couch, and watch a movie?"

"That sounds perfect," Helen Louise said. "What do you think, Diesel?"

The cat opened his sleepy eyes and yawned. He meowed once, closed his eyes, and went back to sleep.

"I guess it's unanimous," I said. "Now let's find a movie."

After reviewing the choices, we settled on a romantic comedy we both recalled with fondness. We dozed off before it finished, however, and I woke at some point afterward with a slight crick in my neck. I roused Helen Louise gently, and we headed for the bedroom. We found Diesel stretched out, sound asleep, down the middle of the bed, his head on my pillow.

I took a couple of aspirin to ward off the headache I felt coming, thanks to the crick in my neck, and we went to bed, Diesel snuggled between us.

I woke the next morning feeling clearheaded, with no more soreness. Diesel no longer lay between Helen Louise and me. She lay on her side facing me, and I watched her, marveling how lovely she was, tousled with sleep. One eye opened and regarded me; then the other opened, and she smiled.

"Good morning," she said.

Later on we dressed and went down to breakfast, escorted by Diesel. We had apparently missed most of the group, because the dining room was nearly empty. Only Zac was there, and he had just about finished his breakfast.

"Good morning, Zac," I said, and Helen Louise nodded to him. Diesel meowed, and Zac grinned.

"You two look mighty pleased with yourselves this morning," Zac said. "You have about ten minutes to eat breakfast before you're due to report to the meeting room. Nine o'clock sharp. Orders of General Ducote."

I groaned. "I thought we had gone off-schedule."

"You obviously didn't check your text messages this morning," Zac said. "The general texted everyone at seven this morning to ask that we all assemble at nine."

"We'll be there," Helen Louise said as she helped herself from the remains of the breakfast buffet. "Come on, Charlie. It won't do to keep Miss An'gel and the others waiting."

"Charlie, I'll get with you later on that timetable you wanted me to draw up." Zac downed the rest of his orange juice and sauntered out with a wave and a smug smile.

"Did you know you were blushing a little at what Zac said?" Helen Louise grinned at me.

"I'm too old to blush anymore," I said as I selected a couple of sausage links to go with my biscuit and scrambled eggs.

"Uh-huh," Helen Louise said.

Diesel reminded me that he was waiting for bites of bacon, and I let the matter drop while I alternately fed the cat and myself.

Without gobbling down the food, we managed to get a decent meal before we walked into the meeting room on the dot of nine. Miss An'gel nodded her approval as we took our seats on the sofa with Johnny Ray. Everyone else was present.

Miss An'gel began to speak. "Regretfully, our plans for the week have been overset by these two terrible murders. That is unalterable. If we were free to go I would suggest that everyone return home if any of you are so minded. As it is, however, the lieutenant insists that we remain. I spoke with him this morning to ask for a progress report on the case." She frowned. "He did not say so in a forthright manner, but I am under the impression that an arrest is imminent. Although that might be wishful thinking on my part."

What was she up to? I wondered. Was she trying to provoke the murderer into betraying himself or herself by doing a bunk? I couldn't believe that either Wesner or Kanesha would approve of this. And where was Kanesha?

I wished the killer would lose courage and try to run away. That would simplify matters for everyone. I doubted the killer would get far, if he or she tried it, but perhaps if enough panic were induced, it would happen. I decided to play Miss An'gel's game.

"That's great," I said, trying to sound enthusiastic but not overly so. "The police are really closing in, it sounds like."

"Amen," Johnny Ray said. "I'm ready for this to be over."

"They don't have to look very far," Burdine said in a spiteful tone. I could see that she had her gaze fixed on Zac. Why was she so determined to see him as the murderer?

Zac paid no attention to her. "I'll be glad when this is over. I was really looking forward to seeing the sights of Asheville. Biltmore was great, and I'm glad I got to see it. But there's a lot more to see and do here."

"I've been afraid to go out at night," Celia said. "I have my dear friend Betty Milton I could be spending time with, and another friend, Rosemary Poole-Carter, whom I haven't seen in ages. I can't invite them here, naturally, and put them in danger."

"I don't think the killer would have a reason to harm your friends," Ellie said. "They have no connection to Denis and Cora, surely."

"No, that's true," Celia said. "Perhaps I'll reconsider."

Miss An'gel had listened and watched as the group talked—not missing a thing, I would have wagered. What was she looking for?

The door opened, and Kanesha Berry walked in. "Good morning, everyone. I apologize for interrupting the meeting," she said. "Miss An'gel, could I speak privately with you?"

"Certainly." Miss An'gel rose and accompanied Kanesha out of the room.

"I wonder what that's all about," Miss Dickce said.

"Maybe she's telling Miss An'gel about the arrest," Benjy said. "Maybe the lieutenant is ready to do it."

Miss Dickce and Benjy were obviously in on Miss An'gel's stratagem. I glanced around the room to gauge the effect of their words. Ellie and Celia appeared apprehensive. Melba and Paul looked puzzled, and Elmore and Burdine simply looked blank. Johnny Ray was obviously eager. I knew he would be happy when this was over and he could take his family home.

Diesel didn't appear to be bothered by any of this. He remained quiet, lying by the side of the sofa near me. I stroked his head, and he seemed calm.

"How much longer do we need to sit here?" Paul Bowen asked, sounding impatient to the point of rudeness. "What else did Miss An'gel want to discuss with us?" He directed his question to Miss Dickce.

"I'm sure Sister will be back any minute now," Miss Dickce said. "I don't know whether there is anything else to discuss at the present moment. If you'd like to go, I don't see any reason why you shouldn't."

Paul started to rise, but Melba placed a restraining hand on his arm. He shot her a startled look, but he subsided into his chair again. Melba bent her head near his, and they held a brief whispered conversation.

Miss An'gel returned shortly, without Kanesha. "I'm sorry to keep you all waiting. I did ask the lieutenant if we could continue to go about sightseeing, and he said that was fine as long as we do not leave the city limits and do inform the officer on duty where we are going."

Paul got up immediately with Melba. She threw Miss An'gel an apologetic glance as they walked by her. Johnny Ray followed them. Celia stood, muttering to herself. I suspected she would go visit one of her friends.

The room cleared quickly, leaving Helen Louise, Diesel, and me with the Ducotes and Benjy. Kanesha rejoined us and took a seat near Miss An'gel.

"Were you trying to rattle some cages?" I asked.

Miss An'gel regarded me with her usual calm. "I wouldn't put it in such crude terms, Charlie, but yes, I was hoping to stir things up."

"Did the lieutenant know what you were planning to do?" Helen Louise asked.

"I might have mentioned it to him," Miss An'gel said. "I did speak with him this morning. That, at least, was true."

Kanesha maintained her usual enigmatic expression, but I reckoned she would have happily scolded Miss An'gel if she thought it would have had the least effect. She knew better, however.

"Did you glean any insights from the reactions you got to your announcement?" I asked.

"I hardly expected the killer to prostrate himself before me and confess," Miss An'gel said tartly. "I believe what I said struck home, however. It's entirely likely that the killer will attempt to make a run for it, and the lieutenant and the Asheville police will be ready. They've been tailing everyone who leaves the hotel."

TWENTY-NINE

I couldn't think of anything to say after Miss An'gel's announcement that we would all be under surveillance outside the hotel. I should have realized before now that would be the case.

I stood, along with Helen Louise. "Well, then, I think we will probably go out today."

"Yes, I've been wanting to go back and explore the rest of the Biltmore estate," Helen Louise said. "The gardens, of course, as well as the winery. I'd love to try some of their wines."

"That sounds like a lovely way to spend the day," Miss An'gel said.

"What about Diesel?" Miss Dickce asked. "I don't think they'll let him in the winery or the gardens, either."

"Sister is right," Miss An'gel said. "We got a special dispensation for you to take him through the house with our tour, but that was all."

"I guess we didn't think it completely through," I said, my tone apologetic.

Helen Louise shrugged. "It's okay."

"No, it's not," Miss Dickce said. "You two deserve to have your day out. I'm not feeling particularly energetic today and planned to stay in the hotel. You just leave Diesel with me and go enjoy your day. You'll stay with me, won't you, sweet boy?"

Thus appealed to, Diesel meowed. He loved the sisters and Benjy and would probably be happy with them today. I knew they would take excellent care of him.

"Thank you, if you're sure it's not an imposition." I felt Helen Louise relax beside me. She really had her heart set on visiting the winery today.

"Not at all," Miss An'gel said, and Miss Dickce nodded.

Helen Louise searched in her purse for her room key and handed it to Miss Dickce. "Thank you so much."

Miss Dickce accepted the key. "Don't give it a second thought."

We didn't. After a quick trip back to our suite to collect a few items, we headed for the parking lot and were soon on the way to the Biltmore estate. Helen Louise once again navigated.

After discussions with the ticket seller at the entrance to the estate, we decided to drive to the winery, where we could park. Once we were finished there we could catch a shuttle to the gardens, and then back again to pick up the car later. Our admission included complimentary wine-tasting.

We had a beautiful, clear day for our exploration of the estate. The temperature was relatively mild, but we had come prepared with hats and sunscreen while we were out in the direct sunlight. Frederick Law Olmsted, considered the father of American landscape architecture, designed the gardens at Biltmore. Helen Louise and I enjoyed ourselves thoroughly as we took our time wandering through the different spaces. Biltmore boasted, variously, an Italian garden, a shrub garden, a walled garden, and a rose garden, among others. We didn't tour everything because we were eager to move on to the winery, plus we'd had a surfeit of greenery after several hours.

We decided we should eat, however, before we sampled the wines. I hadn't even thought about making reservations at one of the restaurants that required them, so we ended up lunching in the Courtyard Market, where we had our choice of several eateries.

Helen Louise was in her element at the winery. We took our time and enjoyed the wine-tasting. We ended up with a dozen bottles of wine to take home with us. By the time we finished our visit to Biltmore, it was nearly five o'clock. We loaded the wine in the car and headed wearily back to the hotel.

"I'd love to come back sometime and stay in one of the hotels at the estate," Helen Louise said.

"That sounds like a great idea to me," I said. "We haven't been able to experience as much here in Asheville so far as we both wanted, and I wouldn't mind revisiting Biltmore, perhaps in a different season."

"When it's a little cooler outside," Helen Louise said.

"Yes, I got a bit sweaty by the time we got on the shuttle bus to the winery," I said. "I think I'll have a shower when we get back."

"Not if I get to it first," Helen Louise said. "I'm feeling a bit grubby myself."

We wended our way out of the Biltmore grounds and back to

the hotel. As we parked the car, Helen Louise said, "You know, I almost don't want to go back inside."

I paused in the act of climbing out of the driver's seat. "Would you like to go somewhere else?"

Helen Louise shook her head. "Other than home, no. It's that once we go back inside, we're back in the midst of the murder investigation. I don't know about you, but I get that closed-in feeling in the hotel."

"I know, love. I do, too," I said. "Maybe Miss An'gel's ploy worked, and the killer did try to run. There might be good news inside."

Helen Louise laughed. "You'd have received several text messages by now, and so would I, if that were the case."

"True," I said. "We might as well not postpone it, though. Let's get the wine out of the trunk. Can't forget and leave it out here in the heat."

"No, we certainly can't, not after what I spent today," Helen Louise said.

We managed to get the wine safely up to our suite by using the elevator rather than the stairs. I didn't trust myself carrying things up the stairs, especially not expensive things like wine bottles. Helen Louise knocked on the door and called out to Miss Dickce, and moments later Miss Dickce opened the door.

"Stay back, Diesel," Miss Dickce said. "Don't get under their feet now."

Thankfully for my balance, Diesel obeyed, and we conveyed the wine safely into the room.

"My goodness, looks like you're planning a party with all that wine," Miss Dickce said. "Is it all from Biltmore?"

"Yes, ma'am, it is," I said. "Helen Louise really liked several of the wines we tasted today." Before Miss Dickce could inquire further about the wines, I said, "Tell us, did anything happen today while we were out? For example, did anyone try to run away from Asheville?"

Miss Dickce shook her head. "So far, no. I didn't think An'gel's bright idea would work, you know. There's no use telling her that, though. You know how stubborn she is." Miss Dickce rolled her eyes, and I was hard put not to chuckle at her. Helen Louise shot me a glance full of amusement. Diesel chirped and warbled.

"See, Diesel knows I'm right," Miss Dickce said with a fond glance at the cat. "Now, I'm sure you're both tired after your day out and are ready to rest for a while." She returned Helen Louise's hotel key, and we thanked her profusely for allowing us to have some time away from the hotel.

"It was my pleasure," Miss Dickce said. "Spending quiet time with Diesel was exactly what I needed. My headache vanished within fifteen minutes of settling in here with him." She grimaced. "I have a feeling it will come back soon, however."

"I hope not," I said as I ushered her to the door. "We'll see you later, I'm sure."

I turned to find that Helen Louise had left the room. I went immediately to the bedroom, and I heard the shower start up in the bathroom. "What do you think of that?" I asked Diesel, who had accompanied me. For once he had no comment.

"I know a trick worth two of that," I murmured as I began to disrobe. The quotation from *Henry IV, Part I* might have been somewhat out of context, but it would serve.

Later on, feeling refreshed by the shower, we dressed and contemplated dinner.

"I don't really feel like going out," Helen Louise said. "How about you?"

"Fine with me," I said. "We got our exercise today with all the walking." My phone buzzed, alerting me that I had a new text message.

The moment I saw that it was from Miss An'gel, my heart began to sink. It continued as I read the text.

Please join us in the meeting room at seven for aperitifs and amuse-bouche before dinner.

I showed Helen Louise the message, and she shrugged. "We can hardly decline," she said. "We can go down for a while, and Diesel can come with us."

"You're right." I checked my watch. "That gives us about fifteen minutes before we need to leave the room. I can't help but wonder, though, whether Miss An'gel has another ploy up her more than ample sleeve."

Helen Louise snorted with laughter. "Do you doubt she does?"

I sighed. "No, not really."

We relaxed on the sofa with Diesel stretched out on the floor in front of us. I began to relax a bit too much, as I felt my head nodding. Helen Louise's head already rested on my shoulder. My head lolled against hers, and then I dozed off.

My phone rang and brought me awake. I gently removed Helen Louise's head from my shoulder and woke her. She stared groggily while I answered the call. From Miss An'gel, as I had known it would be the moment I heard the phone.

"Good evening, Charlie," Miss An'gel said. "Did you receive my text? I hope you and Helen Louise are able to join us. And Diesel, too."

"Yes, ma'am, I did get your text, and we're about to head downstairs. We'll be with you in a few minutes." I listened for a moment longer before I ended the call. "We have been summoned."

Helen Louise, awake now, smiled grimly. "Let's get going, then."

I attached Diesel's leash to his harness, and we left the suite. I checked the time when we reached the door to the meeting room. We were only twelve minutes late. I opened the door, and we entered.

I noticed Kanesha immediately. She stood next to Miss An'gel, drink in hand, surveying the room. What was she hoping to spot? I wondered.

Miss An'gel saw us and stepped forward in greeting. We passed a couple of minutes in small talk while I examined the room. Every member of the group was here. Ellie sat with Melba and Paul, chatting in what appeared to be a cheerful mood. Miss Dickce held court with Zac and Benjy, while Johnny Ray, Celia, and the Gregorys made up the final group. Everything appeared harmonious. No one seemed on edge, no feeling of tension in the room. I began to relax. Maybe this was simply a party after all.

Miss An'gel directed us to the aperitifs and amuse-bouche, on a table near the Gregorys and their group. I didn't see anything that I could safely let Diesel have, so he was destined for disappointment. I would give him some extra treats later. I poured myself a glass of sherry, while Helen Louise chose pastis. She pointed out the amuse-bouche I was likely to enjoy, and I picked up several and added them to my plate.

At the expense of my relaxed mood, I decided to ask Miss An'gel whether she had anything particular planned for this get-together. When I posed the question quietly, for her ears only, she regarded me with a bland expression.

"Sister and I thought a small soiree before dinner would be a way to lift morale," Miss An'gel said. "Sister got the idea from you and Helen Louise. She told me about the wine you brought home from the winery at Biltmore."

That was all she would say, and perhaps she told me the complete truth. I began to relax again and enjoy myself as I moved around to the different groups and chatted. People did the same, and the groups changed for the next half hour, and soon I had spoken to everyone in the room with the exception of Kanesha, who remained aloof.

A loud "Excuse me. I'm so, so sorry" not far behind me caused me to turn around abruptly. Elmore was staring at food that had obviously just been deposited in Melba's lap. "My arm got jostled," Elmore said. "I couldn't help it. Really I couldn't. I'll pay for cleaning your dress, of course."

"Yes, thank you," Melba said. "I think I can get most of it off if someone will hand me some extra napkins."

Paul already had several in hand, and he gave them to Melba. We watched as she tried to clean the amuse-bouche from her lap.

There came a sound of something large hitting the floor behind us, and I felt a tug as Diesel pulled hard against the leash looped on my arm. I called to him, but he didn't stop. I pushed past Celia and Ellie with a hurried apology to follow the cat. He burrowed under the sofa, and I sat on the floor beside him to coax him out.

From this vantage point I could see Zac Ryan prostrate on the floor. I thought at first he was out cold, but then he began to retch and groan.

THIRTY

Kanesha immediately went into action. She knelt beside Zac, and Benjy joined her. "I've had CPR training," he said, and Kanesha nodded.

"Someone call an ambulance," she said.

"I'm on it," Paul Bowen said, his phone already to his ear.

"Everyone move back and give them space," Miss An'gel said in commanding tones. Everyone moved back immediately.

I remained on the floor by the sofa, watching and praying that Zac would survive whatever had assailed him. I naturally suspected that he had been poisoned, but who in this room would have been bold enough to poison him in full sight of everyone else? That was a cold-blooded act, and the thought of it made me feel nauseated. Was any of us safe until the killer was caught?

"I'm going to alert the hotel staff," Melba said before she ran out of the room.

Helen Louise huddled beside me on the floor. "I'm terrified,

Charlie. This is crazy. Do you think somebody is trying to kill him?"

I had no comforting answer for Helen Louise. I said simply, "I don't know." I slipped an arm around her and pulled her close. We stayed there and watched the drama in front of us. Celia and Ellie, along with Johnny Ray and Paul, had moved to a spot near the wall, leaving the way clear for Kanesha and Benjy to work on Zac. Miss An'gel and Miss Dickce stood by and watched the proceedings. Burdine and Elmore held each other, both looking ashen as they watched.

I couldn't spot the face of a murderer among them, no matter how hard I tried. Unless Zac had had a seizure of some sort totally unconnected to the two murders, then someone in this room had poisoned him right in front of all of us. But which one of them did it?

I felt Diesel tug insistently at the leash as he attempted to move farther under the sofa. What was he doing?

"Hang on a second," I told Helen Louise. "This cat is about to yank my arm off. I don't know what's got into him."

Helen Louise obligingly moved away so I could turn and get on my hands and knees to peer under the sofa. Diesel appeared to be trying to bat at something. Now was not the time for him to find a new toy. I gave the leash to Helen Louise and asked her to hold on while I crawled around behind the sofa to see what had so excited the cat's interest.

I finally spotted it. A small plastic bottle with a label of some kind. I was about to reach for it to take it away from Diesel, but some sixth sense stopped me. I extracted a handkerchief from my pants pocket and used that to grab hold of the bottle.

I was right to have done that, because when I examined the

bottle it turned out to be a medicine bottle. I looked at it more closely and got a distinct shock. I almost dropped the bottle.

The patient's name on the bottle read Denis Kilbride, and the medication was something called Lisinopril. Had this been used to poison Zac?

Balked of his prize, Diesel meowed plaintively, but he didn't try to grab it back. I turned around and scuttled back to Helen Louise.

"What was it?" she asked.

I showed her but warned her not to touch it.

"Oh my Lord," she said. "Someone used that to poison Zac."

"I think so," I replied in a grim tone.

The EMS personnel arrived and took over from Kanesha and Benjy. I went immediately to Kanesha and gave her the pill bottle, along with my handkerchief. I explained where I'd found it. She nodded in dismissal, and I went back to Helen Louise and Diesel, now on the sofa.

Kanesha conferred with the EMS team and showed them the bottle. I prayed that, if this was indeed what had been used to poison Zac, they would be able to use the information in his treatment and save him if at all possible.

We all watched in tense silence as the EMS team continued to work on Zac, giving him oxygen and trying to stabilize him. One of the team conferred via cell phone, and a few minutes later they had Zac on the gurney and on the way to the hospital.

Kanesha followed them out after giving strict instructions that we were not to touch anything in the room. Perhaps she was going to the hospital with Zac until Lieutenant Wesner or one of his team could get there. She had promised to let us know as soon as she had more information about Zac's condition. Melba returned then and rejoined Paul. She was followed by the police officer on duty, who took up position right inside the door and watched us all.

Helen Louise and I did not tell the others about the medicine bottle Diesel had found. I recalled now that I hadn't heard any rattling sound, so the bottle must have been empty. The murderer had probably poured its contents into whatever Zac was drinking. Again I felt nauseated.

Another realization hit me as I sat there in that silent room. The killer had taken Denis Kilbride's medications after he or she had killed Denis. That explained why none were found in his room once the body had been discovered.

Had the killer planned then to use the medication to kill someone else? Was Zac always the intended target?

I hadn't had a chance to confer with him over the timetable of movements he was working on. Had he turned up some clue during his work on that and attempted to figure it out on his own? Had he somehow alerted the murderer without realizing it?

I had far too many questions incapable of being answered, at least for now. When Kanesha returned from the hospital, hopefully with good news about Zac's condition, I could discuss my questions with her.

Miss An'gel broke the silence by suggesting that we pray for Zac's recovery. She then intoned a brief heartfelt prayer on Zac's behalf, and we all said "Amen" at the conclusion.

Now that the tension had been broken by the prayer, a low buzz of conversation arose. I thought about going back upstairs to await word from Kanesha, but it appeared that everyone intended to stay here. Then I remembered the police officer on duty and realized that we were probably meant to stay put until Wesner or one of his team showed up.

Wesner himself turned up about twenty minutes later. He strode into the room, his expression thunderous. I was afraid that meant Zac had died, but he quickly reassured us on that point.

"Mr. Ryan is so far responding to treatment," Wesner told the group after greeting Miss An'gel and Miss Dickce. "I have no assurance yet that he will survive, however. He is still in pretty bad shape. I will update you as soon as we have more information. In the meantime I will be questioning each of you to discover any information you might have that will help us determine what led to Mr. Ryan's collapse."

Elmore stuck up a hand. Wesner acknowledged him, and Elmore said, "Any idea what he took?"

"We aren't aware that Mr. Ryan took anything himself," Wesner said. "That remains to be determined. He could have been given something without his knowledge. Does anyone know what he was drinking?"

"Vermouth, I think," Benjy said.

Wesner nodded. "Thanks. My team should be here any moment to bag and tag the evidence." He indicated the drinks tray and the remains of the amuse-bouche.

Elmore's question puzzled me. Perhaps he subscribed to his wife's theory that Zac was the killer. Did he think Zac had intended to kill himself in front of everyone to avoid being arrested?

That didn't make a lot of sense to me, but as I remembered all too well, killers in Golden Age detective fiction sometimes chose suicide as a way of avoiding being hanged for murder. I rather doubted that, if Zac were indeed the killer, he would choose that way out.

I thought it much more likely that the real killer wanted everyone to think that, however. After Burdine's outburst in which she accused Zac, the killer might have decided to make Zac the scapegoat. But I couldn't figure how the killer expected that to work without a signed confession from Zac.

"Lieutenant," Benjy said, "could I speak with you privately?"

"Certainly. Come with me." Wesner led Benjy from the room. I caught Miss An'gel and Miss Dickce exchanging concerned looks. Neither of them appeared to know what Benjy intended to do. I couldn't imagine, either, but he might have seen something important that could help solve the case.

The group waited uneasily. Wesner's crime scene team arrived and asked us to remove to the lobby while they worked. The officer who had been watching us shepherded us out and remained with us. There wasn't enough seating to go around, so Helen Louise and I, along with Diesel, found a spot against a wall and sat on the floor.

After a few minutes, Wesner came back, but without Benjy. He asked Miss An'gel and Miss Dickce to accompany him, and he took them back to the study he had used for questioning us before.

Slowly he worked his way through the group until Helen Louise and I were alone in the lobby with the police officer and Diesel. At least we finally had comfortable seats. Elmore and Burdine had been called right before us, and Wesner seemed to be taking a good bit of time with them. I wanted to discuss things with Helen Louise, but there would be time enough for that later. I was all too aware of the officer's sharp eyes and ears fixed upon us. I wondered idly what was going through his mind as he kept watch. It wasn't a job for which I would have the necessary patience.

Finally, at almost nine o'clock, Wesner sent for us. We both rose wearily and followed another officer down the hall to the study. Diesel chirped plaintively, and I told him we would be back in our room shortly.

Wesner gestured for us to take seats, and so we did. Diesel sat beside me, and I kept a hand on his head to soothe him.

"Before you ask," Wesner said, "I'm afraid I have no further news on Mr. Ryan. I can tell you that his condition is critical, and it could go either way, the last I heard."

"That's horrible," Helen Louise said, and I nodded. "We'll continue to pray for him."

"And that you catch whoever did this to him," I said.

"You don't subscribe to the theory that Mr. Ryan intended a public suicide?" Wesner asked.

"No, I certainly don't," I said.

"Miss Brady?" Wesner said.

"I don't, either," Helen Louise replied.

"Thank you," Wesner said. "You must know Ryan pretty well then."

"No, actually we don't," I said, all at once feeling uncomfortable. What was Wesner trying to do?

"He's a smart young man enjoying his life and his career," Helen Louise said. "I can't think of a reason he would want to kill himself."

"Even if he was a double murderer?" Wesner asked.

"Have you been able to prove that Zac is the killer?" I asked.

Wesner gave me a hard look. "What if I told you I have a suicide note in which he claims he killed both Denis Kilbride and Cora Apfel?"

THIRTY-ONE

"I don't believe it."

The words popped out of my mouth before I had time to consider what I was saying. A moment's brief reflection, however, didn't make me want to take back my words.

"How did you obtain this alleged suicide note?" Helen Louise said.

Wesner nodded approvingly. "Nicely phrased, Miss Brady. Young Mr. Stephens gave it to me. Said he found it when he and the chief deputy were working on Mr. Ryan. It was under his body when they turned him over."

"Was it supposed to have fallen out of his pocket?" I asked. "Frankly, that's hard to believe."

"I agree," Wesner said. "We'll be testing the piece of paper, naturally, for fingerprints. We're looking for examples of Mr. Ryan's handwriting as well."

"It was handwritten?" I asked.

Wesner nodded.

"I thought Zac's generation typed everything on the computer and printed it out," I said.

"If he recovers to the point when questioning is feasible, I intend to ask him about it," Wesner said. "Chief Deputy Berry has remained at the hospital to monitor the situation, along with a couple of my officers." He glanced at his notes. "Now, I'd like you both to think about what you were doing and where you were about ten minutes before Mr. Ryan collapsed, and then take me to the point when you realized he had fallen. Mr. Harris, you first, please."

I cast my mind back and tried to work out a point roughly ten minutes before Zac collapsed. "We were all moving about the room, chatting briefly with one or more members of the group. People drifted. I believe I was talking with Helen Louise and Ellie maybe eight or ten minutes before Zac fell." I paused. "We chatted for about five minutes, then I went over to talk to Celia, and Ellie came with me. I was still with them when I heard Elmore say 'Excuse me' to Melba. Right after that, I heard Zac fall. Diesel bolted, and I had his leash looped around my wrist. I had to follow him and try to calm him down. It wasn't until I was sitting on the floor trying to coax Diesel out from under the sofa that I saw that Zac was on the floor."

"Thank you." Wesner jotted away on his notes for perhaps thirty seconds before he asked Helen Louise to take her turn.

"I was talking with Charlie and Ellie," Helen Louise said, "until Charlie went to talk to Celia. I was surprised that Ellie went with him, leaving me standing there by myself, but she said she wanted to ask Celia something. Miss Dickce and Benjy were nearby, so I went over to talk to them. That's where I was when I heard Elmore say 'Excuse me' to Melba, and then the fall. I had my back to them."

"Mr. Harris, did you have your back to Mr. Gregory and Miss Gilley when he dropped his food on her lap?" Wesner asked.

"Yes, I did," I said.

Wesner scribbled a bit more.

"So neither of you had Mr. Ryan in your line of vision right before he collapsed?" he said.

"No," Helen Louise and I said in unison.

"No one seems to have been looking at him for several minutes before he collapsed to the floor," Werner said musingly.

"Not even Kanesha—Chief Deputy Berry, I mean?" I said.

"I wasn't including her," Wesner said. "She gave me her evidence already, and I'll compare it later with what everyone has told me."

That sounded like evasion to me. He didn't want to answer my question, and of course there was no reason he had to. This made me think, though, that Kanesha had seen something—or someone, rather. Had she seen who put the poison in Zac's vermouth?

Vermouth, as I recalled, could have a dry, almost bitter taste. Or so it was in my own experience of it. I didn't care for vermouth, except in a martini. Not a bad choice to disguise the potential taste of poison, though. The killer couldn't have counted on that, surely, unless he or she was conversant with Zac's tastes in liquor.

Wesner was watching me, and for a moment I had the odd feeling that he knew what I was thinking. *Okay, let's see if you're prepared for this question.* "Are there any usable fingerprints on the medicine bottle?"

"We'll be comparing any prints found on the bottle to those we collected from your group already," Wesner said. "Frankly I don't expect to find any other than Kilbride's, but I could be wrong. Surely this group knows about fingerprints."

"Of course," I said, slightly stung by the hint of sarcasm in his voice.

"Do you have any other questions for us?" Helen Louise asked.

"Is there anything you haven't told me before that you think I should know?" Wesner replied.

Helen Louise shook her head, but something did occur to me. "Burdine Gregory accused Zac of being the murderer that first day."

"She did?" Wesner didn't appear all that interested. Perhaps he had heard this already from another member of the group. "To his face?"

"No, after he left the room," I said.

Wesner nodded. "Right. Anything else?"

"No, not that I can think of." I broke off. "Yes, there is one more thing." I had to tell him, though it was more than a bit embarrassing. "Zac came to me yesterday, saying he wanted to work with me to solve the two murders. I agreed, reluctantly, though I was not planning to work on the murders in any formal sense. I know that's your job."

"Go on," Wesner said.

"I suggested to Zac that he might work on a timetable of

events based on his own movements and encounters with others of the group. He seemed enthusiastic about it, and he told me earlier today, I think it was, that he wanted to talk to me about it." I shrugged. "Maybe he had figured something out, I don't know. He was going to do it on his laptop, he said."

Wesner finished jotting something down, then looked up. "Thank you, Mr. Harris. That is new information that might be helpful."

"I'm glad to do anything to help," I said.

"Right." Wesner stood. "If there's nothing else, we're done here."

"We're going upstairs to our suite," Helen Louise said firmly once we were out of the study. "I'm exhausted, and I'm sure you are, too, by now. Poor Diesel is probably starving. Do not let Miss An'gel or anyone else waylay us, all right?"

"Fine with me," I said. The amuse-bouche I had managed to eat during the ill-fated gathering hadn't done much to assuage my hunger. If we wanted anything to eat, we'd have to raid the minibar in our suite. The hotel restaurant was closed by now, and neither of us had the energy to go out in search of sustenance.

We made it upstairs to our suite without anyone appearing, and all three of us breathed sighs of relief once we were inside the room. I released Diesel from his harness and leash, and he bolted for the bathroom. Helen Louise and I collapsed on the sofa.

"Are you hungry?" I asked.

"I could eat," Helen Louise replied. "But not if it means leaving this room."

"No," I said. "I was thinking the minibar. I'll go look." I pushed myself off the sofa and walked over to the console that housed the minibar. With the door open, I recited its contents to Helen Louise. This was not the average minibar, thankfully, because it included various cheeses, apples, pears, and bananas.

We decided to feast on the fruit and cheese, along with wine from Helen Louise's purchases of the day. Diesel came back the moment he smelled the cheese and insisted on getting a bite or two. That was all I gave him because cheese could cause severe gastric distress in cats. Two small bites were enough to satisfy him, thankfully.

"I can't stop thinking about Zac," Helen Louise said. "Do you think he really confessed and then tried to commit suicide in front of all of us?"

"On one hand, I'd say that if he was the killer and knew the police were closing in, he'd probably choose to go out in dramatic style," I said. "I don't think he'd ever be one to go quietly, do you?"

"No," Helen Louise said after a moment's reflection. "But I don't think he killed Denis and Cora."

"I don't, either," I said, "but I'm darned if I know who did. Ellie is still the only person in the group who has a strong motive, with the possible exception of Johnny Ray."

A knock at the door put an end to our deliberations. I was tempted to ignore the knock, but then the person knocked again and called out, "Charlie, are you in there?"

"Melba," I said with a groan. "What on earth does she want at this time of night?"

"One way to find out," Helen Louise said.

I went to the door and let Melba in. "This had better be important," I told her.

Helen Louise greeted Melba and offered her wine. Melba shook her head. "No, thanks. I won't take up much of your time."

I resumed my seat on the sofa while Diesel moved his attentions from me and my cheese to Melba. She pulled a chair closer to the sofa. Diesel put his head on her knee, and she cooed to him for a moment and stroked his head.

"What's up?" I asked.

Melba hesitated, then seemed to come to a decision. "What do y'all think about Paul? Is the age difference a problem?"

"Age difference?" I said. "Is he that much older than you?"

Melba scowled. "Are you drunk? Don't be an idiot. You know he's younger than me."

"Not by much, surely," Helen Louise said. "I don't see it as an issue."

"Almost six years," Melba said.

"Don't be silly. What's wrong with that?" I asked. "He really seems to like you, and it seems to me that you like him."

Melba glared at me for a moment; then her expression softened. "Trust you to bring me back to earth."

I grinned at her. "That's what I'm here for. Seriously, though, forget about age."

"Charlie's right," Helen Louise said. "If you two really care about each other, go for it."

Melba all at once looked pensive. "I'd really like to, but there's something I'm afraid of."

"What on earth are you afraid of?" I asked her.

Her hands twisted in her lap, and Diesel meowed, sensing her sudden distress. She took a deep breath.

"I'm afraid that Paul was personally involved with Denis Kilbride."

THIRTY-TWO

I almost spit out my cheese at Melba's words. Hastily, I swallowed instead. As soon as I could, I said, "Why on earth would you think that?"

"Has he said anything to make you think this?" Helen Louise asked at the same time.

Melba stared at us for a moment, probably trying to sort out what we had each said to her. "No, he hasn't exactly said anything to me directly. It's more what he doesn't say."

"What do you mean?" Helen Louise said.

"Anytime I mentioned Denis's name, he starts acting evasive," Melba said. "You know me—I'm curious about these murders, and I'm wondering what Denis could have done to make somebody want to kill him. Paul worked with him on some of his finance deals, so I figured he might have picked up a few things along the way."

"If he did, though, he doesn't want to talk about it with you," I said.

Melba nodded.

"Have you considered the fact that the details of Denis's business with the bank are private, and Paul is ethically bound not to talk about them with you?" I said.

"Denis is dead, for Pete's sake," Melba said. "Why shouldn't he tell me at least a little bit? It's not like I'm asking for a full rundown on how much he borrowed and all that crap that I couldn't care less about."

"What is it you want to know, then?" Helen Louise said.

"Personal stuff that Paul might have picked up," Melba said. "I know they went out to dinner sometimes, and Denis was a drinker. Maybe he was indiscreet and let something slip. He was that kind of guy."

"Basically Paul is refusing to gossip with you about Denis, and you're interpreting that to mean that he possibly had a physical or romantic relationship with Denis." I tried to keep the sarcasm out of my voice, but from the look Helen Louise shot me, I was pretty sure I failed.

"I'm sure Charlie is sorry that what he just said came out that way," Helen Louise said.

Melba glared at me. "I doubt he's sorry."

"Blame the wine," I said. "Look, I'm sorry if I hurt your feelings, but, honestly, don't you think it's a bit of a stretch?"

"I understand how she feels," Helen Louise said. "You're at the stage in the relationship where you want to be able to confide in each other, and Paul is obviously holding back on you."

"That's it exactly," Melba said.

"Oh," I said.

Diesel warbled, and Melba stroked his head. "You understand, don't you, sweet boy?" The cat warbled again, and Melba shot me another look of irritation.

"I think Charlie might be right, however," Helen Louise said. "Hear me out. Paul has struck me as a man who's serious about his profession, and that includes ethical business practices. Paul may simply feel uncomfortable because he thinks you're trying to get him to gossip about Denis's business interests. Nothing to do with his personal life."

Melba didn't appear completely convinced. "I just don't know."

"You need to be more direct with him, then," Helen Louise said. "Ask him point-blank if he had any association with Denis other than his professional one. You can judge by his reaction whether he has anything to hide."

"I think you're right." Melba sounded decisive. "I'm going to do that right now. Thank you, Helen Louise." She looked at me and sniffed. "Good night, Charlie."

"Good night," I replied.

Diesel accompanied Melba to the door, but as soon as she was gone, he came back to me, hoping for more cheese. By now, however, I had finished it. I showed him empty hands. He gave me a plaintive meow before he turned hopefully to Helen Louise. She, too, showed him empty hands, and with that, he had to be content.

"Not one of your shining moments," Helen Louise said, her tone mild.

"No, I guess not," I said, feeling chagrined. "I didn't mean to offend her, but was I wrong in thinking she was blowing the situation out of proportion a teeny-tiny bit?"

"Probably not," Helen Louise said. "I think the issue here is that Melba is really serious about Paul, more serious than I've seen her before about other men she's dated. Maybe that scares her a little."

"So she's looking for an excuse to back off from Paul?" I asked.

Helen Louise shrugged. "Subconsciously, perhaps. It's been a long time since she's had a serious relationship."

"I would be so happy for her to find someone worthy of her, who'll treat her well," I said.

"So would I," Helen Louise said. "She deserves happiness."

"I guess we'll find out about Paul before long," I said. "She won't thank us, though, if our advice backfires somehow."

"We'll have to wait and see," Helen Louise said. "I'm ready for bed. How about you?" She yawned.

"Definitely," I said. "I'll clear this away and join you in a few minutes."

"Thanks." She kissed my cheek. "Come on, Diesel, bedtime."

The cat followed her out, and I tidied up. While I did so, I found my thoughts alternating between Melba's dilemma and Zac's condition. Melba would handle her situation with strength and determination, I had no doubt, but Zac had no control over his, poor guy. I paused for a moment in my cleaning to offer up a fervent prayer on his behalf. I really couldn't bring myself to believe that he was a killer, despite what evidence there might be to the contrary.

I never really wanted to believe that anyone was a murderer. That was the problem. Eventually, however, the facts would confront me in a way that gave me no quarter. I had yet to reach that point with these two murders and a potential third one.

"Charlie, what's taking so long?"

Helen Louise's voice brought me out of my reverie. "Almost done. Be there in a minute." I hastily finished what I was doing, turned out the lights in the sitting room, and headed for the bedroom. Helen Louise and Diesel were in bed, the cat curled up next to my beloved, his head on her pillow. *Love me, love my cat*, I thought. I was fortunate indeed that Helen Louise did love Diesel. I couldn't care so deeply for someone who didn't love animals as much as I did.

I changed into my habitual nightwear, shorts and T-shirt, and slipped into bed with them. Helen Louise and I kissed over Diesel, and he meowed. I patted his head and laughed. "Go to sleep, silly boy." He yawned.

"Good night, love," Helen Louise said, and I bade her good night in return. The lights off, we all settled down to sleep. That sleep was interrupted not long afterward, however.

"I'll go," I said. "But I may yell at whoever it is knocking on the door this time."

Helen Louise mumbled something, and Diesel didn't stir. I forgot that I was wearing only shorts and T-shirt until I opened the door and saw Kanesha's expression. I glanced down at myself and sighed.

"Come in." I stood back to let her into the suite. Once I closed the door behind her, I said, "Make yourself comfortable while I go throw on some clothes."

"Sure," Kanesha said. "Sorry to wake you up, but I think you'll sleep better once you hear what I have to tell you."

I hurried to the bedroom without responding. I pulled on the pants and shirt I had been wearing previously. Helen Louise appeared to have gone to sleep, so I pulled the bedroom door shut behind me when I returned to the sitting room.

"Okay, what's the good news?" I plopped down on the sofa, my head now clear again.

"Zac Ryan is going to recover," Kanesha said.

"Thank the Lord," I replied. "But did he really confess to killing two people?"

"No, he didn't," Kanesha said. "We showed him the so-called confession—with only an initial as a signature—and he denied that it was his."

"Do you believe him?" I asked.

"I do," Kanesha said. "I have Wesner's permission to tell you this, but it goes no farther than this room, understand?"

"Can I tell Helen Louise?" I asked.

"Yes, because I know you will, no matter what I say," Kanesha replied tartly. "But no one else."

"What about Miss An'gel?"

"She knows," Kanesha said. "We don't want the rest of the group to be aware of this. It's better that the killer thinks he or she still has a chance of Zac dying and being labeled as the murderer. Unless another member of the group does something stupid, of course, to bring attention to himself and draw the murderer's fire."

She looked straight at me as she gave that warning, and I couldn't blame her, although it did rankle a bit.

"Message received," I said.

"Good," Kanesha replied. "Sorry I woke you, but I thought you'd want to know about Zac."

"We hadn't been in bed long," I said, suddenly fighting the urge to yawn.

Kanesha rose to go. "Get a good night's sleep, and I'll see you in the morning."

"Wait a minute," I said as she walked toward the door. "I have a question."

She stopped and turned back. "Yes?"

"It's about Paul Bowen," I said. "Do you have any knowledge of a personal connection between him and Denis Kilbride? Other than the banking connection, that is?"

Kanesha frowned. "What is this about?"

"Melba," I said reluctantly. "She's worried that Paul and Denis might have been connected outside the bank."

"Not that I'm aware of," Kanesha said. "Good night."

I didn't detain her, and she departed.

I turned the lights off again and went back to bed. I was going to share the good news with Helen Louise, but she was sound asleep. I debated waking her but thought the news could wait until morning. I got comfortable and tried to go to sleep.

Instead, I thought about the conversation with Kanesha. I felt relieved for Melba's sake, and for Zac's as well. I really wasn't surprised to hear that his confession was a fake, although I realized that this was subject to further examination before the police would accept it as fact.

Kanesha didn't think Paul Bowen had had any kind of personal relationship with Denis Kilbride (i.e., a sexual one), so that left Ellie Arnold as the most likely suspect once again. Ellie was so mild mannered as to be practically comatose sometimes. I found it hard to envision her aroused with enough passion to kill not only once, but twice, and attempt a third murder.

She was the one who knew about Denis's medications, though. I couldn't figure out why she would have taken them from his room. That made no sense to me. His death would have been more likely ruled as natural if the EMS team had found heart medication in his room. The medical examiner might have done a more cursory autopsy in that case. Probably not, but the killer could have thought that might happen.

Now I had a headache. I slipped out of bed to go into the bathroom and find some aspirin. I took a couple, washed them down with water, and crept back to bed. Helen Louise didn't stir, nor did Diesel. Maybe now I could go to sleep. Aspirin usually helped me with that.

If I were to go for the most unlikely suspect, I mused, I would have to pick Celia. I wondered on what pretext Celia could have gone to his room and been let in. Denis must have been pretty well lit at the time, so it might not have mattered if she had a believable reason for accosting him that late at night.

In this case, I thought, the least likely suspect was probably not the killer. With that decided, I soon drifted off to sleep.

I slept soundly and didn't wake until Helen Louise tapped me on the shoulder and Diesel stuck his nose in my ear and sniffed. That combination never failed. I turned over, yawning. "Good morning. What time is it?"

"Good morning to you, too." Helen Louise dropped a kiss on my lips, and Diesel stuck his nose against my cheek. "It's nearly nine o'clock, sleepyhead."

"How long have you been up?" I asked.

"About thirty minutes," she replied.

I took a good look at her and realized that she was already dressed. I pushed myself up and threw the bedclothes back. Diesel didn't appreciate it that I threw them over him. He protested loudly and quickly extricated himself. "Sorry, boy," I said. "Let me take a quick shower and get dressed. Go on down to breakfast if you want. I won't be long."

"I'm hungry, so I think I'll take you up on that," Helen Louise said. "I desperately need coffee."

"Go, and I'll be down soon." I headed for the shower.

Not until I was in the shower, scrubbing myself with soap, did I remember that I had good news to share with her. That would have to wait until after breakfast now. I couldn't tell her any of what Kanesha had told me in public.

I discovered that Helen Louise had taken Diesel down with her. I was almost dressed and ready to leave when my phone rang. It was Stewart. I debated letting it go to voice mail, but I figured Stewart wouldn't be calling unless it was important.

"Good morning," I said. "How are you?"

"Are you sitting down?" Stewart said. "Have I got a juicy one for you. I think I've found you a really good motive for Denis Kilbride's killer."

THIRTY-THREE

I almost dropped the phone at Stewart's triumphant claim. I scrabbled to keep hold of it and put it back to my ear.

"I'm not sitting down," I said, "but go ahead anyway."

"Right. I found out about more of Denis Kilbride's playmates," Stewart said. "A couple of guys I know in Memphis knew Denis and dished up some good dirt on some of his prior relationships."

"That's good," I said, "and I suppose one of them is either someone in the group or related to someone."

"Exactly," Stewart said. "Do you know who Todd Gregory is?"

I knew I'd heard the name, but in my coffee-less state it took me a moment to dredge it up. "Burdine and Elmore's son?"

"Yes, that's him."

"What happened to him?" I asked.

"He died earlier this year," Stewart replied. "He was really unhappy, had been for years, because of depression. He was a frequent visitor to the bars in Memphis from the time he was about seventeen years old. He was fifty-one when he died, according to the obituary."

"I'm sorry to hear about the depression," I said. "Was it severe?"

"I believe so, especially as he got older," Stewart said. "From what I managed to harvest from the Athena grapevine, Todd was pretty wild in his youth, like a lot of kids testing their sexuality at that age. He grew out of that phase by his mid-twenties and had a couple of long-term relationships with guys based in Memphis."

"Why Memphis?" I asked, slightly puzzled.

"He didn't want his parents finding out he was gay."

"Surely they must have known," I said.

"Knowing and acknowledging it are two different things," Stewart said. "Todd was their only child and could do no wrong where Mummy was concerned. He was the perfect son, handsome all-American type. He even dated a few women in Athena to keep his parents happy."

"That's so sad," I said. "He couldn't be himself with his parents, and that has to weigh heavily, especially in someone who suffers from depression."

"Yes, I think it did in his case," Stewart said. "There's a bit more to the story, and it involves Denis Kilbride." He paused. "Even though they had apparently known each other from the bars in Memphis, it wasn't until about two years ago that Todd and Denis connected. Apparently, Todd fell hard for Denis, but Denis wasn't interested in a long-term relationship with another man. He was intent on finding a wife and keeping up his image as the proper straight businessman. That's where Ellie Arnold eventually came in."

"How did Todd react to this?"

"Not well," Stewart said. "This comes from a friend of mine who knew Todd pretty well because of his parents' chiropractic clinic. Todd really loved Denis, but Denis couldn't handle it. Todd got more and more depressed." Stewart paused. "According to my friend, Todd killed himself. His parents got it hushed up, though."

My heart went out to Burdine and Elmore. I couldn't imagine how painful it had been for them to lose their son, especially through suicide. Todd's own pain must have been agonizing for him to end his life.

"You really have been busy," I said around a lump in my throat. "You've dug up a lot. I knew I could count on you." I paused. "If necessary, do you think your friends would share this with the police here?"

"Now, that I don't know," Stewart said. "If it has any bearing on the case, maybe they could be persuaded. But it might not be necessary if you flush out the killer soon."

"Based on this information, I can see Burdine and Elmore as suspects now," I said. "Do they blame Denis for their son's death?"

"I should think it's possible," Stewart said. "I'm figuring that Todd might have finally left his parents a letter telling them why he was taking his own life. He could have indicated that Denis was partly responsible for his decision, or Burdine and Elmore could have construed it that way."

"That's a distinct possibility," I said. "Or Burdine and Elmore could have found out some other way about their son's sexuality.

I find it hard to believe they were completely oblivious to it, but then some people are willfully blind to things, like you said."

"Yes," Stewart said. "Haskell told me Kanesha is there with you. Is that true?"

"Yes, she's here by arrangement with the sheriff, courtesy of Miss An'gel," I said.

"Naturally," Stewart replied. I could see him grinning into the phone.

"Is there anything else?" I asked. "Helen Louise is expecting me downstairs for breakfast, and I'm getting desperate for caffeine."

"Nothing else," Stewart said cheerfully. "Ring me back when you get a chance and bring me up to date on everything."

"Will do." I ended the call and hurried downstairs, hoping there would still be enough food for breakfast on the buffet.

I found Helen Louise and Diesel alone in the dining room. Helen Louise filled my coffee cup the moment she spotted me. "What took so long?" she asked.

"Stewart called," I said. "Let me grab some food, and I'll tell you."

The pickings were rather sparse, but I managed to score a couple of biscuits, scrambled eggs, and the last few slices of bacon. I looked at the remains of the cheese grits with great regret. Perhaps tomorrow.

Diesel immediately demanded bacon, but Helen Louise shook her head. "He's already had two pieces."

"I'll give him one bite so he doesn't pout." I broke off a small piece and held it out to him. He sniffed it before he accepted it and inhaled it. "That's it."

He meowed plaintively, but I stood firm. "No. That's it."

He turned his back to me and stayed that way until I finished breakfast. I chuckled as I prepared my coffee with cream and sugar. I took several appreciative sips. "Ah, that's better." I started on my food.

Helen Louise watched me, and I knew she was burning to find out what Stewart had told me.

First, however, I wanted to share the good news about Zac. There was no one else about, not even a member of the hotel staff, so I told her.

"Wonderful," Helen Louise said. Then her face clouded. "What if he staged this in order to make everyone think someone else tried to kill him?"

"He could have done that, I guess, but he was taking an awful risk. He could have died if Diesel hadn't found that medicine bottle."

"True," Helen Louise said. "Now, what did Stewart have to say?"

In between bites of my breakfast, I told her. When I finished, she looked appalled and sad.

"What a terrible story," she said. "Poor Burdine and Elmore. I knew their son had died, but that was all. I don't believe there was any kind of service, and I only heard about it through the grapevine. I know a woman who was one of their patients at their chiropractic clinic."

"Yes, their clinic. I've never been to a chiropractor. Have you?" I asked.

"No," Helen Louise said. "I have friends who swear by them, though."

"I think my mother went to one for a while," I said as the memory suddenly surfaced.

"Given this information, I suppose it's possible that either Burdine or Elmore, or maybe both of them together, decided to kill Denis because they blamed him for their son's suicide," Helen Louise said. "Horrible situation all the way around."

"Yes, it is," I said, my appetite suddenly gone. I pushed my plate away and picked up my coffee. I drained it and reached for the pot to refill it.

Helen Louise said, "You've got to tell Kanesha and Wesner about this. This puts a new spin on everything."

"Yes, it does," I said after a sip of coffee, "but do you really think Kanesha doesn't already know about Todd Gregory?"

"She may be aware of some of the facts," Helen Louise said, "but she doesn't have Stewart's connections in Memphis. Stewart probably picked up some bits that Kanesha doesn't know about."

"You're right. I planned to talk to Kanesha," I said. "Surely you realize that."

"I do," Helen Louise said. "Sorry, I'm feeling antsy. I want this to be over. I'm tired of feeling like I have to look over my shoulder all the time."

"Me, too." I pulled out my cell phone and called Kanesha. She answered promptly. "Good morning," I said. "I have things to tell you. Where are you?"

"I'm with Wesner downstairs in the hotel."

"Okay. We're finishing breakfast. I'll be along in a minute." I stuffed my phone back in my pocket. "Do you want to come with me?"

Helen Louise nodded. "It may sound silly, but I'll feel safer. I'd rather not run into Burdine and Elmore right now."

"Can't say as I blame you." I downed the rest of my coffee. "Let's go and get this over with."

Helen Louise handed me the leash, and I led Diesel with us as we walked down the hall to the temporary headquarters for the investigation.

I knocked on the door, and Wesner called out for us to enter. "Good morning," I said as I shut the door behind us.

We advanced into the room and took the usual seats in front of the desk. Kanesha occupied a chair to Wesner's left.

"What information do you have for me?" Wesner said.

I proceeded to tell him what Stewart had told me, after first explaining who Stewart was. Wesner glanced quickly at Kanesha, who nodded at the mention of Stewart's name to indicate he was reliable, I supposed.

When I finished, I sat back and waited for Wesner to comment. He regarded me impassively for what seemed like minutes but was probably only about ten or fifteen seconds. "Thank you, Mr. Harris."

"That's all?" I said. "No comments other than that? Did you already know all this? Did I waste my time and yours in coming to you?"

Helen Louise laid a restraining hand on my arm, and I forced myself to calm down. I reminded myself that Wesner was in charge, and he knew how to do his job best. I couldn't expect him to take my word without checking things out. "I guess we'll be going, then," I said as I rose. "Come on, Helen Louise."

"Hold it," Kanesha said. "Stay where you are, if you don't mind."

I settled back into my chair. Helen Louise once again put her hand on my arm as a reminder for me to keep my temper. I smiled at her to let her know I appreciated her support.

Wesner cleared his throat. "Your information is appreciated, Mr. Harris. You were able to corroborate some of what Chief Deputy Berry told me, but you did supply details that we didn't know about."

"Particularly the detail that the Gregorys might have held Denis Kilbride accountable for their son's suicide earlier this year," Kanesha said. "And I can confirm that it was a suicide."

"Do you think Todd Gregory's activities in Memphis were well known in Athena?" I asked.

"I have no reason to think so," Kanesha said. "Not well known anyway. I'm sure it wasn't completely secret, however. He wasn't the only man in Athena going to the bars in Memphis looking for company."

"What did Todd Gregory do?" I asked.

"He worked in his parents' office. Managed their business for them," Kanesha said. "They were very successful. They sold their business about a month after Todd Gregory died."

"Do you think that the Gregorys killed Denis Kilbride?" Helen Louise asked.

Something that had been niggling in the back of my mind suddenly managed to get through.

"I know how one of them got to Denis that night," I said.

THIRTY-FOUR

"Well, go on," Wesner said impatiently. "How did one of them get to him, as you call it?"

I turned to Helen Louise. "Do you remember how Denis Kilbride complained about his back?"

Helen Louise thought for a moment. "You're right, he did. Twice, in fact."

I turned back to Kanesha and Wesner. "When Denis Kilbride stormed into our meeting that night," I said, "he complained about his back in front of the group. Burdine or Elmore could have used that as an excuse to go to his room to offer to give him a treatment. He was drunk, according to you, so he might have let them in without thinking about it. That gave them the perfect opportunity to kill him."

"Why would they take his medications from the room?" Wesner asked. "That's one thing that I haven't been able to figure out."

An answer to that occurred to me, too, though I would have to admit that it sounded far-fetched when I said it aloud.

"In our group discussions, Burdine often harps on the facts in the case. She always likes to claim that she figures out who the killer is way before the detective in the book does." I paused to take a breath. "I think she might have done it to confuse the issue, to make it harder to figure out. Plus, she had drugs in her possession she could use later if necessary on someone else."

"When did she find the pin that was used in both murders?" Kanesha asked.

"That I don't know," I said, "but I'm sure y'all have information on everyone's movements, even Cora Apfel's. Was Cora assigned to the Gregorys' floor?"

Wesner said, "She was."

"There you are," I said. "Cora could have lost her pin in the Gregorys' room, and Burdine or Elmore held on to it. Chiropractors have to know about anatomy, so they would have known how it could be used to kill someone."

Wesner remained impassive, frustrating me. Had I managed to give him a new angle on the case, or was he merely indulging me?

"Those are good points," Kanesha said. "The problem is, we have no evidence that places either or both of the Gregorys in Denis Kilbride's room that night."

"What about Cora Apfel's murder?" Helen Louise asked. "She was found next door during the morning. Someone could have seen one or the other of them coming out of the meeting room."

Kanesha and Wesner didn't comment. I had to wonder, though, if Kanesha had been on her own, if she would have been more forthcoming. She was not in charge of the investigation, however. Wesner seemed to be determined to be as noncommittal as possible. Dang his hide!

I stood, and Helen Louise followed suit. "We'll be going now."

Wesner rose. "Thank you, Mr. Harris, Miss Brady. I appreciate your cooperation in this investigation."

I tried, and probably failed, to sound gracious in my reply to that. "You're welcome."

We walked out of the room, and Helen Louise shut the door, not quite gently, behind us.

"He's certainly infuriating, isn't he?" she said lightly.

"He is," I said. "If only Kanesha were in charge."

"She's not, unfortunately for you," Helen Louise said as we reached the foot of the stairs.

"Nothing I can do about that," I said. "I want this to be over for all our sakes. I hate feeling like I'm stuck in suspension, and when I'm pretty sure I have the answer, I'm frustrated that the cops don't seem to be acting on what I told them."

"Pretty sure isn't enough," Helen Louise said. "Are you coming upstairs or not?"

"I'm coming," I said, and followed her and Diesel back to our suite. Once inside, I took Diesel out of his harness and leash and let him roam. I flopped on the sofa while Helen Louise disappeared into the bedroom.

If I were Nancy Drew dealing with Chief McGinnis, I thought, I'd have gotten more respect from Wesner. Or the Hardy Boys dealing with Chief Collig. At least he welcomed the boys' help sometimes. I supposed I should be grateful that Wesner had at least listened to me. After all, I wasn't an Oscar Smuff. At that thought I had to laugh, picturing myself as the ineffective private detective from the Hardy Boys books.

I was taking this too seriously, I told myself. *You're spoiled, thinking you're such a hotshot*, my inner saboteur jeered at me. *Wesner isn't going to put up with you posing as the Great Detective who's never wrong.*

"Oh, shut up," I said.

"Excuse me?" Helen Louise stopped in front of me. "What did I say?"

"Not you. Me," I said. "I was talking to myself."

Helen Louise sat beside me on the sofa. "Is this a private conversation between the two of you, or am I allowed to participate?"

I quickly explained, and Helen Louise smiled. "Don't be too hard on yourself, love. You're caught up in the mystery, like probably others of the group are, if they're innocent. This is like our secret fantasy, being in the middle of a Golden Age detective story, but who is the great detective?"

"It's turned into a bit of a nightmare, too. Zac wanted to be the great detective," I said, "and look what happened. That should be a lesson to me. I'm sure that's what Sean would tell me."

"He probably would," Helen Louise agreed. "He loves you and wants to keep you safe, and I can't blame him for that. I'd like you to be around at least long enough for us to be married."

I laughed. "All right, I get the point."

Diesel climbed onto the sofa and spread out across our laps, his head in mine. He meowed loudly, indicating that attention should be forthcoming and preferably immediately.

"You're so spoiled," I told him, and he responded with a warble as we stroked him.

"He certainly is," Helen Louise said, "but he's worth it." The cat warbled again, and she chuckled. "Nothing like conviction, is there, Diesel?"

I only half heard her last remark, because my attention was suddenly caught by an idea, suggested by what Helen Louise had said about our group. I turned it over and over in my mind, and I decided that I couldn't bring it about on my own. Miss An'gel would have to be the one to instigate it, and I thought I knew her well enough to predict how she would react to it.

"I need to talk to Miss An'gel," I said, startling Helen Louise and Diesel as I made a move to get up from the sofa. Diesel grumbled with me as I raised him up to make my escape possible.

"What have you got to talk to Miss An'gel about?" Helen Louise said, sounding slightly annoyed.

"Oh, an idea I've had," I said vaguely. Now that I was off the sofa I could get to my cell phone. I called Miss An'gel, crossing my fingers that she would answer and I wouldn't be stuck with voice mail.

My luck held. Miss An'gel answered. "Good morning, Charlie. How are you?"

"Doing fine," I said. "Are you available for a talk right now? I have an idea to propose to you."

"That sounds intriguing," she replied. "As a matter of fact, Sister and I were about to go out, but we can postpone that. Would you like to come to our suite, or should we come to you?"

I shot a quick glance at Helen Louise. "I can come to your suite, that's no problem."

"All right, then. We'll expect you in a few minutes," Miss An'gel replied.

I put my phone away. "I'm going to Miss An'gel's suite. Would you like to come with me?"

"You'd rather I didn't, I'm pretty sure, so you can discuss whatever harebrained idea you've come up with without me." Helen Louise shook her head. "Charlie, I've got half a mind to call Sean right now so he can lecture you."

"Now, don't be that way," I said. "My idea isn't dangerous, I promise you. Miss An'gel won't go for it if she thinks there's any real danger, you know that."

"I'm not so sure about that," Helen Louise said. "Miss An'gel has never been afraid of taking a risk, based on my knowledge of her. Neither has Miss Dickce, not the way she drives."

"Would you like to come with me?" I said again.

"You can tell me about it later," Helen Louise said with a resigned smile. "I've got a new book I want to start, so I may as well get on with it."

"All right, I won't be long. I'll leave Diesel with you, I think. He looks comfortable where he is. See you in a bit."

Miss Dickce admitted me into their suite immediately. To my surprise, Kanesha was there. I almost made my excuses to leave, but Miss An'gel insisted that I join them. Reluctantly, I entered the room.

"Charlie, I'm glad you called." Miss An'gel indicated that I should take a chair near hers. Miss Dickce rejoined her sister on the sofa. Benjy was not in the room. "Kanesha came up a few minutes ago, and we've been discussing the murders. I think it's fair to say that Kanesha is a bit frustrated with the way Wesner is handling things."

Kanesha didn't appear in the least happy with Miss An'gel's statement. I wouldn't have dared look at Miss An'gel like that, but Kanesha lived with danger more than I did. Miss An'gel caught the look and smiled.

"I have to say myself that he seems a bit on the cautious side," Miss An'gel continued. "Kanesha is certain of the identity of the killer and so am I." She held up a hand to forestall any comment from me. "The problem is evidence to link the killer irrevocably with the murder of Denis Kilbride. Then we can hope to link the killer to the second murder. Our killer has been clever, Charlie, no doubt about it."

"That's where my idea comes in, the one I mentioned on the phone," I said. "We came here to have a week of discussions about mysteries, with a lot of the focus on the Golden Age. This whole situation with the two murders and a third one attempted is like something out of a Golden Age novel. Helen Louise said a little earlier to me that we were like a group in which no one knew who was supposed to be the great detective."

"Yes, I see your point," Miss An'gel said.

"I've always seen Sister as more of a Miss Silver type, while I'm Miss Marple," Miss Dickce said with an impish grin. "Celia would be like dear Miss Seeton, don't you think?"

I wasn't aware that Celia Bernardi had any artistic abilities, unlike Heron Carvic's unusual spinster, Miss Seeton, but I let that pass. Instead, I glanced at Kanesha. Her enigmatic expression seemed glued in place.

Miss An'gel threw her sister a repressive glance and urged me to go on.

"I thought we could bring the situation to a head by resorting to one of the conventions of the Golden Age mystery," I said. "Bringing everyone together and telling them that All Would Be Revealed. You know the drill."

Miss Dickce squealed with delight. "Splendid, Charlie. And you can play Hercule Poirot."

"I'm flattered, Miss Dickce," I said, trying not to chuckle, "but that's not exactly what I had in mind." I looked at Miss An'gel.

"I suppose you cast me in the role of Poirot," she said dryly.

"If you like," I said. "Or Nero Wolfe, perhaps. Even Miss Silver, though I've never seen you knit."

Miss An'gel looked at Kanesha. "My dear, I know you only read mysteries occasionally, but I'm sure you understand what Charlie is suggesting."

"I do," Kanesha said. "I will remind you that this is not the first time Charlie has done this."

"No, it's not," I admitted. "But you have to admit that, when I have done it, it has been effective."

Kanesha shrugged.

"Come on, my dear," Miss An'gel said. "Will you work with us on this?"

Kanesha looked at her. "I might as well, because I know you'll do it anyway."

"Excellent," Miss An'gel said. "Now, here's how we'll do it."

THIRTY-FIVE

Miss Ang'el had set the meeting for five o'clock, to which Kanesha had agreed. She needed time to do some prep work. Zac was not well enough yet to leave the hospital, but she was going to set up a video monitor in the meeting room so Zac could appear virtually. He was well enough to talk, at least briefly.

When I made it back to our suite, I found Helen Louise stretched out on the sofa, reading. Diesel, I discovered, had gone to the bedroom and taken over the bed. He roused long enough to warble at me before going back to sleep.

I picked up Helen Louise's feet, inserted myself under them on the sofa, and then let them down into my lap. She put down her book and peered at me over it. "All set?" she asked.

"All set," I said. "I think this will make you feel better about the whole idea. Kanesha was there. Apparently she's a little frustrated with Wesner, too, and thinks my idea, capably managed by Miss An'gel, will bring about the results we need to get this over with.

"Actually I got the idea from you, so you deserve a lot of the credit," I said.

"And all of the blame if it goes wrong," Helen Louise said wryly. "Okay, what idea did I give you?"

I explained, and Helen Louise shut her eyes. "Lord have mercy, what have I wrought?"

"I think it's a good idea, and I think it will appeal to the competitive instincts of the group. The killer can't refuse to play along because that would send up an immediate signal. He or she will have to participate and hope they can outwit the rest of us."

"I suppose," Helen Louise said with obvious reluctance. "Kanesha will be there?"

"She will, in the room with us, and she'll make sure a couple of Wesner's officers are waiting just outside the door," I replied. "Kanesha said there's no evidence of a gun in anyone's room, so that's good."

"I thought our room had been searched," Helen Louise said. "I should have expected it, I guess. Are we taking Diesel with us?"

"Yes, because I don't want to leave him alone. Miss An'gel volunteered Benjy, but I think he should be with the group."

"All right. How about lunch, then? I don't want to go into this evening on an empty stomach."

Helen Louise, Diesel, and I entered the meeting room five minutes before five. Miss An'gel, Miss Dickce, Benjy, and Kanesha were there. The others came in not long after us. Miss An'gel had arranged for drinks to be available, and we all served ourselves. Once everyone had a drink and had found a place to sit, Kanesha moved to a position near the door, and Miss An'gel called everyone to attention.

"Thank you all for being here. I promise this meeting won't interfere with your evening plans, if you are planning to enjoy one of the many fine restaurants here in Asheville," she said with a benign smile.

"What brought this group together is a mutual love of mystery and detective fiction," Miss An'gel said. "Sister and I have been impressed by the depth and breadth of the knowledge of the genre that you all have collectively displayed. I thought we ought not to miss this opportunity to put our collective knowledge together and try to figure out the plot that we are currently in the midst of."

I had been watching the expressions of group members while Miss An'gel talked. Johnny Ray caught on quickly, I thought, and Celia almost as fast. Melba cut me a sideways glance. She had probably figured it out the moment she received Miss An'gel's text. The others didn't seem to catch on until Miss An'gel's final sentence, and then the truth hit them. I couldn't watch everyone at once, but I saw that Elmore didn't seem bothered, while Burdine looked briefly alarmed. Ellie, too, seemed uneasy. Paul simply appeared blank. I wondered idly if he played poker.

Melba caught my eye and nodded. I thought that meant her talk with Paul had gone well, and she was no longer worried. I hoped that was the correct interpretation, but I would have to verify it later.

"All right, then," Miss An'gel said after a suitable pause to hear objections. "Then let us pretend we are in Nero Wolfe's office in the brownstone at 454 West 35th Street. I will be Nero, and Charlie will be Archie."

I heard a couple of coughing fits, quickly suppressed, and I suspected that Melba was the source of one of them and Johnny Ray of the other. I simply smiled and dipped my head in acknowledgment of Miss An'gel's statement.

"Let us begin." Miss An'gel resumed her seat in the large armchair supplied by the hotel. There was no desk, but the armchair was suggestive enough, I thought, of Wolfe. "Elmore, let's start with you."

Elmore's eyes almost bugged out. "Me? Why me?"

"You're as good a place to start as any," Miss An'gel replied blandly. "Think back over the last few days. If I remember correctly, you mentioned seeing Denis Kilbride in a bar the night he arrived. Tell us about that."

Elmore frowned. "I don't know that I have much to tell. Burdine and I went out for a walk like we often do at home before we go to bed. We walked down the street a ways, and we saw this bar was open. Burdine said she wouldn't mind a drink before bed, and we were going to go in and have one. She spotted Denis Kilbride through the window, and we decided against it. So we walked a little farther, then turned around and came back to the hotel. We went upstairs and got ready for bed."

"About what time was this?" Miss An'gel asked.

Elmore glanced at his wife as if seeking the answer. Burdine didn't respond. "I reckon it was somewhere between ten-thirty and eleven when we got back to the hotel."

"Which way did you go when you left the hotel for your walk?" Miss An'gel said.

Elmore considered that, then said, "We turned right outside the hotel and walked that way."

"Burdine, do you agree with what Elmore has told us?" Miss An'gel asked.

"I do, except that I think it was a little after eleven when we got back to the hotel," Burdine said. "Why would we lie about something so ordinary?"

"That's a good question." Miss An'gel smiled. "Kanesha, I believe you have a contribution to make."

Kanesha stepped forward. "The Asheville police canvassed all the bars within a mile radius of the hotel. None of the bartenders recall seeing Denis Kilbride before when they were given a picture of him."

"So what does that prove?" Burdine said. "He might not have stayed long enough in the bar for anyone to remember him. We saw him."

Kanesha shrugged and stepped back in place by the door.

"I saw him, I tell you. I don't care what the police say," Burdine insisted.

"Would you believe what the medical examiner had to say about the time of death?" Miss An'gel asked.

Burdine nodded. "Maybe."

"The medical examiner places Denis Kilbride's death as early as eleven o'clock, give or take a few minutes," Miss An'gel said. "If he was killed around eleven, then how could you have seen him in the bar, twice, when you say you didn't get back to your room until eleven or a little after?"

Elmore looked stunned by this information, but Burdine scowled. "As early as eleven, you said. But how late? Isn't there usually a range of an hour or more? The medical examiner couldn't pinpoint it that accurately, surely. There would have to be other evidence fixing the time at eleven."

"Good point," Miss An'gel said. "The range of possibility is between eleven and twelve or twelve-thirty, I believe. Is that correct, Kanesha?"

"Yes, the medical examiner was able to narrow it down. I'm not at liberty to tell you how," Kanesha said.

This was news to me, of course. Burdine had obviously lied about seeing Denis Kilbride in the bar. Trying to establish an alibi for herself. By Elmore's reaction, I wondered whether he had been involved in the murder.

To my surprise, Miss An'gel addressed Ellie. "You saw Denis after the incident in this room, didn't you, Ellie?"

"Yes, you all saw me leave with him," Ellie said. "I went up to his room with him and fixed him an ice pack for his jaw. I talked to him for about five minutes, I guess. I was begging him to leave the next morning and go back to Athena. There was no point in his staying here."

"Why did he burst into the room and accost Zac Ryan?" Miss An'gel said. "Did he tell you?"

"We had talked about Zac over dinner. I didn't really want to have dinner with Denis, but he begged me, and I finally just gave in," Ellie said. "I guess the more he thought about Zac, the angrier he got. He wanted to blame Zac for the problems between us. He thought Zac had been trying to turn me against him by talking about their relationship. He said Zac kept pursuing him, though Zac swore he wasn't interested." She hesitated. "I guess I did sort of blame Zac, too, but I know it wasn't Zac's fault, not really. It was all on Denis for being unfaithful."

"Then why did he try to kill himself?" Burdine asked. "We all saw him, right here in this room."

"I'm glad you asked that. Kanesha," Miss An'gel said. "I believe we're ready."

Kanesha walked to the back of the room, behind Miss An'gel's armchair, and rolled out a cart with a computer and monitor on it. "Just a moment while I get us hooked up," she said. "Charlie, the lights."

I hurried to dim the lights so that any glare on the video screen would be reduced. We waited in tense silence while Kanesha fiddled with the equipment. Suddenly, Zac Ryan appeared on the screen, and a number of the group gasped or exclaimed. He was quite a sight with various tubes attached to him, but I think the primary shock was because he was still alive.

"Thank goodness he didn't die," Celia Bernardi said.

"Amen to that," Melba said.

Miss An'gel turned to the video screen. "Good evening, Zac. How are you?"

I had moved closer to have a better view of the screen. Suddenly the camera zoomed in on Zac's face, and I could see his wry smile.

"I've been better, Miss An'gel," he said. "But I'm alive."

"I'm thankful that you are, Zac," Miss An'gel said. "I'm sure you know by now that Benjy found a suicide note that fell out of your pocket when he and Kanesha were doing CPR on you."

Zac gave a weak laugh. "Yes, I heard about that note," he said. "I didn't write any such thing, and I don't know how it got in my pocket. If it ever really was in my pocket."

A ripple of murmuring ran through the group. I focused on Burdine, and she was obviously shocked.

"Do you remember who you were talking to just before you collapsed? Or who might have been near you?" Miss An'gel asked.

"No, not really," Zac said, and in the silence that followed, I would have sworn I heard someone exhale.

"Thank you, Zac," Miss An'gel said. "We don't want to tire you any further. You concentrate on recuperating."

"Will do," Zac said. "It's on you, Charlie." The screen went blank.

"What did he mean by that?" Melba demanded.

"Private joke," I said.

Miss An'gel reclaimed everyone's attention.

"As you have probably figured out, Zac was nearly murdered," she said. "Only the killer knew about the planted suicide note. It really was a rather clumsy device, don't you think? Surely a member of this group could have come up with something better."

There was no response to the disdain in her voice. If she had hoped to goad the killer into giving himself away, it didn't work.

Miss An'gel eyed the group for a moment.

"Very well, let us move on," she said. "There was one fact in Denis Kilbride's life that most of you were unaware of. He had affairs with both men and women, and I believe that is connected to his murder."

"No, you can't do this." Burdine burst into sobs.

THIRTY-SIX

Burdine continued to cry, and Miss An'gel watched her with a tremendous amount of sympathy, and that surprised me a little.

"I'm afraid we must," Miss An'gel said gently. "We can only get at the truth by discussing it."

I glanced at Ellie, not surprised to see her body rigid, her expression blank, as if she were trying to make herself invisible.

Miss An'gel took a deep breath before she continued. "Archie—I mean Charlie—will now tell you more about Denis Kilbride's secret life."

"I must preface what I'm about to tell you by saying that a lot of this rests on information from persons outside the group. I believe the information is reliable and that it bears strongly on what happened here. If necessary, I'm sure the authorities will be able to verify it all." I paused to survey the room. Burdine's head was bowed, and Elmore's attention seemed focused on his wife. Everyone else was watching me intently.

"Denis met other men from Athena in Memphis." I took a steadying breath and stole another glance at Burdine and Elmore, both now watching me. Their faces were ashen, and I thought Burdine might break at any moment.

"Denis wasn't interested in forming a lasting attachment with a man. But one man made the mistake of falling in love with Denis, only to get spurned as a result. That led directly to his death."

"You can't do this," Burdine said again. "My son was not gay; he wasn't in love with another man."

Elmore regarded her pityingly as he slipped an arm around her. "It's no use, honey. You can't change the facts no matter how much you deny it."

"Denis didn't cause your son's death. He perhaps didn't act honorably in the way he treated Todd, but he didn't kill him," Miss An'gel said gently. "I know we all grieve with you for the loss of your son, but Todd made his own decision, didn't he?"

"Are you saying that Burdine killed Denis in revenge for causing her son's death?" Melba asked. "How horrible. And that poor maid, too."

"I didn't kill Denis," Burdine said. Elmore remained mute beside her. I thought he had withdrawn completely from the rest of us, locked in a private hell.

"Then why did you lie about seeing him in that bar down the street?" Miss An'gel asked.

Burdine suddenly seemed to collapse in on herself. I could think of no other way to describe it. "Because I was in his room around eleven. He was drunk, and he actually had the nerve to call me about his back. He used to come to our clinic, and he wanted me to give him an adjustment."

"Feeling about him the way you did," Miss An'gel asked, "why did you go to his room?"

"My hands are still very strong," Burdine said unexpectedly. "I thought he'd given me the perfect chance to kill him and get away with it. I went to his room prepared to choke the life out of him. He had left the door open for me, and I went in." She paused to swallow. "He was passed out on the bed, and I thought, well, it will be easier this way." She burst into tears again and covered her face with her hands.

Miss An'gel waited for her to recover a little. "And then you killed him?"

Burdine shook her head. "I couldn't. I wanted to, but I couldn't bring myself to touch him."

I was thunderstruck. I was so sure that Burdine had killed Denis Kilbride because she thought he was responsible for her son's suicide. I couldn't deny the power of Burdine's confession, though. I believed her. She didn't kill Denis because she couldn't bear to touch him. Her homophobia obviously ran really deep. I felt even more compassion for her son.

So who killed him and Cora Apfel?

Miss An'gel nodded at Elmore. "What do you have to say to all this?"

Elmore shifted uneasily in his chair. He surprised us all, I thought, with his next words. "I figured Todd was gay by the time he was a teenager. Burdine was blind to it, but the signs were all there. It wasn't what I wanted for my son, but he was a good boy, and I loved him." He paused to pull out a handkerchief and wipe his eyes.

"I knew he was getting up to mischief in Memphis," Elmore said, "but I couldn't stop him once he turned eighteen. He dated girls occasionally, brought some of them home, and we thought he might settle down and get married. He never did, though. Just didn't seem to love any of those girls."

Burdine sobbed loudly, and Elmore took a moment to try to comfort her before he resumed. "He never mentioned any boys, though. Later on, as he got older, he seemed to settle down, but he still didn't marry. A couple of years ago, I overheard him on the phone talking to someone, and I knew it had to be another man. Todd was happy, laughing, in a way I hadn't heard him do since he was a kid.

"Found out later it was Kilbride he was talking to," Elmore continued. "I thought, well, maybe it's time to tell him just to go ahead and be happy, despite the way we felt about him being gay. But later on he wasn't that happy."

"That bastard broke my son's heart." Burdine spat out the words, her expression twisted into a mask of hate.

"He did," Elmore said wearily. "Todd killed himself. He'd always suffered some from depression. Got it from his mother. He finally couldn't bear the pain anymore."

"Did you kill Denis Kilbride?" Miss An'gel asked quietly.

Elmore nodded. "I went up after Burdine came back. She told me where she'd gone and what she planned to do. I decided to finish it. For Todd."

"What about Cora Apfel?" Miss An'gel asked. "Why did you kill her?"

Elmore shook his head. "I didn't, and I didn't try to kill Zac, either."

We all looked at Burdine.

"What about Cora?" Miss An'gel said, her voice hardening.

Burdine looked up at the ceiling as she spoke. "I had kept the pin after Elmore used it on Denis. I'd told Elmore I had found it, after he dropped it on the top of the bureau when he came back from Denis's room. I should have hid it in my purse but I didn't. That maid found it that morning. I caught her snooping in our room. She had found her pin, and she also had a small brooch of mine in her hand, one of the last gifts Todd had ever given me. I followed her downstairs to this room and was telling her I wouldn't complain to the manager about her going through my things.

"I asked her about her narcolepsy, and she laughed. She told me she faked it when she thought she was going to be caught. She even offered to show me how she did it. Right here on the sofa. I had asked to look at the pin more closely and so she'd handed it to me. She went into her fake-sleeping routine and I stuck her pin in her heart. I knew once the autopsy results were in, she would know what Elmore had done. She had to go."

"You removed Denis's medications while you were in his room, didn't you?" Miss An'gel said.

"I did." Burdine frowned. "I'm not sure why I did it. I guess maybe I thought he might have a heart attack without them. Then Elmore told me he had killed Denis. I guess I should have flushed the drugs, but they came in handy later. I crushed some of the pills up and poured the powder into Zac's drink. He would be the perfect scapegoat. I hated him, too. I saw the way he flirted with men." The venom in her tone sickened me. With that kind of hatred in her, I fully understood Todd's despair.

Kanesha came forward and stopped in front of Elmore and Burdine. "You need to come with me now." The Gregorys stood, and Kanesha escorted them out.

After the door closed behind them, Miss An'gel spoke again.

"I know this was traumatic for all of you, and I apologize for any distress this has caused, but we had to get to the truth."

"It's okay with me," Johnny Ray said gruffly. "We were all under a cloud until this was finished, and now it's over."

"Yes, it is," Celia said, "and I feel so sorry for Burdine and Elmore. How much they suffered, losing their son like that."

"I get that," Benjy said. "I would be upset, too, but they went too far. If only Burdine had been more understanding." He shook his head. "Elmore sounded like he was more tolerant."

"Betrayal was a huge factor, too," Melba said. "Denis betrayed Todd, who was in love with him."

"Denis was good at betrayal," Ellie said, her expression sad. "Poor Todd. I had no idea about him."

"Denis was a cad," Helen Louise said angrily.

"You'll get no argument from me," Miss An'gel said.

"Nor me," Miss Dickce added.

"He was a jackass," Paul Bowen said. "I agree with the ladies. That's not how you behave. I wish he'd had the courage to be who he was, openly. He caused a lot of heartache, and I'm sure he suffered it himself."

"But he didn't deserve to be murdered," I said. "And Cora certainly didn't. The police might have eventually gotten around to her hatpin, if Burdine had simply let her have it back. But chances are they wouldn't have. Cora needn't have been killed. I can't forgive that, Burdine's outdated attitudes, or her attempt to kill Zac. I understand her rage about her son's suicide, but murder wasn't the way to handle it."

"No, you're right, it wasn't," Helen Louise said.

Diesel rubbed himself against my legs. I knew he must be confused to some extent by all the emotions in the room, and I was thankful he hadn't freaked out in the middle of everything. It was time, though, to take him upstairs and let him be quiet and feel safe.

"I don't think there's any more to be said." I held out my hand to Helen Louise. "We're going upstairs. We'll see you all later."

Helen Louise rose and followed me to the door. I looked back to see the others getting up to follow us. I think we all needed the quiet of our rooms to let our emotions find some kind of equilibrium in the wake of what we had witnessed.

Thomas the bellman, whom I had seen only in passing the past couple of days, surprised me by coming to our room later that evening. He had changed out of his uniform into his street clothes.

"Good evening, Mr. Harris," he said when I opened the door.

"Good evening, Thomas," I said. "What can I do for you?"

Thomas smiled. "It's the other way around. It's what I can do for you. Miss Ducote happened to mention that you've been looking for a pet sitter, and I came to offer my services."

I was completely taken aback. This wasn't what I had expected. "Come in."

Thomas entered the room, and Diesel sauntered over to him. Thomas held out his fingers. Diesel sniffed them, and then allowed Thomas to scratch his head. He even warbled.

Thomas smiled down at Diesel. "He's beautiful. I'm sure you want to know whether I'm reliable before allowing me to take care of this guy for you." He reached into his pocket and withdrew his wallet. From that he extracted a business card and handed it to me.

The card identified him as a bonded pet sitter, and he worked for a small agency that helped people find the sitters they needed.

I handed the card back to him. "I think that's sufficient."

We discussed rates, Diesel's food, and general habits, and Thomas said he was available immediately. I called Helen Louise from the bedroom with the good news. She walked out, smiling, and extended her hand to Thomas.

"You'll never know how grateful we are," she said. "I am ready to get out of the hotel and, well, just get out of the hotel."

"I understand, ma'am," he said. "We know what happened."

I nodded. "It's over, thankfully."

"Y'all go on and have a good time," Thomas said. "Diesel and I will be right here when you get back."

We needed no further encouragement. Helen Louise already knew the restaurant she wanted to try, and we took a cab there. Over an excellent meal with even better wine, we talked a little about what had happened here in Asheville.

"I feel so sad for everyone involved in this mess," Helen Louise said. "I had no idea Burdine was in so much pain. And all those months she evidently spent blaming Denis Kilbride for her son's suicide."

"Ironic to a tragic degree," I said. "I can't imagine what it is like, losing a child, no matter the cause. I don't know how I would cope if something happened to one of my children or my grandchildren."

"I pray that we'll never find out," Helen Louise said. "I feel sad for Ellie, too. I think she might really have been in love with Denis. But when she found out about Zac, and that Zac wasn't the only time Denis had been unfaithful, she must have been devastated."

"I can only imagine her state of mind recently, poor kid," I said. "She must really have felt alone."

"There was no one she felt close enough to, I think," Helen Louise said. "I wish I could have helped her."

"No family to speak of, except an elderly aunt in Mobile, I think she said."

Helen Louise nodded. "I'm so thankful you're in my life. You and your family. You've all made me feel loved and valued. I never feel alone the way I used to before you came back into my life."

I smiled at her, my heart so full despite the sadness and the waste of lives we had encountered here. "You have made me feel less alone, too. We are lucky to have each other, and our family."

Helen Louise smiled and lifted her glass. "To home and family."

I touched her glass with mine. "Home and family."

ACKNOWLEDGMENTS

Michelle Vega continues to be the best editor I could ever have wished for. Every writer should be so lucky. The team at Berkley/Penguin Random House continues to shine: Jennifer Snyder, Brittanie Black, and Elisha Katz. Thank you for all that you do.

Nancy Yost and her able colleagues, Sarah Younger and Natanya Wheeler, make a formidable team, and I deeply appreciate all they do to help me continue to be published. I couldn't ask for better representation.

As always, my friends have supported me through the vicissitudes of life. Stan Porter and Don Herrington prop up my morale and help me get the job done. Elizabeth Foxwell, a friend of three decades, greets me every morning with e-mail, and without it, I don't know how I could start the day. Patricia Orr and Terry Farmer, my tirelessly enthusiastic beta readers and dear friends, never fail me. Carolyn Haines and Julie Herman, well, you both know how much I appreciate the unfailing love and support of my sisters. Finally, my pals, the "Cozy Mystery Share a Palooza" gang, are the delicious icing on top of the cake: Victoria Abbott, Ellery Adams, Heather Blake, Leslie Budewitz, Peg Cochran, Kay Finch, Mary Kennedy, Molly MacRae, and Leann Sweeney. Thanks for letting me be part of the sorority!